FREED

THE TORN SERIES BOOK THREE

J.A. OWENBY

1

Spring 1990

"My God, I thought I'd lost you forever," he said as he wiped his tearstained cheek and pulled his chair closer to my hospital bed.

My eyes rested on his face as I reached out and trailed my fingers down his face and across his jawline, unsure if I was dreaming or if he was real. My fingers wrapped around the oxygen mask and pulled it away from my face.

"You're really here?" I asked.

"Yes," he said and nodded. "Although the mask isn't comfortable, your lungs need it after the fire." He reached for it and gently placed it over my face again.

I pulled it away as soon as he let go, my eyes widening.

"You know about the fire?" My voice raspy from the smoke.

Walker ran his hand through his hair and frowned. Confusion clouded my exhausted mind. I didn't understand. How did he know about the fire?

"Tell me everything you know," I demanded, trying to push myself up into a sitting position, but my body betrayed me and I sank back into the bed.

"You should talk to the doctor, Lace," he said and stood up.

My eyes traveled down his body. The last year and a half had changed him. His shoulders filled out his T-shirt and his jeans no longer hung on his hips the way they had when we'd first met. Muscles rippled through his arms as he crossed them in front of his chest. Disbelief washed over me. Was he really in the same room with me? Even as my gaze drifted across his face, a hollow ache pulsed through me with every beat of my heart.

My thoughts were interrupted as the door opened and two police officers marched into my room.

"Walker Farren?" the taller, dark-haired cop asked.

"Yeah, that's me," Walker replied.

"You're under arrest for the attempted murder of Xander Koffman."

My mouth dropped. What the hell was happening?

"What? No, there must be some mistake!" I said, attempting to sit up again. "Walker?"

Walker's face fell, and he stared at his feet as the officer handcuffed him. The click of the metal echoed throughout the room.

"No, wait! Please." Tears spilled down my cheeks, and I collapsed into my pillow as the police officers led Walker out of my room. My cries came out in muffled, choked sobs.

Attempted murder? Xander? I clutched at my stomach. Was I still pregnant? I needed some answers, and right this second wouldn't be soon enough.

"Stop your crying."

I peered up from the pillow as Mama walked through the door and approached my bed.

"Mama?" I asked, reaching for her hand. "Thank you," I whispered.

"For what? What are you talking about?" Mama asked, irritated.

"It was you. You came into the house and saved me. I remember what you said—you said you loved me and were proud of me." My tears silently fell down my cheeks as I squeezed her hand.

"Well, that should've been your first clue you were hallucinating.

Not sure I would've chosen those words. Lacey, I wasn't there with you."

"What?" My eyebrows knitted together. "You carried me out of the fire. But I don't know if I lost the baby."

"Baby?" Mama spat. "No wonder you were left to burn in the house. You got pregnant out of wedlock, and God was going to destroy you both. I didn't save you, and I would've never interfered with God's plan. He allowed this fire so you would stop living in sinful disgusting life."

"Not another word! Enough!" came a voice from the doorway.

Mama spun around and I sat up as much as I could, my eyes widened with shock.

"Get out right now, or I'm calling the cops," Emma said as she held the door open and pointed toward the hallway. "How dare you say something like that to her. Get out, and don't come back. You're no longer welcome anywhere near Lacey."

I'd never seen Emma's face turn as red as it was at this moment. She'd also never raised her voice to an adult that I was aware of.

Mama got up and walked out the door without a word. She might have left for now, but I didn't trust her not to return. Especially if she believed I deserved to die.

Emma closed the door and flew across the hospital room toward me. "Lacey! Oh my God!" she said as she wrapped me in her arms. I settled my head on her shoulder and sobbed.

"I'm here. It's okay," she said as she patted me on the back.

I cried until my head throbbed, and then pulled away as Emma sat on the edge of my bed. Reaching for a tissue, I wiped the tears from my cheeks. Movement caught my eye, and I glanced toward the door as it opened.

"George!"

"Hey," he said as he approached me. I grabbed his shirt and pulled him in for a long hug. "I'm so sorry. I'm so, so sorry," he whispered, hugging me as tears slipped down his cheeks.

"I'm okay, or I think I am. Not really sure of anything really." Fear bubbled up inside me. "I need some answers."

"Hon, I think we should call the doctor in for you," Emma said as she held my hand.

"I'll go get someone," George said as he wiped his nose on the back of his hand and walked out of the room.

"You're really here?" I asked Emma.

"You're in the hospital. Where else would I be? As soon as George called me, I got on a plane," Emma said.

"George called you? I'm so confused. And they arrested Walker! Oh my God, what's happening?"

"They arrested Walker? I knew he was here, but what did they arrest him for?"

"Wait, you knew he was here?"

"Yeah, but I'll get to all that in a minute. What did the cops say?"

"Something about the attempted murder of Xander," I muttered, attempting to piece everything together.

"Hi, everyone," the doctor said as he entered my room. He pushed his glasses up his short nose as George walked in and sat down. "Lacey, I know you have some questions, but first I'm going to check your vitals. Would you like your friends to leave the room or stay? It's up to you."

"Stay," I whispered.

I lay still as he took my pulse and listened to my breathing. When he was finished, he replaced the oxygen mask on my face.

"Okay. You're exhausted and you've suffered from some smoke inhalation, but you'll make a full recovery."

I stared at him and impatiently waited for him to continue.

"The bad news is . . . I'm so sorry, Lacey, but you lost your baby."

I slumped forward, putting my face in my hands as I started to sob again.

"Shit," George muttered in the background. "I'm so sorry. Is?—Is that why you decided to stay?"

I nodded, continuing to cry.

"I'm going to send in a grief counselor for you to talk to," the doctor said. "You should make yourself comfortable—we're going to monitor you for a few days. You're lucky you made it out of the fire alive." He patted my arm and then left me with Emma and George.

"You were pregnant?" Emma asked as large tears streamed down her face.

"Not anymore," I said, pulling the mask off again and rubbing my stomach where my baby should have been. I wasn't sure how it was possible to experience such enormous loss. I'd only known I was pregnant for a few days, but as the harsh reality of what I'd lost sunk in, agony permeated me. A piece of myself had shattered, and there was nothing left to fill the emptiness.

George approached the other side of my hospital bed and pulled up a chair. He took my hand in his.

"We were terrified when we heard," he said gently. "We thought you were gone. I'd just stood on your front porch yesterday. How did I not realize you were in trouble?" He shook his head in disbelief.

"I couldn't tell you yet since I'd barely had time to process it myself."

"It all makes sense now," he replied.

I turned toward Emma and took a breath. "What happened? How are you here? Why is Walker here? Who took me out of the house? I'm so confused."

Emma grabbed a tissue and dried her tears. Her face clouded as she gathered her thoughts. "Well, do you remember the other night when I called you and said I had something to tell you about Walker?"

I nodded. How could I forget? Xander had flown into a rage over the message.

"I was trying to tell you he and Brittany got divorced a few months ago. He showed up at my apartment and begged me to tell him where you were, saying he'd made a horrible mistake. I know he screwed things up, but there was something different about him, and I caved. I told him you were here in Oregon. He said he was going to book a flight this week and find you."

Emma paused, glancing at me, and I nodded for her to continue.

"I gave him as much information as I could—George's name, the university, everything I knew. He said he'd take it from there. I guess he wasn't kidding, either. Lacey . . . Walker was the one that saved you."

My mouth dropped open as I tried to wrap my mind around what she'd just said. I shook my head. How could I have thought it was Mama? Not only had I seen her, she'd talked to me.

"I don't have all the details," Emma went on. "I just heard he showed up before the fire department and ambulance. He was carrying you down the stairs when they arrived. At this point, I have no idea where Xander is or what happened to him. All I know is Walker saved you. And if I hadn't told him where you were, you'd be gone, and we'd—we'd be making funeral arrangements instead." She hiccupped as she grabbed another tissue.

George reached over me and patted Emma's arm. "It's okay. She's safe now," he said.

Nothing felt safe. My skin prickled with fear, and I jumped at every little noise. I wasn't sure who was going to walk in the door next, Mama or Xander. I bit my lip, leaning my head back and staring at the white ceiling. I'd lost my baby, and I'd lost myself. But this time, I wasn't sure I had the strength to come back from it all.

"How did the house catch fire?" Emma asked, her voice barely above a whisper.

"Xander," I replied. "He taped my hands and feet with duct tape, kicked me in the stomach, and set the house on fire. He left me in his bedroom," I said as despair tore through my chest.

Emma covered her mouth in an attempt to muffle her gasp.

"He's not just mean, he's fucking crazy," George said. He shot a glance at Emma. "Oh, sorry. Lacey is used to my mouth."

"It's okay. I hate to say it, but I agree with you," Emma said.

"Yeah. I figured out just how crazy a little too late," I muttered.

"You should come home with me," Emma said so softly I almost didn't hear her.

George glanced at her.

My face fell as the reality set in—I had no money and no place to live. How was I going to work? I wasn't even sure how I was ever going to sleep, much less go to work and be around people again.

"Okay."

"Really?" Emma asked, surprised.

"Where else do I have to go? You and your parents are the only family I have."

"You have me," George said.

I squeezed his hand. "I love you. You're awesome, and I wouldn't have made it this far without you. I have to go home, though," I said. "Not only is Mama here, but Xander is too. Between the two of them, I don't have a chance of staying alive."

"My God, that's the most fucked-up thing I've ever heard," he mumbled.

"It's way messed up," Emma said as she pushed her glasses up on her nose. "Lacey, I'm going to step out in the hallway and find a phone so I can call Mom and Daddy. They were worried sick, and I need to let them know we'll be home as soon as the doctor clears you to fly."

"Wait, what about Lisa?" I asked as Emma stood up and walked toward the door.

"Well, your timing is good. She just moved out. She and her boyfriend got a place together, so it just so happens your bedroom and furniture are waiting for you."

I nodded. Never in a million years had I planned on returning to Arkansas. My stomach rolled at the idea of going back. I loved Oregon. I loved the green trees and grass all year round, I loved the rain, and I loved my friends.

"What am I going to do without you?" George asked.

"No clue," I muttered, too exhausted to try and make him feel better. "You could come with us."

"Ha! I'm not sure the South could handle me."

"You might have a point."

"Maybe you can come back?"

"Yeah. Maybe someday." But I couldn't think about the future when I could barely hold myself together in that single moment. I stared at the ceiling tiles and willed the tears to stay away.

"He kicked me over and over." My voice hovered just above a

whisper. "He knew I was pregnant and he laughed as my jeans soaked up the blood."

George didn't say a word as he crawled into my hospital bed and wrapped his arms around me. His lips brushed my cheek, and we lay there together as tears streamed down our faces.

2

My last few days in Oregon were a blur. I couldn't sleep, and I refused to eat. The doctor kept the IV in and ordered something to help me rest. The bad dreams of flames and smoke engulfed me, and I scared the crap out of Emma and George on more than one occasion. As horrible as they were, the nightmares broke through the shock and numbness.

Mama was right. I was incapable of making good decisions where guys were concerned. Maybe I should find her and surrender. Maybe she'd been right all these years. Maybe I should stop running and give in.

"Are you ready?" Emma asked, interrupting my thoughts.

"Sure." I wanted to tell her no, I wasn't ready to go back to Arkansas, but my choices were severely limited.

I turned toward George and felt the weight of his gaze travel over my face. His thin shoulders sagged, and his eyes glistened. I couldn't believe that less than a year after meeting him, I was telling him good-bye. It wasn't supposed to happen like this. If I could, I'd reach up and wipe away the pain etched into his face.

"Please be safe," he said as he hugged me.

"I will," I whispered in his ear. Releasing him, I walked backward out the door, giving him a small wave before I turned and left my hospital room.

Unfortunately, I half expected Xander or Mama to jump out at me as we walked down the hall. Every part of me was on edge, jumpy. Emma cleared her throat, and my nerves calmed for a minute. At least I wasn't alone.

"This is probably a dumb question, but I have to ask," she said.

I turned to look at her as the main hospital doors whooshed open and we stepped out into the late spring air.

"Are you curious about what happened to Walker?"

Shocked at her question, I stopped walking and stared at her. Maybe I should wonder what happened, but I didn't care anymore.

"Really? You're worried about *Walker* right now? You do realize Mama or Xander could be just around the corner, right?"

"Sorry, bad timing. I just . . . you didn't see him the day he came by the apartment begging to know where you were."

"What are you saying, Emma?" I asked, not bothering to hide my irritation. Something inside me had snapped, and I was sick and tired of acting like nothing was wrong. I'd said what others wanted me to my entire life.

"Ya know, you're right. I shouldn't have said anything about him. I'm just worried after you had said he was arrested. Who would I even call to find out?"

"He's grown. I'm sure he can take care of himself."

"Yeah, I guess so," Emma said.

We walked through the hospital parking lot without saying another word. I knew I shouldn't have been sharp with Emma, but Walker was the furthest thing from my mind.

Emma unlocked the blue Nissan Sentra, and we loaded our bags into the trunk and hopped in the car. Fortunately, George had brought me the clothes I'd snuck out of the house before the fire.

The silence drew me in like a warm blanket. If I tried hard enough, maybe I could disappear inside it. I'd spent the last year running from Mama and right into the arms of a man who almost killed me. I was tired of being seen.

I stared out the window and once again said goodbye to everything I cared about. My only hope was Xander Koffman would rot in hell for what he'd done to my baby and me. Even that would be too good for him.

MAY WAS BEAUTIFUL IN EUGENE, but I knew it would already be warm and humid in Arkansas.

Emma and I stepped off the late-afternoon flight and walked into the crowded Little Rock airport.

"Emma! Lacey!"

I turned to see Jim and Linda. Linda bobbed up and down on her toes as she waved to us.

"Guess they're glad we're home," Emma said and nudged me with her elbow.

The minute we reached them, Linda wrapped her arms around me. Her tears tickled my face as she squeezed me so tightly I almost stopped breathing. "Oh honey, you're so skinny. I can feel your ribs. Jim, let's get the girls some food. By the time we reach Hot Springs, it'll be time for dinner anyway."

Linda released me, grabbed Emma, and pulled her in for a hug. I glanced sideways at Jim, afraid to see his expression. I'd been a big disappointment, and I wasn't sure I could face him.

"Come here," he said. He wrapped his arms around me as I leaned my head against his shoulder. I couldn't fight it anymore. I broke down. All the fear and anger balled up inside me came rolling out like a tidal wave. My shoulders shook as Jim hugged me.

"It's okay, Lacey," Jim said as he patted my back. "You're home and safe. We're here to help you. You're not alone, ever."

Pulling away, I wiped my nose on the sleeve of my shirt. A moment of awkward silence hung in the air. I knew they loved me, but this wasn't how I'd ever intended on coming back to Arkansas. My eyes burned as I rubbed my eyes and attempted to smile.

"Alright girls, let's find something to eat," Linda said as she dabbed at her own tears. "I'm just so grateful you both made it home safely."

We walked through the airport and grabbed our luggage. As the airport doors whooshed open, we stepped outside, and I sucked in a quick breath of air as. The humidity smothered me. I hated it. I might have missed my friends, but not the muggy Southern weather.

My shoulders sagged while I followed them, and they located the car. And once again, I tossed our luggage into the trunk. Nausea filled my stomach while it dawned on me I was really back in Arkansas. A scream stuck in my throat, and I struggled not to release it in the middle of the airport parking lot. I'd left for a reason. I didn't want to be here.

I should be in Oregon right now with George, Adalyn, and Megan. I should be finishing finals and making plans for the summer. I should be . . . pregnant.

But instead, here I stood, stripped of everything I cared about. Scared. Angry. And other times, an empty shell, void of emotion. How would I ever move past this?

A tight fist clenched around my heart. An empty darkness seeped inside me, and I let it. At least I knew what to expect.

I stared out the window as Jim drove us back to Hot Springs. It wasn't long before he pulled the car into Rod's Pizza Cellar. I wasn't sure I could even eat an entire piece. My diet had consisted of mostly Pepsi and rum over the last six months.

We settled into a booth and ordered. I glanced up at the movie screen. The Three Stooges was playing. Rod's always played black-and-white movies without sound. I used to find it annoying, but now I was just like them—unable to find my voice.

"Girls, I wanted to let you know we paid your rent for three months. We didn't want you to be stressed, Emma, and we also thought it would give you some time to heal before searching for a job, Lacey."

"Daddy! You and Mom didn't need to, but thank you! Oh gosh, I can focus on finals, and then I start my new job. Thank you!" Emma squealed. She hopped out of the chair and hugged them.

"Thank you," I whispered. "It will help a lot." I glanced at Emma. It hadn't dawned on me I would have to pay my half of the bills. My heart pounded against my chest at the thought of going back to work. I didn't trust people anymore. How was I going to deal with them at a job again? How was I even going to get out of bed in the morning?

"Lacey?" Linda asked. "You okay, honey?"

"Yeah, sorry. I—I guess I'm just a little overwhelmed right now."

"I think it would be a good idea if you saw someone—a counselor. You're going to need some help, more than we can give you. It's going to take some time to get back on your feet. And—and losing a baby is something you never fully recover from."

My head snapped up at her words.

"I've had two miscarriages," she continued.

"You have?"

"I was depressed for months. Jim wasn't sure what to do for me. Although it was too soon, I kept insisting on trying again. Eventually, I did move forward. It was easier when Emma came along, but it's one of the hardest things I've ever gone through," she said as her voice trailed off.

Emma reached over and grabbed her mom's hand.

"We're just so glad you didn't—we're just happy you're still with us," Linda said.

I wasn't. Anger flickered through me that I hadn't died in the fire and I was sitting here instead.

A tear had snuck down my cheek and I swiped it away, and then, I lied. "Me too."

3

The sun had set by the time we arrived at the apartment. My stomach rolled as we ascended the stairs. The pizza wasn't sitting well.

We hugged everyone goodbye, and Emma closed the door behind us.

"Come on, I'll help you put your stuff away," she said and lugged my suitcase down the hallway.

I followed her and turned the light on in the master bedroom. Memories flickered through my mind while I stared at the same furniture, beige carpet, and adjoining bathroom I'd left a year ago. Nothing had changed. Nothing except me.

Emma walked over and opened the curtains. The city lights twinkled underneath the night sky.

"You have a great view," she said.

"Yeah," I muttered. She tossed the suitcase on the bed, unlocking the latches, and flipping the lid back while I opened the drawers and began putting clothes away Emma handed to me. She knew me well and realized I wasn't in the mood to talk. But she probably didn't know what to say anyway. Guess it worked out for both of us.

The drawer closed and broke the silence in the room. Emma tucked the suitcase away in the closet and released a sigh.

"I'm exhausted," I said, staring at the floor. It wasn't that I could sleep, but I wanted to be alone.

"Sure, okay. If you need anything, let me know," Emma said as she hugged me. "I know this isn't what you wanted, but I'm so glad you're here."

She left me standing in the middle of my bedroom. I walked across the room, closed the door, and turned off the light. Even if I only managed to toss and turn, I wanted to crawl into bed anyway. After I pulled the covers over my head, I burrowed down. There was no way in hell I planned on leaving this spot anytime soon.

Unfortunately, morning came, and Emma flung my bedroom door open.

"Coffee and waffles are ready. Come on," she said and motioned for me to get up.

I glared at her, slipping out of bed.

"I know you'd rather stay in here all day, but classes start in an hour, and I wanted to see you before I left."

There was no point arguing, so I followed her down the hallway and into the small dining room. I pulled the chair out from the little round table and sunk into it. The newspaper sat on top of a few magazines. I almost picked it up, but then I remembered sitting in the same place almost a year ago, reading about Susan dying and Walker getting married. No thanks, I'd pass.

"Here ya go," Emma said and placed a plateful of waffles in front of me. She followed with a cup of coffee.

"I can't eat all this," I muttered, poking at my food with the fork.

"Well, try. I don't know how you did it, but you've lost weight since you moved. Mom and Daddy made me swear I wouldn't let you lie in bed all day, and I'd feed you."

My eyes narrowed, and then I glanced up from my plate. I wasn't sure why it pissed me off, but it did.

"Alcohol. Lots and lots of alcohol," I snapped.

"What? What do you mean?" Emma asked as she peered at me.

"I mean I drank rum and Pepsi more than I ate. That's how I lost weight."

"You were drinking?"

"That's what I said." I folded my arms in front of me as we stared at each other.

"Why did you disappear, Lacey?" Emma whispered, her voice thick with pain.

I leaned back in my chair. Deep down I realized Emma wasn't trying to pry, but it felt like it.

"Because you were right."

Emma waited for me to continue.

"You were right about Xander. I figured it out too late and wanted to call, but I couldn't. Not only did he monitor the phone bill, but I was too embarrassed to pick up the phone and ask for help. By then, I figured I deserved what I got, and I should just stay with him."

Emma's eyes widened as the words left my mouth. Maybe this was too much for her to hear over breakfast. "That's not true! You don't really believe that, do you?"

"Why wouldn't I, Emma? What in the hell makes you think anything that's happened in my life has shown me any different? I'm not like you. My family isn't like yours." My voice stepped up an octave. "I don't have good things fall in my lap and parents who love me more than life itself. So, yes, when I realized how much I'd screwed up, I figured I deserved it," I said. The chair scraped across the floor as I scooted the dining room chair away from the table and stood up.

"Where are you going?" Emma asked. Worry spread across her face.

"Not hungry." I stomped down the hall and slammed my bedroom door behind me in case she hadn't gotten the message. I closed my curtains and crawled back into bed. Minutes later I heard the front door close. I stared at the wall until my eyelids grew heavy, and I drifted into a fitful sleep.

I wasn't sure what time it was when I woke up, but it was dark, which meant it was most likely after 9 P.M.

The low rumblings of the TV floated down the hall as I peered around the room. My stomach growled loudly, but I ignored it and decided to wait until Emma went to bed to find some food. I preferred something to drink, but Emma hadn't seemed too crazy about the idea. It wasn't her choice, though. She hadn't just survived losing a baby and almost being murdered by her boyfriend. And I sure as hell hadn't asked anyone to save me.

I pushed the blankets off and walked over to the window. If I remembered correctly, we'd passed a liquor store when Jim brought us home, and it was right up the street. My thoughts raced with possibilities while I planned my escape.

As Emma's footsteps approached, I hurried back to bed. My bedroom door cracked open, and a small stream of light peeked through. I lay still so she'd think I was sleeping. She closed the door again.

After I waited for twenty minutes, I changed into a clean T-shirt and shorts. I put my tennis shoes on, grabbed my purse, and tiptoed down the hallway, checking for my key before slipping out of the apartment and into the muggy night air.

Lightning bugs lit up across the lawn as I quietly made my way down the stairs and across the parking lot. Most of the complex was quiet, and the majority of people's lights were off.

I walked through the grass and stayed close to the street lamps so I could see. Memories of walking across the university campus for the first time came tumbling back. My heart ached to be back there.

My lungs filled with the night air as I kept walking. Minutes later, I opened the door to the well-lit liquor store. I nodded at the female cashier, who looked like she was barely over twenty-one, and located the cheapest rum they had. My eyes scanned the brands and then I grabbed three bottles and a six-pack of Pepsi. Maybe if I drank enough, I could fall asleep for a while without the nightmares. I'd thought they were bad after Mama, but nothing compared to the memories of the fire and Xander's foot repeatedly hammering into my stomach.

I took my items to the counter, praying I wouldn't get carded. I was a year away from being twenty-one, but luckily, Hot Springs wasn't big on asking for ID.

A quiet sigh of relief escaped me as the cashier rang me up. She cast occasional glances at my hair, though. I hadn't bothered inspecting myself in the mirror lately, nor had I brushed my hair since I'd been back.

"Hang on a minute." I grabbed a Budweiser baseball cap on the nearby hat stand and returned to the counter.

"Good idea," she said and rang it up. "Fourteen twenty-eight." She grabbed a brown paper bag and placed my rum and soda in it.

"Leave the hat out, please," I said.

"Another good idea," she said, smirking as she handed it to me.

Placing the hat on my head, I laid my money on the counter. "Pretty sure you don't get paid to insult your customers," I said and glared at her. I picked up my bag and walked off before she had time to reply. I wasn't in the mood to deal with anyone's shit.

As I let myself back into the apartment, I leaned on the front door as quietly as possible until it clicked into place, then I turned the deadbolt as slowly as I could. My eyes darted down the hall, but didn't see any lights coming from Emma's room. I grabbed a tall glass from the kitchen before once again tiptoeing down the hallway.

The bedroom door closed softly behind me, and then I walked to my bathroom since the apartment walls were so thin. There was no way I could take a chance of her hearing the paper bag as I lifted my soda and rum out of it. I took the rum slid out of the bag, opened the bottle, and poured a third of the alcohol into my cup. Then I pulled out a can of Pepsi and topped off the rest of the glass.

My shoulders slumped as I lowered the toilet seat, sat down, and sipped my drink. It had been a few weeks since I'd had any alcohol. I stared at the fizzy bubbles and remembered the last time exactly. I'd already been drinking the night I took the pregnancy test, so I figured one more wouldn't hurt, even after the results came back positive. But I hadn't touched anything since. In some ways it seemed like yesterday, and in other ways, it seemed like it had all happened a lifetime ago.

I took a big drink and winced as the rum hit the back of my throat. Maybe it wouldn't take long before the alcohol took effect. I was ready to not feel anything and get some sleep. If I wasn't in control of the ongoing rollercoaster of fear, depression, and anger, then it was safest to smother it with rum.

After I took another long drink, I set the glass on the tiny bathroom counter. My thoughts wandered back to how large the bathrooms were at Xander's house and bit my lip. When would I stop seeing him everywhere I looked? With great care, I put the rum back in the paper bag, opened the cabinet door, and shoved it under the sink. I rearranged the toilet paper rolls, soap, and tampons in front of it. Later I'd think of a better way to hide it.

I took my cup and pulled open the curtain in the bedroom. I leaned against the wall and stared out at the city, wondering if anyone else was looking out their window, or if I was alone.

My muscles began to relax in my neck and back, and a quiet sigh escaped me. The familiar tingle of the rum traveled through my body. Oblivion wasn't too far away.

My drink was almost finished as I closed my eyes, but the moment I did, the visions came rushing back. The flames catching the curtains on fire as I lay on the floor with my hands and feet bound. My eyes shot open, and my breath quickened as I tried to focus on the stars in the sky. I took another drink. Anything to make it stop.

4

I woke up sitting on my floor with my back against the wall. My empty glass had fallen over. At some point, I'd pulled the blankets off the bed and wrapped myself in them.

Grabbing the edge of my dresser, I pulled myself up slowly. My head throbbed as I found my balance. What in the hell had happened? Why couldn't I remember anything after the first few drinks? I sure as hell had never experienced a hangover. And not to mention my room reeked of rum.

The bright sunshine rushed in as I opened my curtain and pushed the window up. I grabbed the fan and faced it out the window, turning the knob to high. Silently swearing to myself, I stumbled to the shower and turned it on. Hopefully the fan and the smell of my shampoo and body wash would do the trick. Maybe I'd crack the window next time. If Emma walked in now, I'd be in deep shit.

By the time I'd dried my hair and dressed in a clean shirt and shorts, my bedroom smelled much better. My head still pounded, but I hoped drinking some water would fix it. Apparently, after not drinking for a while, I'd managed to experience my first hangover. George would be disappointed.

I removed the fan from my window and leaned against the wall, realizing I needed to write George a letter. But I didn't know what to say. He already knew I missed him. Maybe I could find a "Hello from Hell" postcard.

A light knock on my door jolted me from my thoughts.

"Yeah?"

"Hey," Emma said as she pushed open my door. "How're you feeling today?"

Emma was using her gentle voice, which meant something was up.

"The same," I answered and bit my lower lip.

"Well, someone's here to see you."

"Who?" I asked and turned to face her.

"Before you say no, I really think you need to talk to him."

"Who is it, Emma?"

"Walker's here."

My mouth dropped open, and then I shook my head.

"No. I'm not interested."

"You need to see him. Ask him what happened, Lacey. This is your chance to get some answers. I'm telling you, he's different. You should at least hear him out."

"I'm different too. I'm not the person he used to know."

"I can't even begin to imagine how you're feeling, but he did . . . Lacey, he saved your life. Don't forget how much it affected him too. Please, just listen to what he has to say. For me?"

"Fine. But when did you become Walker's number-one fan?" I asked, almost surprising myself with the amount of sarcasm that dripped from my voice.

Emma held her hands up in surrender as she backed out of my room. I turned to look out the window again, but I could sense the moment he stepped into my room. My heart split between telling him I hated him and hugging him and never letting go. But the moment the thought finished inside my head, I remembered he'd married Brittany. I definitely hated him.

"Hey," he said softly.

My breath caught in my chest at the sound of his voice.

"Hey," I said, turning toward him. His blue eyes darkened with concern as they traveled over my face and body. Maybe he'd expected something different, not the dark circles under my eyes and the weight loss.

"I wanted to stop by and see how you're doing."

I frowned. How did he think I was doing?

"When did you get back?" I asked.

"A few days ago. I've been on the Air Force base in Little Rock."

I paused as I realized he'd driven almost an hour to see me.

"So, they really arrested you?"

"Yeah," he said as he ran his hand through his hair. The familiar scent of his Polo cologne reached me, and I stopped myself from inhaling deeply.

"I'm not sure I really want to know, but what happened?"

"What has Emma told you?" he asked as he shoved his hands into his pockets.

"Nothing, really, just that you called her and then flew to Oregon to see me. I guess it was you who got me out of the—the house," I said as my voice cracked with emotion.

Walker sighed heavily. I wondered if he was reliving those moments like I was. The smoke, the heat of the flames as they grew closer, and my vain attempt to get free from the tape. I shuddered and wrapped my arms around myself. Seeing him again was just a reminder of that horrible night. I didn't want him here, but for some unknown reason, I couldn't tell him to leave.

"Can I sit down?" Walker asked, pointing toward the bed.

"Sure."

"I flew out to Oregon to find you. My divorce had just been finalized, and . . ." his voice trailed off.

"And you thought we could just conveniently pick up where we left off?" I asked, my voice thick with frustration and anger.

"No, it wasn't like that at all."

"So, you showing up with Brittany to tell me what a piece of shit I was at the mall that day wasn't enough for you? You thought you'd just hop on a plane and—and what, Walker?" I spat.

"I get you're angry, and you should be. But please, let me at least tell you what happened when I got there. I'm hoping it'll give you some closure."

My silence and glare were the only responses I gave him.

"It was late in the afternoon when I landed, and I went straight to the university and found George. I'm not sure how, but he knew who I was."

I chewed on my lower lip. No way would I admit to Walker I'd told George about him. I stared out my window and waited for him to continue, and then it dawned on me.

"Wait," I said. "I know Emma gave you a little bit of information, but there's no way you could have tracked George down. The university is huge."

"I had everything I needed before I got there. After I talked to Emma, I hired a private investigator. We had a tough time finding you, but we were able to locate George."

"Holy shit, are you serious?" My cheeks flushed with anger.

"I had no idea where you were, and Emma couldn't tell me much. She tried, but you weren't speaking to her, so I did what I had to do."

"You had no right!" I fumed at him.

"I know, but if I hadn't tracked you down, you'd be dead," he said. He rubbed his face as a frown line creased his forehead.

I clamped my mouth shut, realizing what he'd said was true.

"George said something was wrong and he was really concerned about you. He told me you were going to leave Xander, but you didn't show up to meet him and your other friends. When he went to your house to see if you were okay, he said you'd changed your mind and weren't going to leave. He knew something wasn't right. I think he actually said he was scared something really bad was going to happen."

A tear rolled down my cheek as he talked. The images flashed through my mind: the last time I talked to George, the beautiful spring day, and how I couldn't force the words out of my mouth to tell him about the baby.

"He gave me a description of Xander and told me how to get to his house. I drove straight there. As I came up the driveway, I could see the flames and smoke. I parked the car behind some trees and ran up the steps. Just as I was about to kick open the front door, Xander walked out with an overstuffed duffle bag."

My heart pounded so hard my chest ached. He was there. Emma had told me he was, but hearing him say what he saw made it more real. Heart-crushingly real. While he and Xander were on the porch, I was gasping for my final breaths upstairs.

"After I asked him where you were, he rushed at me. It was in that split second I knew you were in the house. I can't explain it, it was just my gut instinct, and then I went after him. I mean, I beat the shit out of him, busted his lip, nose, and eye . . . he was a bloody mess. The moment the bastard was finally unconscious, I ran inside. I pulled off my shirt and covered my nose and mouth. Smoke was filling the house as I searched downstairs but didn't find you. I knew I didn't have a lot of time, and I carefully made my way upstairs and found you in the last bedroom. You were in and out of consciousness when . . . I was almost too late," he murmured.

I wiped my tears away as he paused.

"You thought I was your mom," Walker said.

"Yeah, I remember," I muttered through my tears.

"The fire trucks and ambulance weren't far behind. I guess neighbors saw the smoke and called 911."

"I called 911."

"How?"

"I don't want to get into it right now. Let's just finish this conversation."

Walker paused, studying my face. Then he nodded.

"Right before I stepped outside with you, you passed out, and my entire world stopped. I thought you'd died in my arms. I was shaking so hard I almost didn't make it out the door. One of the EMTs took you, and another one took me aside and examined me. All I could do was watch as they hauled you away in the ambulance. After they'd finished making sure I was okay, I left to find you at the hospital. At that point, I wasn't sure you were alive. I thought I'd lost you for good," he whispered.

I blinked my tears away. He needed to leave. I couldn't handle him being here any longer. He was making everything worse.

"So, what's your point?" I asked. "Do you want something? Do you want me to thank you?" His eyes were rimmed with red, and I knew mine were puffy from crying.

"Lace," he whispered. He ran his hand through his hair and took a deep breath. "I wanted to tell you my firsthand account was enough to put Xander behind bars. He won't be coming after you."

My jaw dropped as his words sank in. "You stayed to talk to the police?"

"If I hadn't, you would've had to go back and face him in court, and I couldn't stand the thought of you going through anymore."

I stood speechless for a minute as my mind wrapped around the information he'd given me.

"Oh my God," I hiccupped. "Thank you. I don't think I could've even looked at him again."

"I know."

"Were you charged with anything?" I asked, wiping more tears away.

"No. It was self-defense, so all the charges were dropped."

I nodded and walked into my bathroom, closing the door behind me. My pulse raced, and I needed a moment to catch my breath and process the fact that Xander couldn't come after me.

The faucet handle squeaked as I turned on the cold water and splashed my face. A minute later, I opened the door and resumed my place at the window. I dared a glance at Walker. Even though he knew Xander couldn't come after me again, his face was filled with worry.

"Why did you come to Oregon for me?" I asked and fixated on the trees outside my window.

"I—I wanted to ask you to forgive me. I made a horrible mistake with Brittany. So much has happened, and I had to see you."

How was I supposed to respond to him? An awkward silence hung in the air between us, and then I heard the springs on the bed squeak as he stood up.

"I'll go. I just wanted to tell you not to be scared anymore, and I'm sorry for everything that's happened," he said as he walked toward the door. "I guess deep down, I was hoping for a second chance."

"I never stopped loving you, even when I was with him," I said softly.

Turning away from the window, I faced him. His eyes lit up with hope.

"But don't come back. I don't ever want to see you again."

Walker's face fell, and his shoulders slumped as he turned and walked down the hall. I closed the door after him, slid down the wall, and crumpled to the floor.

Unsure of how much time had passed, I eventually went to the bathroom and grabbed my stashed bottle of rum and another can of Pepsi. I filled my glass with alcohol and a splash of soda, sipping at it as the fizzy bubbles tickled my nose. Would I be able to sleep tonight without nightmares about Xander? Would seeing Walker enough to give me a shred of peace, knowing he'd stayed in Oregon long enough to put Xander behind bars?

Anger coursed through me as I recalled Walker's words. What had he been thinking? That he'd just hire a private investigator, find me, and we'd live happily ever after? What the hell?

I grabbed the blankets off my bed and sat down on the floor. The corner between my bed and closet worked the best, since I could see if someone walked through my door. One lesson Xander had taught me was to position myself where I could see my surroundings. No one would ever sneak up on me again.

I settled in, drained my cup, and leaned my head back against the wall. My heart ached for a moment at the thought of Walker's face as he left my room. I knew my words hurt, but I wasn't kidding. I didn't want to see him again. I wasn't sure I could ever forgive him.

My breath quickened as a fresh pang of darkness surrounded me. I hated myself for the things I'd said to him. I hated him for leaving me with Mama. But I hated him the most for saving me from dying.

Peering into my empty cup, I grabbed the rum. I unscrewed the lid and took a big drink straight from the bottle. A few seconds later, I took another swig and somehow managed to replace the top on the bottle before I slipped into a fitful sleep.

5

I'm not sure how I made it into my bed, but somehow, I'd managed. I rubbed the sleep from my eyes and stared into the sunlight that streamed through my curtains. The clock read: 8:11 A.M. which meant Emma had already left for school, or at least I hoped she had.

It was a miracle I wasn't hungover. I poked my head out of the bedroom door and looked around. Not seeing Emma anywhere, I padded down the hallway in my bare feet. The smell of coffee tickled my nose as I made my way into the kitchen and poured a cup. It was still hot. I sipped at the bitter liquid and sat at the kitchen table. My stomach growled, reminding me I didn't eat anything substantial yesterday. That wouldn't go over well with Emma and her parents.

I opened the fridge and almost laughed. Emma had wrapped up my waffles from breakfast and saved them for me. It seemed gross, but it still beat a frozen Eggo anytime. I pulled them out, warmed them up in the microwave, and then sat down, nibbling on one as I grabbed the newspaper, wondering if anything had changed in Hot Springs over the last year.

After another bite, I opened the paper to the obituaries. Was it wrong I wanted to see Mama's picture and information listed? I tossed my half-eaten waffle onto the plate, disgusted for thinking something so awful. But another part of me wondered if I'd ever really be free of her unless she died. Would she follow me around the country? I had no idea where she was right now. Oregon? Arkansas? And which was worse: sharing a house with her, or being hunted like an animal?

Suddenly, I remembered Walker had stopped by yesterday. There was no more Xander, he'd taken care of him. But I struggled with the other things he'd said. Had he really thought one visit to Oregon would make everything okay between us again? And a private investigator? Seriously? Was I surrounded by crazy people who stalked me?

I struggled to control the ball of emotions before it exploded, but it was too late. I leaned my head back and screamed at the top of my lungs. I screamed until my voice was raw. I screamed at Walker, Xander, and Mama until my voice faltered. Then I laid my head on the table unable to stop the tears even if I'd wanted to.

What if Mama could see me now, broken and terrified to wake up and face another day? She would laugh in my face and cast demons out of me. I could hear her voice in the corner of my mind, and Xander's wasn't far behind. My arms covered my head as I curled up in the kitchen chair and sobbed. I hated them both, but even worse, I hated myself for being stupid enough to have loved them.

MY RUM HAD LASTED for more than a week. Somehow I'd managed to hide it from Emma, but I knew how the game was played. If I didn't act the part, things wouldn't go well for me. More than anything, I wanted to be left alone, but Emma wouldn't allow it for long.

After a shower, I spent fifteen minutes brushing the tangles from my long blond hair. For a brief moment, I pondered applying makeup when I saw the dark circles under my eyes. I looked like shit, and my cheekbones were more prominent than they were six months ago. My shoulders sagged, and I tossed the makeup back in the drawer and closed it. Screw it. I just didn't give a rat's ass.

I dried my hair and pulled it up in a ponytail. I snuggled into the corner of the brown sofa and turned the TV on to the five o'clock news right as Emma opened the door.

"Hey! How are you feeling?" she asked and grinned. She was probably happy to see me out of bed. She set her purse and keys on the kitchen table.

"Okay," I said and attempted a smile.

"I figured you needed your sleep, so I tried to be quiet around the house."

"I appreciate it," I said. You would think Emma was my mother the way she acted.

"So, can I ask how things went with Walker yesterday?" Emma asked gently as she sat down next to me.

"Ummm, no."

"Really? You won't even tell me why he stopped by?"

I bit my lip and frowned. I really didn't want to talk about it. "He was held for questioning and released, but then he stayed behind to give his witness testimony against Xander. He wanted to let me know the information he gave to the police was enough for them to charge him. He didn't want me to have to go back and testify."

"What? Oh my gosh! That's wonderful," Emma squealed as she pulled me into a hug.

"Yeah, I guess I hadn't even thought about it. When we left Oregon, we didn't know where Xander was. I'd hoped hell, but I wasn't that lucky. I'll take jail for now. How were your classes?" I asked, changing the subject before she could say anything else.

"Good, I'm almost finished. I can't believe it. I begin shifts at the hospital in a few weeks."

"Wow, I'm happy for you," I said, smiling.

Emma turned toward me as she propped her head up on her hand. I recognized the expression on her face. She had something important to say.

"Well?" I asked.

Emma sighed.

"As you say, spill it," I said and motioned with my hand for her to talk.

"I have to go out of town for a week." She waited for my reaction. I'm not sure what she expected, but this was the best news I'd heard in a long time.

"Why?" I asked.

"Well, I've been selected to participate in a nursing program in Kentucky. Only the nurses with honors get the chance to participate, and even then, you have to be chosen by a panel."

"What happens if you don't go?" I wasn't sure why I asked her that. There was no question in my mind, I wanted her to go. I would have the house to myself for a week, without her watching my every move.

"If I go, it puts me ahead in multiple ways, including pay. I want to go, but I'm worried about you."

"That's sweet of you, but I'm here. I'm okay. I can make it for a week. We spent almost a year apart, and I managed to stay alive. Barely, but I made it." *What the hell was wrong with me? How was I poking fun at almost dying?*

"I'll have Mom and Daddy check on you."

"Emma, I'm grown. Besides, you're going to be too busy to worry about me. I promise to call your parents if I need anything, but I doubt I'll even leave the apartment."

"I don't know," Emma said as her eyebrows knitted together.

"I promise. If I need anything, even toilet paper, I'll call your parents."

"You'll have my car too, in case you want to get out for a while."

"Really?"

"Yeah, we're carpooling to the airport. I didn't want to leave you without a car for so long."

"Thanks. And listen, you have to go. This is your future we're talking about. You've worked too hard to let this opportunity go to waste. I'll be okay, I promise. I think some time alone will do me good."

"You're sure? I have to take your word for it. I'll be so busy I might not have a chance to call and see how you're doing," Emma said as she peered at me over her glasses.

"Never been more sure."

"Okay, but you promise you'll call Mom and Daddy if you need them?"

"Promise," I said and attempted a smile.

"After I get back and before I start work, we should go to the lake for a day and get out of the house."

"Sounds good." I had no intention of going to the lake, but she didn't need to know it.

"I've gotta start packing," Emma said as she stood up.

"When do you leave?"

"Tomorrow morning."

"Oh wow, that's fast."

I followed her down the hall and into her bedroom. It wasn't that I really wanted to chat, but it was what she expected. And if I wanted to have this time alone, I had to reassure her I'd be okay on my own.

Emma's room was decorated in shades of blue, with a picture of Elvis hanging on one wall and a large, round clock on the other. She'd never really gotten into posters like I had. I smoothed out the deep-blue bedspread and sat next to her suitcase as she began taking clothes from her closet and dresser.

"How many of you are going?" I asked.

"Only one other student and our instructor."

"How many students did they have to choose from?"

"I'm not sure of the exact count, but only four in the state of Arkansas were selected."

"That's a really big deal. And to think—a year ago, we were sitting at the student center and you were asking me to remind you why you chose nursing."

Emma stopped packing and stared at me. Her face grew serious.

"Do you miss those days?" she asked.

"The ones at college together or the ones when Mama was crazy and drugged me?"

"Geez, do you have to be so rude?" She paused. "Crap. Lacey, I'm sorry. You're just so different. I don't know what to do to help you get back to normal."

My back stiffened at her comment.

"Emma, I'll never be normal again. I'll never be the same Lacey you knew. When you're drugged by your mother and held against your will, when your hands and feet are taped together and you're kicked in the stomach by your boyfriend until you're lying in a puddle of blood . . . when you're left to die as the house you live in burns, there is no normal after that. You need to accept I will *never* be the same person you used to know."

Emma gasped as my sharp words sunk in.

I stood up and walked to her bedroom door.

"Have a good trip," I said, walking across the hall. I slammed my bedroom door behind me.

6

<hr>

I heard Emma get up the next morning, but I didn't. Instead, I lay in bed until I heard the front door shut. No pretending, for anyone, for a week. I wasn't sure what it would even feel like. I'd been acting like people had wanted me to for years. First Mama, then Xander.

Alone. At last. I walked around in my long T-shirt and made some coffee. I grabbed the meatloaf and heated up a piece for breakfast. Although I didn't have an appetite, I knew I should eat something.

Noon rolled around, and the sunlight warmed the living room. I glared at it and shut the curtains. I figured it was late enough, and I walked to my bathroom, opened the cabinet, and dug the paper bag out. After rinsing my cup, I filled it halfway with rum, topping it off with Pepsi. I took a drink and carried the bag to my dresser. I'd need to make another trip to the liquor store today. My eyes rolled as I thought about the rude cashier. I'd be sure to brush my hair this time, which meant I could leave my hat here.

I wondered how many bottles I could carry home at once. There was no way I wanted to make multiple trips and driving Emma's car after drinking wasn't an option. I stared at the amount left in the bottle and topped off what was in my glass.

An hour later, I closed the apartment door behind me and stumbled down the stairs. I located the trash bin and tossed the empty rum bottle into it. My chest heaved with a deep breath, and I adjusted my sunglasses. It took less to get me drunk these days. I wasn't sure why, unless it was the weight loss or the fact I didn't eat much. At least it was cheaper this way.

I'm not sure how I made it to the liquor store, but I suspected it wasn't in a straight line. I opened the door of the store and glanced at the cashier. I smiled. My buddy wasn't there today.

I grabbed my bottles of rum and Pepsi and paid for the items, shifting the bag from one side to the other. It was heavier than I'd expected. Pushing against the door with my hip, I stepped out onto the sidewalk. I peered over the bag, stepping off the curb and into the parking lot. Tires screeched as a body slammed me backward, onto the pavement.

"Hey! Watch where you're going, lady!"

I glanced up from the ground to see a man shaking his fist at me from a car window. What the hell had just happened?

"Are you okay?" came another male voice.

"Uh, yeah. Where's my bag?" I asked, sitting up slowly.

"It's next to you," the voice said.

My vision blurred as I squinted and attempted to see his face. I finally focused on his short, light-brown hair and hazel eyes.

He kneeled down and slipped my sunglasses off. "You stepped right in front of the car. Thank God he was going so slow. You could've been really hurt."

"And you came rushing to my safety?" I asked, slurring my words. I eyed his clothes. "Wait, are you wearing your pajamas?"

He chuckled as he helped me up and grabbed my bag. "I'm Jared. I teach at the karate dojo next door to the liquor store."

"Oh. Well I'm glad the guy who saved me wasn't running around in his pajamas. It might make for a good story, though."

Jared smiled. "At least you're a happy drunk."

"Don't think happy describes me, but I'll take it."

What's your name?" Jared asked as he led me to the safety of the sidewalk.

"Hmmm, I'm not supposed to talk to strangers," I said, wagging my finger at him as I leaned against the side of the liquor store and tried to regain my balance.

"I'm not a stranger. I just saved your life."

"Yeah, what the hell is up with that shit? That's twice now. Twice, in like, a month."

"I'm sorry?"

"Nothing." I slid down the wall and sat down.

"Do you live around here?"

"Yeah, over there," I pointed.

"Do you live in a house? Apartment?"

"Yup." I reached for my bag.

"Let's hold off on the alcohol for a few minutes until I can figure out how to get you home safely," he said and moved the bag away from me.

"Yeah, sounds good. I think I'd like to go home now," I said, squinting up at him.

"Okay. I can take you there. What's your name?"

"Lacey," I said as I tried to focus on his face again. "You said your name is Ryan?"

"Jared. I'm Jared."

"Well, Jared. It's been nice talking to you, but I need to get home now. I don't really like to be in public anymore since the fire."

"What? You were in a fire?" Jared asked as he tilted his head.

"Who was in a fire?" I asked and attempted to stand up.

Jared helped me up, and I stood still for a moment as I gained my balance.

"Where's home, Lacey?"

"The apartments over there." I pointed.

"Okay, so you're really close. Hang on just a minute," he said as he propped me up against the wall. The tinkle of a bell rang as he stepped into a building and disappeared. I held on to the wall, managed to pick up my bag, and peered inside. Nothing seemed broken. I would've been pissed if the stupid driver had ruined my rum.

Jared reappeared and smiled. "Hang on to me," he said as he guided my hand through his arm. "Don't let go."

I walked with Jared to his car. He unlocked it and opened the passenger door for me.

"No."

"No?" he asked.

"I'm not getting in your car. Didn't you go to kindergarten the day they taught us about stranger danger?"

Jared frowned, but closed the car door.

"Okay, but you're really drunk and you have to cross a busy intersection. Please, let me at least walk with you."

I bit my lip and tried to think through the fog of my alcohol-muddled brain.

I stepped around him and teetered as I attempted to step onto the sidewalk.

"I'm fine."

I walked away from him, but he fell into step next to me. He gently grabbed my arm and raised his hand as he halted the oncoming traffic. A horn honked at us as we slowly crossed the street.

"Come on," he said as he guided me into the apartment parking lot.

"Thank you, but this as far as you go," I said.

"Are you sure you won't let me walk you to your door?"

"Yup."

"Is anyone home with you?"

"I have a roommate."

"Good. You probably shouldn't be alone."

"Yeah. So, thanks, Ryan. It was nice meeting you, I guess?"

"Jared. And you're welcome."

I left him alone, turned away, and staggered across the parking lot.

I entered the apartment and set my bag on the kitchen table, sighing as I opened the cabinet and grabbed a clean glass. After I made myself a new drink, I opened the fridge, and grabbed a bottled water and took a long swallow.

My feet felt heavy as I stumbled to the couch, turned on the TV, and curled up on the sofa. I didn't remember anything else until I woke up the next day.

"SHIT!" I said, rubbing my face. I either had to stop drinking entirely or drink more water. Hangovers were a bitch. I held my head in my hands and placed my feet on the floor, wondering what day it was. My eyes focused on Emma's wall clock as it struck 11 A.M.

I stood up, grabbed the newspaper off the front porch, and checked the date. I'd slept until eleven the next day. Was that a good thing or bad? I needed the sleep, but it wasn't like I felt safe enough to close my eyes without the help of my best friend, rum.

Oh God, what was that smell? Was it the trash? I peeked at the trash, but it was empty. Emma must have taken it out the day she left. I chewed my bottom lip until I realized it was me. Frowning, I made a beeline straight for the shower.

7

Although I wanted the week to pass slowly, it had other plans. Saturday had already arrived. Emma was due back home tomorrow afternoon.

The majority of my days were spent in and out of consciousness. When I wasn't passed out, I ate a little bit, but after the second day, I didn't even bother showering. I vaguely remembered meeting some guy at the liquor store, but I wasn't sure if I'd dreamed it. It sounded crazy, but I could've sworn he was wearing his pajamas.

After I sobered up enough, I made another trip to the store. I needed to stock up before Emma got home. This time, I managed to not step in front of any moving cars.

I lugged the bags of rum and soda back to the apartment and made a new home for my stash in the corner of my closet. As I tossed dirty clothes on top of the bags, I stared at the pile and realized I hadn't done any laundry in over a week—I was out of anything clean to wear. Maybe it should have bothered me, but I shrugged my shoulders and staggered to the living room. I enjoyed watching TV when I wasn't passed out. This living arrangement was much better. Emma should stay gone.

I squinted at the clock, counted the hours on my fingers, and groaned as I snuggled into the corner of the sofa. There were only fourteen hours left of peace and quiet without someone nagging me. I didn't even care what her intentions were anymore. I just wanted to be left alone.

Unscrewing the lid of the rum bottle, I took a drink, shuddering as the alcohol slid down the back of my throat. The shit tasted nasty, but I didn't want to sober up until I had to. I sighed as a thought tickled my foggy brain. *I should get my own place.*

I'd never lived by myself, and the freedom to do what I wanted was a huge motivating factor. I had furniture, and I could pick up a TV at Wal-Mart. I mulled it over and finally decided it was what I wanted. Then I realized no one would rent to me if I didn't have a job. My heart dropped at the thought of being around other people again. I wasn't ready.

My plan wouldn't work right now, but I'd keep it in my back pocket for later.

IT WAS three in the afternoon on Sunday when I woke up, grabbed my bottle, and stumbled to my bedroom. I pulled the blankets off my bed and huddled in the corner, tipping the bottle up and taking a drink as I tried to focus. My eyes squeezed shut, and then I opened them, but there were still two dressers in my room.

My eyes narrowed against the bright sunlight, and I swirled the rum around in the bottle. I searched for my glass but didn't see it, so I just drained the remainder of the bottle. A heavy sigh escaped me as my head rolled against the wall and I floated into oblivion once more.

"WHAT THE—SHIT!" I threw the blankets off and scrambled out of bed. "What the fuck?" I screamed.

"Lacey Anne! Watch your mouth," Emma said as she ran into my bedroom.

My knees threatened to give out as I stared at the man in my bed. My gaze was returned by tired, bright-blue eyes.

"What is this?" I yelled.

"Calm down and I'll explain. Besides, you're in hot water, so you're not in any position to make demands," Emma said.

"Emma, for God's sake, I have a right to know why Walker is in my bed and why I'm in a T-shirt, panties, and nothing else."

I glared at Walker as he sat up and leaned his back against my bedroom wall.

"I've got this Emma," he said as he ran his hand through his rumpled hair.

"Are you sure?"

"Yeah."

"Behave, Lacey," she said, pointing at me as she left the room.

"What the hell is this?" I asked, my voice gaining an octave.

"Before you continue with your attitude, you should know you scared the shit out of Emma and me. She came home, and you were passed out in your own vomit. She couldn't wake you up. She even smacked you in the face a few times. After she checked your vitals and realized you were passed out from drinking, she called me. I rushed over as fast as I could, but I couldn't wake you up either. You were probably on the edge of alcohol poisoning. And my God, you smelled bad," Walker said as his eyebrows pinched together.

"Seriously?" I asked, my hands resting on my hips.

"Yeah, it was bad. I put you in a warm shower, clothes and all."

"You what? If I was passed out, I couldn't stand in the shower. Try again," I said and crossed my arms over my chest defiantly.

"You're right. You couldn't even stand. I held you so you wouldn't fall. You never fully regained consciousness, even with water in your face. You muttered a few things, but that was it. I couldn't make anything out."

"So, you're telling me I was passed out, Emma was scared, and you rushed to my rescue once again?"

"Well, sounds a lot nicer than how it really happened," Walker said as he ran his hands up and down his face.

"Shit," I said, my forehead creased in frustration. I didn't remember any of it. Nothing. I reached up and ran my hands through my damp hair. "You washed my hair?"

"I tried. It wasn't easy, and I finally just sat down with you in the tub."

My eyes narrowed while I shook my head in disbelief.

"There's no way I was that drunk. I've never passed out like that before. You're lying."

"I wish I was, Lacey. You were in bad shape. We almost took you to the hospital. That's why Emma called me instead. She knew I was strong enough to get you in the shower and cleaned up. She changed your clothes, and I stayed up and watched you most of the night. I guess I dozed off right before you woke up."

"Night? I remember coming to the bedroom around three, I think. Wait, what day is it?"

"Monday."

"What time did you come over?"

"Around eight last night. Emma called me right after she found you."

"I slept all day and through the night?"

"From what I could tell," Walker said. "You should put some shorts on and eat. I'll make you something."

I stared at him as he slid out of my bed fully clothed.

"So, you just waltz right in and tell me what to do now?"

"Pretty much."

"Absolutely not. I told you to never come back," I said, my voice thick with anger.

"You'll get over it."

I bit my lip. He wasn't playing.

He stood up and stretched as I looked for some shorts. I backed up a few steps, scanning the few remaining items that were left on my closet floor.

"Where are my clothes?"

"They're in the washing machine. Emma cleaned out your closet and started your laundry. I guess you left the door open. She said it looked like a liquor store in there."

A flush crept up the front of my neck and across my cheeks. *She found my stash. Dammit.*

"I can tell by the expression on your face you're wondering if she poured your rum out. She did."

"What the hell is wrong with you people? She had no right!" I said and stomped my foot on the floor.

"Really?" Walker asked as his eyebrow rose. I could have sworn I saw a small smile pull at the corner of his mouth "If you're not in the kitchen in five minutes to eat, I'm coming in with food and I'll feed you myself."

I clenched my fingers into a fist. They couldn't treat me like this.

He walked to the door and slowly turned back toward me. He paused as he searched my face.

"When I put you in the shower, your T-shirt slid up your back. I saw the bruises," he said gently.

My eyes widened, and I inhaled sharply. Although they'd mostly faded, my body was still marked from Xander beating the shit out of me. Tears pooled in my eyes.

"Also, I counted your ribs while you leaned against me," he said. "I get that you don't want to be here. I get that you're pissed at the whole damned world, but you're not going to kill yourself on my watch."

"I'm not your responsibility," I hissed. "You should've let me die! You're so stupid! You think you saved me, but I'd rather be dead than live like this!" I yelled.

Walker winced as the words left my mouth.

"I won't apologize for saving you, ever," he said as he left my bedroom and disappeared down the hall. I could hear him in the kitchen as Emma poked her head into my room.

"Don't be mad at us," Emma pleaded. "You scared me so bad. I panicked."

"He's lying, right? Tell me he just made all of this up."

"He's not. I came home later than expected last night and I couldn't wake you up. I knew I wasn't strong enough to get you into the shower on my own. So, I asked for his help."

"Emma, you allowed him in the shower with me when I was pretty much unconscious? How could you?"

"How could *you?*" Emma asked as she threw her hands in the air. "After everything Mom, Daddy, Walker, and I have done for you, this is how you say thank you?"

"I—" I clamped my mouth shut.

"You told me you've changed and you weren't kidding, but if you want to continue to live here, you have to get your crap together. No more drinking, and no more acting like an angry brat to the people who are doing everything in their power to help you. It's your choice, but I won't watch you kill yourself. I love you too much."

My mouth dropped, and I stared at her, speechless. Then Emma turned her back on me and walked out of the bedroom. She'd never talked to me like that. Ever. I rubbed my face and let out a big sigh. She was right. I hadn't given a shit about anyone else. All I knew was I didn't want to be here. I wasn't strong enough to pick up the shattered pieces of my life and put them together again. I'd tried after Mama drugged me, and I'd managed to not only dig my own grave but bury myself in it.

Frustrated, I picked up my shorts off the floor and slipped them on. I wasn't sure what Walker was cooking, but my stomach growled in anticipation.

My bare feet didn't make any noise on the carpet as I walked down the hallway and into the kitchen. I grabbed a coffee cup and filled it, glaring at him as I sat down at the table. My eyes squeezed shut and tried to erase the memories of him cooking with Garrett. Garrett. I shook my head as my heart ached. It had been two years since I'd seen him. Where was he? How was he? I wanted to ask Walker, but I was too mad at him.

"Here," Walker said and slid a plate in front of me with eggs, bacon, and toast on it.

"I can't eat all this," I said, glancing up at him.

"Yes you can," he replied and returned to the stove.

I stared at the eggs and nibbled on the bacon while he rinsed the dishes and loaded them into the dishwasher.

"I'll check on you in a few minutes."

He disappeared back down the hall, and I took a bite of my eggs. Although I wouldn't admit it to him, I was starving, and Walker could cook well. I took a bite of my toast and stopped mid-chew as I strained to hear Walker and Emma's conversation.

"I hate to say it, but I think you're right," Emma mumbled.

"Then it's settled?"

"Yeah, thank you. I couldn't have done this without your help."

"Thanks for calling me," he said.

I began chewing again as Walker returned to the kitchen.

"Keep eating," he said and grabbed his car keys from the kitchen table. Then he nodded at me, opened the front door, and closed it behind him.

8

Emma and I barely spoke over the next few days. I stayed in my bedroom most of the time, only coming out to eat. As hard as I tried to keep my door closed, every time she passed by she opened it back up. Unfortunately, I'd kissed my privacy goodbye the moment they found me passed out. But I knew it couldn't last forever. Emma had to start her new job.

The front door closed behind her Monday morning, and I jumped out of bed and squealed. Finally, I had some space again. I ran to my closet, grabbed some clean clothes, and glanced at the clock: 9:52 A.M. *Dammit, would the liquor store even be open yet?* If not, I'd go to the grocery store and grab some wine coolers to tide me over.

I grabbed my keys and purse and almost sprinted down the hallway. I stopped short as the door swung open. *Shit, did Emma forget something?*

"Morning, I see you're up and dressed. That's a good sign."

My keys clattered on the floor as my mouth hung open.

"I see Emma stuck to our agreement," Walker said and chuckled.

"What in the hell are you doing here? Don't you understand I do *not* want to see you again?"

"You've made it clear," he said as he walked into the living room

46

and plopped down on the sofa. He picked up the remote and turned on the TV.

"What are you doing?"

"Watching TV."

"Shouldn't you be on base?"

"The Air Force only cares that I'm on base when I'm working. I don't have to ask permission to leave afterward. And what are you doing? I'd almost think you were off to the liquor store as soon as Emma left."

"You're not funny." I folded my arms over my chest. "You need to leave." I opened the front door. "Outcha go," I said, pointing out the door.

"Sorry, I'm here until Emma gets home."

"You're what?" I asked, anger flashing through me. "You're babysitting me?"

Walker shrugged his shoulders as he continued to flip through channels. "Man, daytime TV sucks. Do you guys have any movies?"

I glared at him as I slammed the front door and then stomped down the hallway to my bedroom.

THERE WERE ONLY SO many days I could stand to be sober and stay in one room. The middle of June had rolled around, and every time Emma left, Walker came over. I'd managed to not speak to him for a few weeks, but he didn't seem to care. I was pretty sure he was going to suffer brain trauma with all the TV he was watching, though.

I stared at my ceiling and listened to the hum of the fan. For whatever reason, the full heat of summer hadn't arrived yet. It was hot, but I could tolerate it. I had my window open all the time; it was my only connection to the outside world. If something didn't change, I was going to go even crazier, but I had no idea what to do.

Cracking open my bedroom door, I could hear Walker's low chuckle. He'd show up in the mornings with movies and a few books. He had no problem making himself comfortable. I sighed as I walked down the hall and into the kitchen. The one thing that had improved was my appetite, and I was starting to gain some weight. My cheeks weren't as sunken, and my color had returned. But I didn't care. I still wanted my rum and wasn't sleeping well without it. Hell, I wasn't sleeping, period.

I made sure to clang a pan on the stove and make as much noise as I could in the kitchen. Maybe Walker would get tired of me and leave, but nothing I did seemed to bother him. I decided I didn't want to cook and poured a bowl of cereal instead.

"Don't you have a job or something?" I asked, shoveling a spoonful of Grape Nuts into my mouth. It was the noisiest cereal in the world.

"Yeah, I do."

"And shouldn't you be at said job?" I asked, crunching my cereal with my mouth open. If I wasn't so pissed I probably would've laughed at how immature I was being, but I wanted him to leave. Apparently, I'd stop at nothing to irritate him.

"I work nights on base," he replied without taking his eyes off the TV.

Shit. I hadn't even thought of that.

"I don't need a babysitter," I said and narrowed my eyes at him as he continued to stare at the TV and ignore me. "Walker. Walker! Did you hear me?"

Walker calmly reached for the remote and pushed the pause button on the movie. "I heard you. I'm not going to be here all the time, only when Emma's at work. You're gonna have to get used to me being around."

"I don't need you here," I snapped, placing my cereal bowl on the table.

"From where I'm standing you do. And it's okay after everything you've been through. I made the mistake of leaving you once. I'm not doing it again," he said as our eyes locked.

My stomach flipped at his words. He was serious, he wasn't going to leave. Obviously Emma wanted him here too. Maybe *they* should get together.

I huffed and wrapped my arms in front of my chest as he started the movie again. I glanced at the clock. Emma would be home in two more hours. We were going to have to talk about this arrangement.

I went back to my bedroom and stared out the window. My bottom lip stuck out as I realized it was the only fresh air I'd had lately. If Walker weren't here, at least I'd be outside going to the liquor store. Sometimes I wanted to grab him by the shirt and shake him. I hated him.

Five fifteen rolled around slowly. Emma and Walker's voices floated down the hallway. I couldn't make out what they were saying, but I'm sure it was about me. A knock on the front door interrupted their conversation, and a familiar voice had me running down the hallway.

"Joss?"

"Hi!"

"Oh my God, I'm so glad to see you," I said, hugging her.

"Girl, you're too skinny. Are you eating?"

"Yes." I glared at Walker. "Isn't it time for you to go?" I said to him as my eyebrows rose in anticipation of seeing the door close behind him.

"Lacey, stop being so rude," Emma said.

"It's okay," Walker said, "I've gotta go. Joss, it's good to see you. Emma, have a good night." He stopped as he stared at me. A flicker of sadness appeared in his eyes. I frowned. Walker had been almost void of emotion since the night he'd nursed me back to consciousness. I didn't understand what I'd just seen.

He nodded at me and then disappeared out the door.

"What was that about?" Joss asked.

"I have no idea," I said.

"I'm going to give y'all some privacy and go shower," Emma said.

"That's mighty kind of you," I muttered under my breath.

The moment Emma was out of earshot, I sat down at the kitchen table.

Joss pulled up a chair. "How are you?" she asked, her eyebrows knitted in concern.

"They're driving me insane, Joss. I can't have a moment of peace. Walker is here the minute Emma goes to work!"

"You do understand why they won't leave you alone, right? When Emma told me what happened . . . Lacey, you scared the shit out of everyone who loves you."

"You don't get it. I can't do anything without them. I have no privacy. Emma insists on my bedroom door being open when she's here. Walker watches an unhealthy amount of TV, which leaves me to hide in one room in the entire apartment."

"What's so bad about him being here?"

"Holy shit, are you serious?"

"Why wouldn't I be? You're safe with him. No one can hurt you."

"Xander is in prison anyway. The only person . . ." my voice trailed off.

"I think you're looking at this wrong. They're trying to keep you safe so you can heal."

"I'm in prison," I snapped.

"No you're not. You can do anything you want."

"I can't drink!"

"Yes you can. No one is stopping you from going to the liquor store right now, except you."

"No, they won't let me."

"Lacey, I know you've gone through hell and back. No one is blaming you for wanting to drink and hide, but there are consequences. We're here to help you get your feet back underneath you, to feel safe, to heal. Don't blame them if you don't want the same thing."

I stared at my feet, not wanting to see the expression on her face. A part of me knew she was right, but I didn't want the same thing. "I don't. I don't want to be here."

Joss took my hand.

"We know, and it's why no one will leave you alone. We're scared and doing the best we can under shitty circumstances. Walker saved you and whether you want to believe it or not, there's a reason you're here at this table right now instead of six feet under the ground."

My head snapped up as her words sunk in. Tears pooled in my

eyes. "The only time I feel any peace is when I'm drinking. Do you know what it's like to have the smell of your own blood stuck in your nose? I can't get rid of it. I can't stop the memories of Xander kicking me in the stomach until I lost our baby, or the tape cutting into my wrists as the curtains caught fire around me. Every time I close my eyes I see his face, his sneer as he snorted cocaine while I was bleeding on his bedroom floor," I whispered.

"You're not alone with him anymore. Please, let us in."

I wiped my tears away with the back of my hand. "What if I can't? What if it's too late for me?"

"Hey Joss, do you want to stay for dinner?" Emma asked as she entered the kitchen. "Oh, shoot. I'm sorry. I'll let you guys finish talking."

"It's okay. I don't have anything else to say," I said.

"Thanks, Emma, but I have to get going," Joss said.

"Okay, well don't be a stranger. I'll make dinner for everyone next time," Emma said.

"I'll walk you out," I said as Joss grabbed her purse.

"See ya later, Emma," Joss said and raised her hand in a small wave.

I followed Joss down the apartment stairs and to her car.

"Are you going to be okay?" she asked. "Be honest with me, no bullshit."

I kicked at the pebbles on the asphalt, struggling with whether to tell her the truth or not.

Finally, I glanced up. Her gaze was fixated on me as she waited for my response. "No idea. I'm terrified one minute, angry the next, and I don't want to be here. So, honestly, I don't know how to answer you."

"Well, at least you told me the truth," she said as she hugged me. "You know we love ya."

"I know, but I'm not sure it's enough."

"Then find out what is. What's important enough for you to get through this? Right now, you can't see the big picture because you're stuck in the pain," she said.

"Big picture? What big picture?"

"Something bigger than you. Think about this. If you were the only woman to ever go through a situation like yours, there wouldn't be counselors and domestic violence shelters. This is a huge problem. You've walked through hell and come out the other side. Now, what are you going to do with it? Personally, I think you should get your shit together, go to a counselor, and figure out how to move on. Once you do that, you'll realize you have something amazing to share with other people."

"What? What the hell can I possibly offer someone?"

"Hope," she said and paused. "I've gotta go. I'll be by again soon, but call me. I miss you."

9

I nodded as Joss got into her car and pulled out of the complex. My shoulders slumped as a heavy sigh escaped me. Then, I realized I was standing unguarded in the middle of the parking lot. Walker and Joss were gone, and Emma was cooking dinner. This was my chance.

My feet propelled me forward and I bolted across the freshly mowed lawn and down the street. I slowed as I rounded the corner to the liquor store parking lot, jogging to the sidewalk and stopping short in front of one of the storefronts. Holy shit, I hadn't dreamed it. The guy in his pajamas stood in front of a group of people. Approaching the large rectangular window, I watched him move across the floor. I had no idea what he was doing, but his movement was slow, precise, and powerful. He bowed slightly to the group and walked across the room toward me.

I stepped backward as he opened the door.

"Hey, would you like to come in?" he asked. A warm smile spread across his handsome face as he held the door open for me.

"I, uh, I was just . . ."

"I'd love for you to come in, Lacey."

"You know my name?" I struggled to put the pieces together. I vaguely remembered him, but I didn't remember telling him my name.

"Do you remember me? I walked you home about three weeks ago."

The godforsaken flush crept up my neck and across my cheeks as I realized he'd seen me three sheets to the wind.

"Kind of," I stammered.

"Well, you seem to be doing better today. Come on in. I need to get back to my class."

I nodded as I entered the dojo and found a green plastic chair in the back of the room. I eyed the walls that sported full-length mirrors. The white-tiled ceiling was a stark contrast to the dark wooden floors.

"Okay, everyone back to the kata," Jared said as he took his position in front of the group again.

I watched as the class moved together. Jared walked around and corrected people's arms and standing positions. My eyes scanned the room and fell on him again. He stood about five feet eleven, and he was lean. I couldn't make out his full shape in his pajamas or whatever his outfit was called, but my guess was he was a powerhouse. My eyes traveled to his black belt and then around the room. They all had black belts.

I jumped as the group members all made a noise at the same time, and then they bowed to Jared as he dismissed the class. He grabbed a towel and patted the sweat from his face as he approached me.

"What did you think?" he asked as his hazel eyes searched my face.

"Wow, I—I'm not sure. Everyone has a black belt on, though. What does that mean?"

"We have a belt system like other martial arts, and black is next to the highest you can achieve, but there are multiple levels of black. I'm a fifth-degree black belt. The guy with the short brown hair over there just received his black belt last month, so he's new to this class. A few of these students are second-degree black belts. We're all different."

"Are you the highest in this class?"

"I am," Jared said and flashed a smile. "There's one other fifth-degree here, but she doesn't teach."

"She?"

"Yeah, she's pretty badass. Hey, why don't you come back tomorrow night at six o'clock? I have a free class for beginners. You're welcome to wear shorts and a T-shirt and see if you like it."

"Really?" Apparently I'd been reduced to two-syllable words. I wasn't sure if it was because he was gorgeous or because I was embarrassed he'd taken me home so drunk I didn't even remember it.

"Okay, um, yeah. I can do that," I said as I stood up.

"See you tomorrow then," Jared said.

I walked out of the dojo in a daze. Had I just gotten talked into going to a karate class? What the hell had just happened? It had to have been that smile of his.

This time, I looked both ways before I stepped off the curb into the parking lot. I walked slowly back to the apartment and thought about the group of guys I'd just watched. They'd moved so gracefully, but with a lot of power. There's no way I'd mess with any of them. Could this be good for me? Could I learn to protect myself and feel safe? What would it feel like to not be afraid of Mama showing up and kidnapping me? What would I do when Xander got out of prison? They wouldn't keep him forever. I wasn't sure if this was something I could do or not, but maybe it wouldn't hurt to at least show up.

I walked up the apartment stairs and opened the door. Emma and Walker stood in the middle of the living room.

"Hey," I said as I walked into the kitchen, opened the fridge, and grabbed a bottled water.

"Are you okay?" Emma asked. Concern spread across her face as she approached me.

"Yeah, I just needed some air. It gets claustrophobic being inside all day."

I set my water on the table, then pulled out the chair and sat down. Walker leaned on the wall and crossed his arms over his chest while Emma sat down with me.

"Did it help?" Emma asked.

I bit my lip as she leaned across the table, realizing she was trying to see if she could smell alcohol on me. Honestly, I couldn't really blame her. I'd literally run right to the liquor store when Joss had left.

"You were gone for more than an hour," she said. "I was starting to worry."

"No, I—I ended up at a dojo," I said. My eyebrows knitted together as the words left my mouth. "I'm not sure how, but I did."

"A daja what?" Emma asked.

"Dojo," Walker said as he approached the table. "It's where they practice and teach martial arts."

I nodded in agreement. "I'm going to a class tomorrow night for beginners. Maybe this will help me feel safe. I don't know, but it can't hurt to just go to one class I guess."

"Anything that helps you get better has my full support," Emma said and sighed. "Just, next time you go, can you let us know? We thought . . . we were worried you weren't coming back."

I glanced at her and Walker. For a moment, my heart ached for what this must be like for them. "Yeah. I can," I said.

"So, everyone's okay?" Walker asked.

I peered up at him. "Yeah, I'm okay. Sorry," I muttered.

"Alright, I'll see everyone tomorrow."

"Thanks, Walker. Have a good night," Emma said.

The door closed softly behind him.

"You had us scared," she said.

"Sorry, I didn't mean to. I wasn't planning on going anywhere, but when I walked Joss to her car, and I realized I hadn't even been outside for a while. That's nuts. When did I become someone who doesn't even . . ." I shook my head, struggling for the words to sum up what I'd become. A broken, angry, suicidal someone.

A pang of fear shot through me as I realized I really had died in the fire. Walker might have carried my body out that day, but I'd left everything else behind, and it had burned to the ground.

"Joss told me there's more than what I'm going through. There's a bigger picture," I muttered.

"She did?" Emma asked as her eyes widened.

"Yeah. I don't think she was trying to be rude or anything. She just reminded me I'm not the only woman to go through this. Emma, I survived and I—I don't even know what to do with that," I said as my voice cracked with emotion.

Emma stayed still and quiet.

"How do I even talk to you anymore? I don't even know what I feel. One minute I'm so angry I think it's going to rip me apart from the inside out. The next minute, I'm trying to figure out how to kill myself, and the next, I see flashes of myself lying on the floor with blood-soaked jeans and the house on fire. Xander laughed. He *laughed*. How fucked up is that? I don't know what to do anymore or how to go on. It's not like I want to be sitting in front of you so screwed up. But tonight, when Joss said that to me, and then I watched the karate class, I wondered for a tiny second if I could come back from this."

I buried my face in my hands and let the tears flow. I cried for my baby, I cried for the Lacey that was still bound and left in the fire, and I cried for the part of me that had survived.

"Lacey, I don't know how, but if anyone can come back from this, it's you. You're stronger than anyone I've ever met. If you think this karate class will help you, go. I'll drive you and pick you up if you need me to."

"It's okay, I can walk, thank you," I muttered.

"I just want you to know you have our love and support. We just want to help you through this until you can love yourself again."

Lifting my head, I accepted the tissue she held out to me. I wiped at the string of snot that was swinging from my nose and laughed. I glanced up at Emma, her eyes widening as a slow smile spread across her face.

"Did you just laugh?" she asked.

"Yeah," I said, laughing again. "Did you see the huge string of snot swinging from my nose?" I giggled.

"Yeah!" Emma said and giggled. "It was this long," she said, holding her hands apart a good two feet.

"No, it wasn't *that* long, maybe more like this," I said, closing the distance between her hands by six inches. "Hell, Tarzan could've swung off that one," I said through my giggles.

"Oh my God! You're making me cry!" Emma said as she wiped her cheeks, still laughing.

"I'm so glad Walker didn't see it," I said, scrunching up my nose.

"Yeah, not sure he'd let you live that one down, no matter what you were going through."

Our giggles carried through the apartment. I'd forgotten what it was like to laugh so hard you cried. I'd forgotten how to laugh at all. And leave it to a string of snot to bring a flicker of life back into me.

"I'm starving. We should order some pizza," Emma said.

"Yeah, sounds really good. I think I could eat an entire one all by myself."

Emma stopped and looked at me. "I'd love to see that," she said. "Maybe we should order extra for Walker tomorrow."

"Oh," I said.

"What? Did I say something wrong?" she asked.

"No, just that Walker will be back tomorrow."

"Sorry. I know you don't like him here, which I'm still a little confused about, but until you're doing better, you're going to have company. Deal with it."

"I don't get it, though. Why is he here? I mean, obviously you guys are afraid I'll hurt myself, but why him?"

Emma leaned back in her chair and searched my face. "You really don't know?" she asked.

"No, I don't get it. I—he's the last person I would expect to be here every day. We have a past, Emma, and if you remember, it ended badly. And every day he comes here, it reminds me of all the bad shit that happened with him and Xander. I still haven't even begun to wrap my mind around it. It's like I'm in a fog and I'm watching someone else's life on TV. I don't even think it's sunk in that Walker is actually here. It probably sounds stupid, but I don't know what else to say."

"You don't have to figure out everything tonight. It's going to take time. You had so much happen so quickly. We studied in class how traumatic events can cause something called PTSD. It stands for post-traumatic stress disorder. You're describing it well. Have you considered going to a counselor?"

"Yeah, but I don't have any money, and the only one I know is Walker's aunt. Talk about awkward."

"Mmm, yeah, not sure she'd be the best one to talk to. I can see if the hospital is connected with counselors who do pro bono work or use a sliding scale if you want me to. I'll even go with you if you need me there."

"Really? You'd go to counseling with me?"

"Sure, why wouldn't I?"

"Why *would* you?" I asked as my eyebrows rose.

"Because it's what family does for each other," Emma replied.

I nodded. "I'll think about it."

"That's all I'm asking. Now, what kind of pizza do you want?"

"Supreme, thick crust, extra cheese," I said. "I'm starving!"

Emma ordered the pizza, and we turned on the TV. She flipped through the channels until she found *Roseanne*. The pizza arrived forty minutes later, and I ate three pieces. My tummy ached a little with all the food I'd eaten, and I leaned back into the sofa and yawned. My eyelids fluttered closed, and I drifted off to sleep.

1 0

I heard the front door open and a murmur of voices floating across the room. Ignoring it, I squeezed my eyes closed, snuggled farther into the couch, and drifted off to sleep again.

MY EYES SQUINTED against the sunlight, and I raised my hand to guard them as my vision adjusted. I sat up slowly, my head pounding, but this time it was from crying, not a hangover.

I started to stretch and froze midair. Walker sat at the end of the couch holding a book. He smiled as he placed it on the corner table near the phone.

"Oh shit," I muttered. "You're back."

"Yeah, I'm here. How are you doing? I thought you were going to sleep all day."

"What time is it?" I asked while attempting to smooth my crazy hair.

"One o'clock."

"In the afternoon?"

Walker nodded as it dawned on me I'd slept the day away. When

60

had my hours gotten so weird? My face fell as I remembered staying up all night waiting for Xander and sleeping during the day.

"You okay?" Walker leaned forward.

"Yeah." Tossing the blanket off me, I entered the kitchen and grabbed what was left in the coffee pot. I warmed it up in the microwave and shot Walker a look as he watched me.

"I'm fine, don't stare. Seriously, I'm just really tired. I don't know if it was the crying or all the pizza."

"Crying?" he asked as he stood up and stepped toward me.

"I'm surprised Emma didn't tell you. You two are pretty tight these days." I cocked my eyebrow at him. The bite in my voice stopped him in his steps. "Gotta go shower."

I turned and walked down the hallway, leaving Walker standing alone in the living room.

My hand shook as I opened the door of the dojo and stepped inside at five minutes to six. Several people stood by the tables in the small, carpeted waiting area. Maybe they weren't any more sure about what to do than I was. I chewed my lip as I stood there waiting for Jared to show up.

My focus traveled around the room as a few more people filed in. They were mostly men; there was only one other female. She looked a little older than me. I eyed the exit as my heart thumped against my chest. No way in hell could I this. I stepped around the chairs and pushed the door open.

"Hey, you're here," Jared said as he walked into the dojo before I could leave. "Thanks for getting the door," he said as a warm smile spread across his face.

Shit. I couldn't leave now. Reluctantly, I followed him onto the wood floor with the rest of the group. After careful consideration, I chose a spot in the back of the room and focused on Jared at the front.

"Welcome, everyone," he said as he clapped his hands together. "This is the free class offered to see if it's the right place for you. We're going to start off with some simple stretches, so everyone spread out and find a comfortable place on the floor."

We all bent over and touched the floor. I was sure my body would creak and moan like a seventy-year-old's.

I followed Jared's lead as the group stretched, and my eyes wandered across the people in the room. Finally, I spotted the other girl at the front.

I stared at the heavyset man standing next to me, guessing he was in his mid-thirties. Two more guys were in front of me. My heart thudded against my chest and a knot began to tighten in my stomach. My vision clouded as images of Agnus pinning me against the house intruded my thoughts.

My hand reached out and balanced myself against the wall, staring at the floor. A muffled cry escaped me as I attempted a deep breath. I glanced up as one of the guys in front of me turned and stared. My cheeks flushed as I bent over at the waist and dug my fingernails into my leg. Maybe it would jolt me enough to give my brain something else to think about.

"Face the front, please. Tiffany, can you take over?" Jared asked.

I hadn't realized he was standing in front of me until he gently touched my shoulder. Flinching, I attempted a step backward, but my legs rebelled. I stood rooted to the floor, my legs trembling and threatening to buckle.

"Look at me, Lacey," he said in a hushed tone. "I want you to keep eye contact with me, okay?"

I nodded and focused on his hazel eyes, but they weren't his, they were Xander's. I closed mine tightly and attempted to clear Xander's sneer from my mind.

"Look at me and take a deep breath."

Prying my eyes open again, I settled my gaze on his jawline. His jaw didn't remind me of anyone else, so I stuck with it.

"Feel your feet on the floor. I want you to wiggle your toes."

I did as he asked, hoping it would work. I was sure I was only seconds away from passing out in front of him and the rest of the class. What the hell had I been thinking coming here?

"I want you to imagine you're connecting with a white light deep in the earth. Let it flow up into your feet, your legs, your stomach, chest, and out through the top of your head. Are you doing that?"

"Yeah," I choked out a few seconds later.

"Take another deep breath and envision the white light splashing down on you, over your head, and down your body. It's warm and gentle."

I sucked in more air, listening to Jared's deep, soothing voice.

"Good. Your shoulders are relaxing, and your breathing is more steady."

I glanced up at him and nodded.

"Thank you." My voice hovered above a whisper.

"Let's have you watch tonight, okay?" he said as he gently touched my shoulder. "I'll take you to the best seat in the house." He guided me off the floor of the dojo and to one of the small tables in the waiting area directly behind the class.

"You can watch in the mirrors. Even when you're not on the floor, you can see me at all times, and I can see you too."

I crumpled into the chair. My body still refused to stop shaking as I wrapped my arms around myself in an attempt to gain control. I needed to leave before I lost it again.

I'd been holed up in the apartment for so long I had no idea how being around a group of guys would affect me. My chin quivered as I watched the class. I wasn't ready. There was no way I could handle being surrounded by people who towered over me. The memories were too fresh.

Although my legs were still wobbly, I crept to the back of the room, located my shoes, and slipped my Nikes back on. I'd hoped to disappear out the door undetected, but the class had ended, and Jared walked toward me.

"Hey, are you alright?" he asked.

"Yeah." My cheeks flamed red. "Sorry. I'm not sure what happened," I said and attempted a smile.

"No worries. Don't leave yet, though. Give me five minutes?"

"Really, I need to go," I stammered.

"Please, just give me five. I promise I'll be quick."

My eyebrows knitted together. Why did he want me to stay? What did he want from me? Had I thought he was a good guy when he was really another Xander?

Fear gnawed at my stomach as I nodded in agreement. I watched him turn toward some students, and then I slipped out the front door. I looked both ways in the parking lot, and then broke into a run as fast as I could. My feet pounded against the sidewalk as the stream of cars sped by me. I dashed across the lawn, rounded the corner of our apartment building, and ran up the stairs. My body slammed against the front door as I turned the knob and burst into the living room.

"Shit!" Walker said as he jumped off the couch.

I collapsed onto the floor, trembling.

"Lace, are you okay?" Walker asked as he reached me. "Lacey?"

Black dots danced across my vision as I struggled to hold on to Walker's voice. His strong arms pulled me toward him, and I settled against his chest as the whimpers escaped me.

"It's okay. I'm here," he said softly as he rocked me. "You're safe. No one can hurt you," he whispered in my ear.

After a long pause, I caught my breath enough to hear his heartbeat over mine and focused on the steady rhythm. The rise and fall of his chest calmed my nerves as I let him hold me. I clutched at his shirt as the tears began to fall. He tightened his arms around me as he rested his cheek on the top of my head. He didn't say anything else as he rocked me.

After a while, I wasn't sure how long we'd been sitting on the floor, but my head throbbed and my tears had finally dried up. Walker hadn't made any attempt to move, so I allowed myself to feel the warmth of his body and the safety of his arms.

I discreetly wiped my cheeks and nose and tilted my head up toward him.

"Hi," he whispered as he tucked a piece of hair behind my ear.

I swallowed, still unable to talk. He leaned down and gently kissed the top of my head.

"Are you okay?"

I nodded and attempted to clear my throat.

"Do you want to talk about it?"

I shook my head no.

"Okay."

I peered up into his blue eyes as his finger gently moved down my cheek. Pain flickered across his face.

"I should get up," Walker said as his voice cracked.

I released his shirt and attempted to stand, but my legs were still weak. Walker stood up, leaned down, and scooped me off the floor and into his arms. I rested my head on his shoulder as he walked down the hallway and into my room. He lay me down on my bed, removed my shoes, and pulled the covers up over me.

"I'm going to sit here until you fall asleep, okay?"

Too exhausted to protest, I nodded.

Emma and Walker's voices pulled me out of a fitful sleep. I squinted at the clock. It was a little after 10 P.M. I stayed still in my bed and attempted to make out what was being said.

"Yeah, I know, but if it's too hard for you I completely understand," Emma said.

"I'll be fine, it was just a bit more than I'd expected. She's been so detached and rude. But—not tonight. It about broke my heart all over again. I'm not sure what happened, but I guess it brought up all the memories."

"Do you think someone tried to hurt her?"

"Don't even go there, Emma. I'll hurt some motherfu—"

"She's not your responsibility," Emma interrupted. "She's mine. Besides, you've had enough to deal with already."

"No. I left her once, and I won't do it again. I can't."

"Okay, I just wanted to make sure. This has gotta be bringing up your own crappy memories. But honestly, I really don't think I could do this on my own," Emma said and sighed.

"You don't have to. I'll be here in the morning."

"Thanks. Have a good night."

The front door closed and I rubbed my eyes as I remembered

standing in the karate class. I couldn't breathe. Fear had wrapped its cold hand around my neck and choked me. And why had Jared been so insistent on me staying after class? I wanted to trust him, but I'd trusted Xander, and it had almost cost me my life.

I chewed my bottom lip and closed my eyes at the thought of Walker holding me. It had been such a long time, and after all the hell I'd been through I never imagined it would happen again. The beat of his heart against my cheek and his muscled arms embracing me gave me a moment of peace. My heart ached as much with fear as it did with pain. The one guy who had saved my life had also broken my heart into a million pieces. No matter how I felt, though, I couldn't let him in again. I had to learn to take care of myself.

"Good morning," Walker said as I entered the kitchen. He loaded a plate into the dishwasher, leaned against the counter, and waited for me to respond.

I ignored him, grabbing a cup from the cabinet and filled it with coffee. After yesterday, no way was I interested in spending the day with him.

"How did you sleep?" he asked.

"Listen. About yesterday, it didn't happen. Got it?"

Walker crossed his arms over his chest. "Well, actually it did."

I whirled on my heel and glared at him. "Let's be really clear about this. I do not want you here. Emma has invited you into our home, not me. So don't get any ideas just because I had a shitty evening. I'm fine."

Not waiting for to reply, I grabbed the newspaper off the kitchen table and walked down the hallway. I closed my bedroom door behind me. It was going to be a long-ass day.

I MISSED OBLIVION. I missed the burn of the rum as it hit the back of my throat and warmed my belly, but more than that, I longed for the dreamless sleep it offered.

Dread trickled down my spine as I sighed and stared out my bedroom window. The sun had begun its slow, summer-evening descent. I'd refused to go out to the living room for the rest of the day. There were moments I almost forgot Walker was there until I heard his deep laugh floating down the hallway.

I chewed my lower lip and recalled the look on his face last night. It almost seemed like holding me was too much for him. But maybe he was remembering the nightmare we'd lived through. He wore the same expression when I was in the hospital—haunted and sad.

I rubbed my arms, not wanting to think about him anymore. That was difficult since he practically lived with Emma and me, though. The logical side of me understood why he was here, but the broken part of me hated him for everything he'd thrown away.

Suddenly, anger swirled in the pit of my stomach at the idea I was a prisoner in my own home once again. I grabbed my keys, opened the bedroom door, and strolled past Walker and out the front door. *Screw them. I can leave whenever I want to.*

"Lacey!" Walker yelled.

I ignored him and kept walking across the apartment complex and down the street. If Walker needed to know where I was going, he could follow me. I swatted at a mosquito as I rounded the corner to my favorite store. Life was bullshit, and I could make my own choices. I was sick and tired of people controlling me.

The air-conditioning of the liquor store smacked me in the face as I entered. I approached the rum aisle and grabbed a few bottles. Next stop, Pepsi.

I walked up to the cashier and placed my items on the counter.

"You can't serve her. She's not twenty-one."

"What the hell?" I asked, turning to see Walker standing next to me.

"Do you have ID?" the cashier asked.

"No," I muttered. "I left it at my apartment, and I walked here."

"Sorry, ma'am. I can't sell alcohol to you then."

I whirled around and jabbed Walker in the shoulder. "Outside. Now," I said, my voice thick with anger.

The moment the door closed behind us, I jabbed him in the arm again. "What the fuck? Are you serious?" I asked, my gaze burning a hole into him.

"Yeah. I am. I really don't care if you drink, but you don't just have one or two. You almost drank yourself to death, Lacey."

"Oh my God! I'm so sick and tired of seeing your face. Get a damned life already and stay the hell out of mine!"

"Is there a problem, Lacey?"

I turned to see Jared in the doorway of the dojo.

"Is he bothering you?" he asked.

My focus traveled to Walker and then back at Jared. "Yes, he is," I said and walked into the dojo with Jared.

I peeked over my shoulder. Walker stood alone on the sidewalk. He ran his hand through his hair as his shoulders slumped forward. He looked at me through the window, then turned and walked away. I was too pissed to care.

"Who's he?" Jared asked.

"Him? Uh, well, long story."

"I've got time," he said as he pulled out a chair for me. We sat at the small table together.

I scanned the dojo and realized no one else was around. I wasn't sure if it was a good or bad thing, but at least the door was only a few feet away.

"My ex-fiancé," I mumbled.

"Oh, well that explains it," Jared said.

"Explains what?" I asked and frowned.

"Whatever you said out there . . . he was obviously upset when he left. Not sure what your feelings are for him, but no way in hell is he over you."

"What? Why would you say that?" I asked, searching Jared's face, unsure if he was teasing or being serious.

"Guys know other guys," he said as he rubbed the stubble of facial hair along his jawline.

"Well, I'm finished with him. He blew it."

"Good to know, then."

"What's that supposed to mean?" I asked, my eyebrows knitting together.

"Nothing. Hey, I'm glad you're here, though," he said changing the subject. "Where'd you run off to last night? I wanted to see what happened in class, and how I could help you understand you're safe coming here."

I chewed my lower lip, debating what to tell him. I really had nothing to lose with the truth.

"I freaked out. It just came out of nowhere and I wasn't prepared, I guess."

"Someone hurt you?"

I sucked in a sharp breath and turned my head away.

"Was it that guy? The one you were arguing with?"

"No," I said and shook my head. "Not him."

"Okay, I don't need to know anything else, but it helps me understand how to work with you. I've seen it before."

"Seen what?"

"My mom," Jared said as he leaned back in his chair. "I would see the expression on her face the day after my dad would beat the hell out of her. The gut-wrenching fear. I saw it again when you were in class."

My anger started to slip away as I listened to him. What had it been like for him to see his mom go through that?

"So, you knew?" I asked.

"Well, I can't say I knew for sure, but I suspected."

"What happened to your mom?"

Jared shifted his gaze to the floor. His eyes flashed with sadness. "We buried her six years ago. My dad beat her to death."

"Shit. Shit, Jared . . . I'm so sorry," I said.

"Yeah, us too. My sister and I tried to get her to leave, but she wouldn't. It's like she believed she had to stay or thought she couldn't do any better or something. I don't know exactly. But after she died, I swore to myself I'd help anyone else who had gone through the same thing. I'd train them to turn around and beat the living shit out of their abuser. I'd help them take control and get their life back."

"Oh," I whispered.

"I trained my sister too. Tiffany? You saw her in class last night."

"She's your sister?"

"Yeah, she's the badass I was telling you about. Hell, she can kick *my* ass."

"Really? I mean, she's smaller than I am!"

"Yeah, and quick as shit."

I smiled at the thought of her putting him on the ground.

"If you want, I can work with you."

"I don't know, Jared. I barely know you."

Jared searched my face for a minute. "I get it. You need to see if you can trust me. Would it help if Tiffany worked with us some too? I think you two would get along well."

I turned as the bell on the door tinkled and Tiffany walked in.

"Hey, we were just talking about you," Jared said.

"Yeah? What about?" she asked as she set her gym bag on the floor next to us.

I eyed her as she slipped her shoes off. She was tiny, and I didn't think she stood any taller than five four, and she'd probably only weighed a hundred pounds if she were soaking wet. I cleared her by a few inches. I had to stop my grin at the thought of her kicking Jared's ass.

"Hey, I'm Tiffany," she said, smiling.

"Lacey. Nice to meet you."

"Rough class yesterday?"

My cheeks heated at her question. "Yeah," I mumbled.

"It's okay. You're here now," she said as she pulled her brown hair away from her face and into a ponytail.

"You got a few minutes, T?" Jared asked.

"Sure, whatcha got?"

"Well, if Lacey would like to learn a few things, I thought we could work with her."

"Sure, I'm in. It'd be nice to have another girl around here."

"Lacey? What do you think?" Jared asked.

I glanced between them as my heart pounded against my chest. "Just us?"

"Yeah, is that okay?" he asked.

"I'll protect you from him," Tiffany said and laughed.

"Thanks, T." Jared rolled his eyes.

"Anytime." She grinned and slapped him on the back.

I couldn't help but smile. Now that I saw them side by side, it was obvious they were brother and sister. They shared the same light-brown hair and hazel eyes, but Jared towered over Tiffany by a good foot.

"Okay, I'll give it a try," I said.

Jared and I stood up, and I followed them to the floor.

"What are your, uh, white pajamas called?" I asked Jared.

"It's a gi. If you decide you want to train, we'll order you one," he said.

I nodded.

"Okay, so you're petite, which means you have some advantages against men and larger women. First of all, like T, you're probably really quick. Don't think because you're small, you can't overpower someone. You'll learn to use their weight against them. T, why don't you show her."

I watched as they moved a mat to the middle of the floor. Then Jared stood behind Tiffany and grabbed her from behind, lifting her off the floor. Her body went limp, pulling his forward. The next thing I knew, Jared was flat on his back. My eyes widened in surprise. A crooked grin spread across his face as he got up and approached me.

"What you need are a few quick techniques to throw your opponent off guard long enough for you to run. There's no harm in running, ever."

"Okay. I can run," I said.

"One of the most important things you need to understand is where your power comes from. Throw a punch at me."

I shook my head. "I can't hit you."

"Yeah you can. You won't hurt me."

"Uh, okay," I said, swinging at him. He stopped my fist in midair before I even reached his body.

"First lesson, your power flows from your core, so every move you make comes from there. Not your chest or arms. T, can you show her?"

"Here," Tiffany said as she lightly placed her hand on my lower abdomen.

I flinched and stumbled backward.

"Whoa, you okay?" Tiffany asked as her eyebrow arched upward.

Sucking in a sharp breath, I nodded. No one had touched my stomach since I'd lost the baby. I put my hands on my hips and stared at the floor for a minute. My eyes squeezed shut and then lifted my head.

"Please, show me again," I said softly.

Tiffany approached slowly and placed her hand on my stomach and the other on my lower back.

"Here. All your power is right here."

"Okay," I said. My forehead creased as I tried to understand what she meant.

"You good to keep going?" Jared asked.

I nodded.

"Good. I want you to throw the punch again but in slow motion, and this time, allow your hips to move with you. Like this," he said as he demonstrated.

I stepped toward Jared and attempted the punch a few times. I tried to let my hips move, but I wasn't getting it. Tiffany came back around, placed her hands on my hips, and guided me through the punch.

"That's it," she said.

"See where my hand is?" Jared asked as he tapped his chest. "One good hit here will knock the wind out of someone. It doesn't take much."

He took my hand and placed my fingers on his chest. "Feel it? And on yours." He tapped my sternum lightly. I winced.

"Any type of hit there will get your opponent to back off. Also, you can use the heel of your hand," he said as he showed me his own. "Swing up and hit the underneath tip of the nose. Their eyes will tear up so bad they won't even be able to see you."

I watched my hand and slowly swung up as he guided my arm to the correct part of his nose.

"Good. Let me see it again and T, can you help her with the correct posture?"

For the first time since I'd come back to Arkansas, I wasn't scared of what or who might be lurking around the corner. Jared and Tiffany worked with me for the next forty-five minutes.

The sun began to drift behind the horizon while I walked home. I glanced at the sky and remembered the sunsets in Oregon. Sadness swirled through me as I walked up the sidewalk and noticed the brown grass. It was different here in so many ways.

I jogged up the stairs and opened the door to our apartment. Emma was standing next to the refrigerator, pouring a glass of iced tea. I searched the living room and kitchen, but I didn't see Walker.

"Hey!" Emma said. "You want some tea? I just cooked some dinner and put it in the fridge. I made lasagna if you're hungry."

"Mmm, I love your lasagna. Thanks," I said, opening the fridge door, leaning in and pulling the glass pan out. "Where's Walker?" I asked nonchalantly.

"Gone."

"Like, gone for tonight and he'll be back in the morning?"

"Not sure when he'll be back, actually," Emma replied.

"What?" I rubbed my forehead, trying to understand what she was telling me.

"It's not like you wanted him here. I figured you'd be relieved."

"Yup, I am," I muttered, putting a piece of lasagna on my plate and popped it into the microwave.

"Well, I hope you don't start drinking again just because no one will be around during the day."

I wondered if he'd left because of our argument at the liquor store. *Shit.* I should have been happy he wasn't here, but instead, my heart sank as I realized I might not see him again. What had I done? How in the hell could he just leave without telling me? Mixed emotions flooded through me as the beep of the microwave interrupted my thoughts.

I walked over to the table and sat down. Emma joined me.

"How are you doing?" she asked as she slid her chair in.

I shrugged and then took a small bite of lasagna. "I worked out at the dojo tonight with Jared and his sister, Tiffany," I said. I'd planned on leaving out the part about the argument with Walker. As much as they talked, he'd probably already told her anyway.

"Yeah?"

"It was good. After freaking out the other night. I was pretty scared to go back."

"What do you mean you freaked out?"

"Walker didn't tell you?" I asked with a hint of sarcasm.

"No. What happened? Are you okay?"

"Yeah. I was just in class, and . . . I was standing in the back, and all these huge guys were around me. For a second, I thought I saw Xander and then I panicked."

"Oh gosh, Lacey. I'm so sorry."

"I ran home, and Walker was here. He just helped me calm down is all. No big deal," I said and shrugged my shoulder.

Emma cocked her head at me. I didn't think she was buying the "no big deal" part.

"But you went back today?"

"Yeah. Jared and Tiffany worked with me when no one else was there. It was better that way. I wasn't as scared."

"Maybe they're good for you. I mean, maybe you taking some karate classes will help you feel better. If they're willing to work with you, then it's awesome. I like them already!"

"Jared told me their mom was beaten to death by his dad."

"What? Oh my gosh!"

"He said he recognized my fear. He flat out asked me if I'd been hurt. I didn't give him any details, but I said yes. I can't imagine how horrible it is to see your mom beaten."

"I can," Emma said softly. "Walker saw you bound and beaten. I saw you afterward. Watching you struggle has been horrible for both of us."

"You mean you? Walker has a nasty habit of leaving me."

"Lacey, you can't have it both ways. You can't treat him like crap and then want him here. It's not fair. He still cares about you, but he does have a life outside of our apartment."

"He did say he's working nights."

"There's more to it than his job, but it's not my place to say anything."

"What do you mean? Is it bad? Is he in trouble?" I asked as scenarios flashed through my mind.

"No, nothing bad. I just wasn't aware you still cared."

I sighed and leaned back in my chair. "Honestly, I don't know how I feel. Most days, I'm just trying to survive."

"You can do this. We can do it together. I think Jared and Tiffany will be good for you too. Let everyone in. Please stop shutting us out."

"I'm trying," I said, staring at the table. "I know my moods have been all over the place, but Emma, I love you. You're my family and . . . thank you for everything. Don't give up on me yet," I said. A tear streamed down my cheek as I glanced up at her.

"I'll never give up on you, ever," she said as she patted my hand.

I nodded and attempted a smile.

The phone rang and startled us from our conversation.

"I got it," Emma said as she stood up and walked into the living room to answer it. A frown creased her forehead as she listened to whoever was on the other end. My stomach churned. Something was wrong.

"Lynn, I don't care if you're in Hot Springs again or not, I'm not telling you where Lacey is. You stay away from her and don't call again," Emma said and slammed the phone down. She tilted her head back, stared at the ceiling, and took a deep breath.

"Shit," I said. "Mama's back, isn't she?"

Emma nodded as she returned to the table and sat down. "It's okay. I mean, we knew she'd come back eventually. She obviously doesn't know where you are since she called me and asked."

I stared at the floor, realizing Emma was trying to minimize the fear that already had its cold fingers wrapped around my heart.

"Look at me," Emma said, leaning forward.

My gaze traveled from the floor back up to her face.

"She doesn't know where you are. If she calls again, I'll threaten her with a restraining order. If she shows up, I'll *file* a restraining order. She can't get to you again. Do you understand?"

I nodded as I attempted to swallow the lump in my throat. *Would she ever leave me alone?*

"You stay focused on you. I'll handle your mom," Emma said.

Silence hung in the air as my thoughts drifted back to the day in the hospital when Emma kicked Mama out of my room. And she had just stood up to her again. Maybe Emma was right; maybe she really could take care of Mama for now.

I had to trust Emma—she was all I had left. I squeezed my eyes closed, took a deep breath, and shoved Mama into the darkest corner of my mind.

THE SUN PEERED through my curtains and woke me the next morning. Mid-stretch, I bolted out of bed, flew out of my bedroom, and down the hall. I searched the living room, kitchen, and hall bathroom, but Walker wasn't here. For the first time since they'd found me passed out, I was alone.

My thoughts raced as I grabbed a mug, filled it with the coffee left in the pot, and put it in the microwave. I half expected the door to fly open at any minute and Walker to stroll in. But he didn't.

I got comfortable on the sofa, grabbed the TV remote, flipped through the channels, not finding anything worthy of watching. Only soap operas. I turned the TV off and took a sip of my coffee. The silence was almost eerie.

What in the hell was I going to do? I was so used to having someone around all the time. For a brief moment I mulled over the thought of going to the liquor store, but I wasn't sure they'd even serve me. I figured Walker had screwed that up for good.

It was after eleven—maybe Jared or Tiffany would be at the dojo.

I finished my coffee, showered, and left the apartment thirty minutes later.

I SLIPPED IN AS QUIETLY AS I could and took a seat in the back of the room, watching Jared as he went through moves I hadn't seen yet. He then walked around helping students. Everyone wore different-colored belts, but they were all men. I wondered why more women weren't interested in training.

Thirty minutes later, the class ended and Jared waved at me as he chatted with one of the students. I sat quietly and hoped he didn't mind me being here. It was the best option I had.

He patted the guy on the back and approached me. A huge smile spread across his face as he pulled out a chair and sat down. "I'm surprised to see you here," he said.

"Is it okay if I came to watch?" I asked.

"Anytime. You can come in every day if this is where you're comfortable. I won't even charge you rent," he said and chuckled. "I'm just kidding. I'm between classes. Do you want to go over a few things from last night?"

"That would be great," I said, smiling. I was relieved he didn't mind me here. Little did he know I'd take him up on his offer. The apartment felt too empty. I thought I wanted more time alone, but too much time to think could be a bad thing.

I slipped off my shoes and followed Jared to the wood floor. We reviewed everything from last night, and I threw better punches at him. It was a bit awkward having someone tell me to hit them, but after a few minutes, I realized it was the best way for him to teach and correct me.

"Okay, I'm going to show you the first kata," Jared said as he glanced at the clock. "I think we have enough time before my next class."

"What's a kata?"

"A kata is a series of moves. Think of it as a routine. Every move has a purpose," he said as he pulled on the ends of his belt. "What I mean is one move is a strike and another is a block. I'll go through it all together so you can watch, and then I'll begin taking you through the moves. Sound good?"

I nodded and took a few steps back to give him some space. As he moved, his gi snapped with the strength and precision of his movements. I watched in awe as he fluidly shifted from one position to the next, wondering if he'd be offended if I compared his grace and strength to a ballerina. But I wasn't sure how else to describe it.

He slid his feet back together and bowed.

"Alright, your turn," he said and grinned. "I'll watch you and see what you picked up."

"What?" I asked and scanned the room to make sure he was talking to me. There was no way in hell I could do any of that.

"I'm just teasing," he said and approached me.

"Oh," I said as my cheeks flushed.

"You'll get used to his stupid sense of humor," Tiffany said as she entered the dojo.

I turned and gave her a slight wave.

"No interrupting, please," Jared said and chuckled. "We'll be done in a few minutes, T."

"It's all good. I'm heading upstairs anyway."

She crossed the dojo and ran up the stairs.

"I live up there," Jared said.

"Oh, I didn't realize there was an apartment above us," I said.

"Yeah, it's easier for me since I teach so many classes. Alright, here's your first position," Jared said as he slid his feet into place and then held his arms up for me to see. "Your turn."

I spread my feet apart and brought my arms up.

"I'm going to adjust your arms," he said as he brought his hands up for me to see. He gently took my forearms and moved them into the right placement.

"Here," he said as he tapped my foot with his. "A little wider. In this stance, you'll want your feet to align with the width of your shoulders."

I glanced down and made the change. "Like this?"

"Uh huh," he said as he took a step back. "Good. Feel your feet anchored to the floor. Again, all your power comes from here," he said as he patted his lower belly.

I nodded.

"So, we move from this position to the next one," he said, adopting the second position's stance.

"Like this?" I asked, mimicking him the best I could.

"Close. I'm going to adjust your arms again," he said as he slowly moved toward me.

Jared took me through four more positions before people began to arrive for the next class. I tried to stay focused on him, but the tinkling of the bell kept throwing off my train of thought.

"Good. This kata is called Kihon. It's the first one you learn here."

"Kihon," I repeated and nodded.

"I've got another class, but you're welcome to hang out. We can work some more afterward if you'd like."

"Really?"

"Really," he said as his eyes softened for a second.

"Thanks," I said. I weaved through the students, reached my table, and got comfortable in my seat at the back of the room.

My stomach growled in protest, and I'd realized I hadn't eaten today. My only choices were to go next door to the liquor store and get a snack or go back home and make lunch. I grabbed my keys and realized I'd left my wallet at home.

I opened the door slowly so the bell wouldn't alert everyone I was leaving. It had grown hot during the short time I'd been working with Jared. The dreaded summer heat had finally settled in. We were actually lucky it had waited until June. Most summers, the air-conditioning was on in early May.

I tried not to count the weeks until fall, but I hated summer here, and I would have to reapply deodorant before I walked back to the dojo. I didn't want to throw a punch at Jared and knock him over with my rank body odor.

Entering the front door, I sighed out loud when I saw Walker wasn't sitting on the sofa. Irritated, I rolled my eyes at myself. Emma was right, I couldn't have it both ways. Deep down, I knew my life was better without him. The fact he'd left without saying goodbye proved it.

I rummaged through the fridge and made a sandwich. My stomach growled as I took a bite. Emma was so good about grocery shopping and keeping food in the fridge. I wasn't sure I'd be eating at all if it weren't for her.

Still hungry, I finished my sandwich and grabbed an apple. The loud crunch echoed through the kitchen. Emptiness washed over me, and I stopped mid-chew. Isn't this what I had wanted? For everyone to leave me alone? My chest ached, and tears pooled in my eyes. No matter what I thought I wanted, now that it had happened, it wasn't what I expected it would be.

Walker and Emma had been right, and I shouldn't be alone after all. There was just one problem with the idea—Walker had waltzed right out of my life again.

After I located my backpack and shoved my wallet and keys into it. I grabbed my deodorant, reapplied, and tossed it in too. My eyes scanned the bathroom counter for a hair tie, and then I put my hair up. Next, I rummaged through my dresser drawers and pulled out another T-shirt and a pair of shorts. It wouldn't hurt to have an extra outfit for training.

I glanced around my room to see if I'd missed anything, and then I took a deep breath and left for the dojo again.

13

The afternoon flew by as I watched classes and trained with Jared and Tiffany in between. Jared continued to try to get me to loosen up. He cracked bad jokes and always let me know before he touched me to adjust my arms. He used his foot to move my legs or feet.

I learned a few more positions of the kata. Tiffany showed me another quick strike, as she called it, in case I found myself in trouble. She seemed pretty cool, and she gave Jared shit whenever she could. I found myself thinking about their mom and what they'd been through. Maybe that was the reason they were close. Krissy and I, we'd never be close.

I pushed the thought of Krissy out of my mind almost as quickly as it entered. All it did was bring up memories of Mama, and I just couldn't deal with those right now. I had to focus on something positive, and right now it was all about learning karate.

"Hey, you wanna grab a bite?" Tiffany asked. "I know this little hole in the wall that serves the best Mexican food."

"Yeah? I could use some food." One thing about training and getting out of the apartment was my appetite was returning.

"Awesome, let me change and grab my purse. I'll be right back," she said as she disappeared up the stairs.

Tiffany returned a few minutes later in jean shorts and a V-neck shirt. "Ready?"

"As ready as I'll ever be," I said.

I followed her out of the dojo to a little red Honda. She unlocked my door first and then walked over to the driver's side. The heat almost flattened me while I opened the door. I stepped back and let the hot air out as I looked at the black leather interior.

"Love my car, but during the summer, it just soaks up the heat. I have to start it and turn on the AC for a minute before I can sit down," she said.

She flipped the key in the ignition, and the car came to life. We waited until the cold air began blowing.

"Maybe you should get light-colored towels to put on the seats," I said as we were finally able to sit down.

"So thought about it, but by the time I'm around the towels, I totally forget. You from here?" Tiffany asked.

"Yeah, I grew up here. I was in Oregon for the last year, though. Unfortunately, I had to come back."

"A guy?"

"Huh?"

"I mean did you come back here for a guy?"

"No. The opposite. I left Oregon because of a guy," I said, peering out the window.

"Jared told me you'd been hurt, but he didn't know any details," she said as she turned out onto the road.

"Oh. You two seem really close," I said, trying to redirect her questions.

"He's my best friend."

"It must be nice to have family you like being around."

"You don't? You're not close to your family?"

"You could say that," I replied.

I knew Tiffany was only trying to get to know me better. Her questions were totally normal, but my secrets weren't. But I didn't know how to steer her away from the many topics that made my stomach turn with bad memories.

"I'm not trying to be nosy. Well, I am, but it's with good intentions."

"Did you grow up here?" I asked.

"Nope. We moved here about six years ago from Minnesota."

I remembered Jared mentioning his mom's funeral around that time. I wondered if that's why they moved, but I didn't know her well enough to ask.

"It explains the accent," I said.

"Yeah," Tiffany said and laughed. "I've been trying to get rid of the damned thing, but it just keeps hanging on."

I smiled, remembering George giving me shit about mine. I needed to reach out to him and see how he was doing.

"I got teased about mine while I was in Oregon," I said. "Have you ever been there? It's the most beautiful state I've ever seen."

"No, but I've always wanted to see the Pacific Northwest."

"You should. We're all brown and burnt here, and Oregon is green even in the summer. I went there for college, and the first few days I swear I just wandered around amazed at all the colors and flowers."

"Doesn't it rain there all the time, though?"

"You get used to it."

Silence filled the car as we pulled into the restaurant parking lot.

"Like I said, it doesn't look like much, but the food is fantastic," Tiffany said. "My treat, come on."

We entered the restaurant, which only held about ten picnic tables. Tiffany picked the table in the corner, and I sat down across from her. I grabbed a menu and realized how dim it was back here, even though the sun was shining outside.

"No windows?"

"Just at the front. They have the best burritos, though. I'm going to get one. What do you want?"

"I'll take your word for it. A burrito sounds good," I replied.

"Great, be right back," she said and walked toward the order window. I watched her as she ordered and paid for our meal. She came back to the table with two glasses of water.

"Water okay?"

"Perfect, thank you. You didn't have to pay for my food."

"I know. You can pay for mine next time."

"Sounds good."

"You wanna talk about it?"

"About?" I asked, confused.

"Who hurt you."

I jolted in surprise that she would even ask me. We barely knew each other.

"I . . . uh."

"It'll help."

"I'm not sure it will. It's still very fresh in my mind."

"Learning karate will make a huge difference. It's good you're beginning to train now. It gives you something else to think about when the memories and flashbacks come."

"How do you know?"

"Been there. My dad."

"Jared mentioned him, but only about your mom. He hurt you too?" I asked. My stomach turned at the thought.

"Yeah, all of us."

I bit my lip. "Me too. My mom," I said.

"Makes sense. It usually starts at home and then when you leave, you tend to find someone to take their place. I've stayed out of relationships the last few years. I don't want to make the same mistake."

"It's probably the smartest thing I've had someone tell me."

"We left Minnesota after Mom died and came here. The one thing Jared insisted on was that we train. He swore no one would ever hurt us again."

"He sounds protective."

"It goes both ways. Just like you, we got into training and worked our asses off. We moved up in belts quickly, made friends with other black belts, and began to feel safe again."

"I hope I can do the same."

"Just keep at it."

We were interrupted by our food being brought out. It was only five thirty, but I was starving. I needed to plan my meals better if I was going to continue to train.

"You like it?" Tiffany asked.

"It's so good," I said around a mouthful of food.

Tiffany laughed and took another bite. She acted as hungry as I felt. "Don't let my brother bring you here," she said between bites.

"How come?"

"He orders two of these and farts for days!"

I somehow managed to swallow my bite of food before I choked on it. I giggled.

"Yeah, you do *not* want to be around him afterward," she said. Her contagious laugh echoed through the small restaurant. I couldn't stop giggling. The more she laughed, the more I did too.

I set my burrito down as she continued to make faces and hold her nose. I guess just the thought of his farts was bad enough to make her smell them. She fanned the air in front of her nose and burst into another fit of laughter. I wasn't sure I'd ever look at Jared the same way again.

"Holy shit," I said as I grabbed a napkin and dabbed at my tears. "I haven't laughed this hard in like, ever. Jeez! And thanks for the mental picture. It's your fault if I start giggling while he's training me. I'm not sure how I'm going to get through that one."

"Yeah, me neither," she said, smiling. "He's a great guy. You're in good hands. You'll see for yourself soon enough."

We paused and took a bite of our food. "But," she said around a mouthful. "I did want to mention something."

I frowned as I waited for her to continue. Where was this conversation going?

"He has a savior complex," she said.

"What?"

"He's going to get attached to you. Just be careful."

"I don't understand," I said and wiped my mouth. I wasn't sure I was hungry anymore.

"I'm not trying to be a bitch. I love my brother, and it's why I brought it up. Don't take what I'm saying personally."

"Is there any other way to take it?" I asked with a hint of anger.

"Wait, you're misunderstanding me. Don't get pissed. Let me explain. He couldn't save Mom. So, when someone like you shows up in his life, it's like he tries to fix everything. You're beautiful and fresh out of whatever hell you've gone through. He'll get attached when he shouldn't. He'll want to save you from whatever you're running from."

"I've learned the hard way—no one can save me."

Tiffany held my gaze for a moment. "It just doesn't get any more real than that," she said.

I nodded in response.

"Don't take it the wrong way," Tiffany said. "If anyone is going to get attached to you, no one better than Jared, but be careful and don't send the wrong message."

"Oh! Oh, no," I said and shook my head. "No, I'm not interested in your brother. He's just training me."

"Actually, he's your sensei."

"My what?"

"Your karate instructor is called a sensei."

"Okay. Got it. But back to the other thing. I'm serious. I'm not interested in Jared like that. I'm too screwed up for a relationship. Hell, I can't even see duct tape without—without having a panic attack."

Tiffany stared at me for a moment. "Where's the asshole now?"

"Prison. In Oregon."

"Good." She didn't press the issue further.

"Okay, so I'm officially changing the topic," I said.

"Noted."

"How old are you?" I asked.

"Twenty-two and Jared is twenty-four. You?"

"Almost twenty," I said.

"When's your birthday?"

I frowned as I realized it was only a few months away. "Shit, it's the beginning of July, right?"

"Yeah."

"It's in early September. I guess it's closer than I thought. I'm not working right now, and my sleep schedule is all sorts of screwed up. I'm losing track of the days."

"You wanting something to do?" she asked as she sipped her water.

"What do you mean?"

"A job."

"No. Not yet."

"I have an idea. Let me talk to Jared first, and then if he thinks it'll work, he can speak to you. He owns the dojo, so all the business stuff is up to him. I figure if you're going to hang out there, he might as well put you to good use."

"Alright, but I'm not sure I'm up for anything yet."

Tiffany smiled as she finished off the last of her burrito.

1 4

The next morning, I pushed the door of the dojo open and gave a little wave to Jared. The moment I saw him I had to bite my lip to stop the giggles that were threatening to break free. No burritos for him.

"Hey," Jared said as he approached me. "I hear my sister took you out for dinner last night."

"Yeah, we grabbed a burrito."

"Man, those are the best burritos ever. Just thinking about them makes me want to run over and grab a few."

I couldn't stop my grin.

"She also mentioned you're not working right now."

"Yeah, but I told her I wasn't sure if I was ready to go back yet either."

"Will you hear me out?"

"I guess it can't hurt, but I reserve my right to say no."

"Fair enough," he said as he pulled a chair out for me at the table. "I need someone around here. It's not difficult work, but it might keep you busy, and I need the help. I can't keep up with my classes and all the paperwork too."

"What kind of paperwork?"

"Sign-in sheets for each class, and then I also need to collect dues at the beginning of each month. Can you balance a checkbook?"

"Sure—I mean, I can balance my own. It's not hard to balance it when it only has a few dollars in it, though," I said.

"It's the same thing, just a little more money. I also need the dojo straightened up, vacuumed, and the bathroom cleaned. You're here during most of the classes anyway. It will give you the availability to take roll and then update the master copy for me. How does everything sound?"

"Sure, I guess it can't hurt. It'll give me something to do."

"It will only take you a few hours each day. I have more work to be done, but I can add it to your list as you get comfortable. I also need help teaching the kids' class."

"What? I can't teach a class! I only know a few things."

"Don't panic," Jared said and laughed. "Most of it's just keeping them focused. You can manage a group, hold the kick bag for them, and help them line up. As you learn, you can help more."

"This sounds like a lot right now."

"It might feel like it at first, but once you have a system down, it'll be easy. I'll pay you three hundred a month and train you."

"Really?" I was surprised at the amount. I could pay half the rent again. "Okay," I nodded. "I'll try it out, but if it doesn't work, please just let me know. My top priority is to still be able to come here and train. It's become my go-to place lately."

"I will. If your work sucks, I'll fire you."

"That's harsh."

"You'll be fine, don't worry." A crooked grin spread across his face.

"I hope so," I said.

"Excellent. Then it's settled. The kids' class is Tuesday and Thursday nights at six thirty. Your first one will be tonight. I'll wait a little longer to order your gi. I don't like to order just one since they charge so much for shipping."

"How much is it? I'll need to wait until I have some money anyway."

"Nope, part of the gig."

"Jared, I need to pay for my stuff. Really."

"Consider it a uniform. You ready to train? Afterward, I'll set you up with the paperwork and you can get started, see a schedule of the classes, and get settled in. You can work down here, or I have an office upstairs."

"In your apartment?" I asked as my voice squeaked.

"Yeah. When you're comfortable. For now, we'll keep you down here."

I nodded as my cheeks heated, and I swallowed, pushing my nerves down. Was I ready? I didn't want to humiliate myself, but maybe this was a good place to start.

"YOU'LL NEVER BELIEVE what happened today," I said to Emma.

It was too hot to cook even with the AC on, so we had opted for a chicken salad tonight.

"What?" Emma peered over her glasses at me.

"I got a job!"

"You did? Lacey, that's fantastic!"

"I know, right? I can start paying half the rent again."

"What will you be doing?" she asked as she took a bite of her food.

"Basically, I'm the dojo secretary. I'll handle the bookkeeping, payments, master sheets of students, and I'll clean and help teach the kids' class."

"Teach? Already?"

"I know, it totally freaked me out. Jared said it would just be keeping the kids focused for now. I guess I'll hold the kick bag for them, help them line up, get in groups, just easy stuff. He said the more I learn, the more he'll have me help. I can handle kids, right? I worked in the children's department at Jack's Department Store, so I'm sure I can," I said as my voice trailed off.

"What is it?" Emma asked.

"I'm scared, Emma. What if I have a panic attack in front of the kids or something? What if I screw up the checking account?"

"It sounds like Jared and Tiffany are becoming your friends, and I don't think they'd ask you to do something you couldn't handle. No matter what job someone is about to start, there's always nerves. Shoot, I thought I was going to toss my cookies the first day at the hospital!"

"Really? What'd you do?"

"I tried to stay near a bathroom," Emma said and laughed. "But it's a good idea for you too. If you start feeling icky, go to the bathroom and splash cold water on your face."

"It might work," I said. "And you're right. I'd be nervous no matter where I went."

"Lacey, I'm so proud of you."

"I haven't done anything except go one week without anyone babysitting me. Besides, I figured going to the dojo was a better choice than the liquor store."

"I agree."

"I'm spending so much time there I don't have as many opportunities for everything with Xander to creep up. But it shows up at weird times. Tiffany took me to dinner the other night, and for a split second, the smell of the kitchen grill reminded me of the fire. I didn't say anything . . . I didn't want her to think I was so fragile I couldn't go out in public."

"But you are."

"That's so messed up, though. I went from living two thousand miles away to being confined to four blocks of Hot Springs. Sometimes I look at my life and I have no clue how I got here or how to change it. I just want to feel better. I want just one night without nightmares or a day without flashbacks. Everywhere I go— I think I see him," I whispered.

"He's in jail, hon."

"For how long? I don't have any idea how long Oregon keeps someone for assault, arson, or whatever they charged him with."

"I have no clue. Walker tried to call and see what he was charged with, but they wouldn't tell him over the phone. But today, right now, you're safe, and Xander isn't anywhere around. You're with friends and learning to kick butt. One step at a time."

"You're right," I said, nodded my head, and paused for a minute. "Have you heard from him?"

"Who?" Emma asked.

"Walker."

Emma tried to hide her smile.

"What?" I demanded. "I was just wondering."

"Lacey Anne, you stay focused on getting your own crap together and let Walker take care of himself."

"I'm not trying to take care of him. I just want to know why he left," I said.

Emma wiped her mouth and tossed her napkin on her plate. She sighed and leaned back in her chair. "Do you still love him?" she asked gently.

"What? What the hell kind of question is that? I just wanted to know why he disappeared again," I said, huffing and grabbing our plates off the table. After rinsing them off, I loaded them into the dishwasher. "I have to get back to the dojo. The kids' class starts soon."

"Okay, I'll see you later then. Love ya," Emma chirped as I closed the door behind me.

I walked across the complex, irritated Emma had asked me if I still loved Walker. Where had it even come from? She'd just told me to take things one step at a time, and then she throws that at me?

And what was so difficult about her answering the question? She either knew, or she didn't. Simple. Why did he leave?

I WELCOMED the cold air of the dojo as I walked inside. My backpack slipped off my shoulder and I flung it in the corner, realizing I'd never used the bathroom here. I crossed the wood floor and spotted the restroom, pushing the door open and poking my head around. It seemed pretty average to me, but I figured if I was going to clean it, I needed to know where it was. I hoped I wouldn't have to run in there because of a panic attack, but Emma was right—a backup plan was a good idea.

"I see you found the bathroom," Jared said behind me. I responded with a blood-curdling scream.

"Shit! You can't sneak up on me," I said as the hot tears spilled down my cheeks.

Jared grabbed me and pulled me in for a hug. "I'm so sorry. I didn't mean to scare you. I thought you heard me come into the dojo."

"No," I sniffled.

"Are you okay?" he asked as he released me and rubbed my arms.

"Yeah," I said, drying my tears. "Be right back," I muttered, turning away and walked into the bathroom.

Once the door closed behind me, I crumpled to the floor. I struggled to gain control over my tears, but they had other plans. After a few minutes, they slowed, and I stood up. I turned the cold water on and splashed my cheeks. My eyes were puffy and my face was red. This wasn't how I wanted to start off my first class.

There was a knock on the door. "Hey, you okay?" It was Tiffany. "Jared said he scared you pretty badly. He feels terrible."

I opened the door to let her in. "Hey, I'm coming. I don't want to be the employee who cries on her first day and doesn't show up on time."

"Don't even worry about it. Jared is the easiest boss ever. As long as you're trying and you get half the shit right with the paperwork, he's happy."

"He hugged me."

"He probably wasn't sure what to do since he was the one who made you cry," Tiffany said and let out a small laugh.

"I just thought about what you said . . . that he gets attached."

"I wouldn't worry about the hug. He's just trying to help."

"I'm just not . . . I'm not."

"I get it, and you're smart."

"Thanks," I said, peering into the mirror to see if the redness had lessened. "I'm ready."

"Awesome. The kids are super cute. They'll take your mind off everything else."

"It would be really nice," I muttered and followed her out of the bathroom and onto the dojo floor.

"Attention please," Jared said and clapped his hands together. Fifteen little ones from ages five to ten all peered up at him.

"We have someone new with us today—she'll be helping with your class. When she asks you to do something, you do it, understand?"

The kids nodded with enthusiasm.

"This is Lacey," he said as he pointed at me. "Let's tell her hi."

"Hi, Miss Lacey," they all said together.

I couldn't hide my smile. Tiffany was right. The kids were the cutest things I'd ever seen.

"Awesome," Jared said. "Let's warm up."

I went to the back of the room and warmed up with the kids. Within a few minutes, they were ready to go.

"Everyone line up right here by me," Jared said as he rallied them all together. "Lacey is going to hold the bag for us, and we're going to do a kick punch combo, okay?"

Jared walked to the corner and picked up a dingy white kick bag. He smiled as he approached me with it. "You okay?" he asked, his eyes filled with concern.

"Yeah," I said and attempted a smile. "Sorry I freaked out on you like that," I whispered.

"Nothing to apologize for. I was just feeling bad."

"No need."

Jared nodded and then patted the bag. "Take it and get into a wide stance like this," he said.

I followed his example, and then he handed it to me. "You're going to rest it against your leg and put your arm through the strap on the back. Then lean your upper body into it. This will help you keep your balance when the kids kick. Most of them don't kick hard, but a few of the older ones have a little bit of power, so just stay rooted to the floor. You got it?"

I nodded. I could do this, right?

The first few kids kicked and punched the bag. Their giggles carried through the room as they got back in line.

"I just kicked a girl!"

"Me too! I'd be in big trouble if my mom knew."

"Boys, pay attention," Jared said and glanced at me. His hazel eyes danced as a smile pulled at the corner of his mouth.

The rest of the class went smoothly, and I let out a sigh of relief as I put all the equipment back. Jared introduced me to a few parents, and I waved goodbye to the kids as they slipped their shoes on and bounded out the door with their parents.

"You did great," Jared said.

"They're super cute in their little gis," I replied, smiling.

"I told you this would be good for you."

"Hope so. I just don't want to let you down. You and Tiffany have been so kind to me. I just want to do a good job for you."

"I know. And you will."

"I told you they were adorable little munchkins," Tiffany said as she hopped down the stairs and joined us on the dojo floor.

"Ha! You're barely taller than those little munchkins, T!" Jared said and laughed.

"Yeah?" she asked as she got into a stance. "Need a little ass-kickin', big brother?"

"You wish." Jared settled into a stance himself. "Lacey, you might want to get off the floor," he said as a crooked grin spread across his face.

I hurried onto the carpeted area and sat down to watch. I figured these two were going to cut loose, and I'd never seen any sparring before. So far in training, it was all technique and individual moves, but these two were about to show me what it was all about.

Tiffany stepped toward Jared and delivered a punch to his gut. He grunted as he stepped back and blocked her kick with his arm. His leg moved quickly as he drove a hit to the back of her knee and dropped her to the floor.

"Nice one," she said as she hopped back up.

She ducked his punch and moved in for one of her own, but pulled back at the last second. Jared never saw her leg coming as she swept his out from underneath him. He landed on his back as she grabbed his arm and forced him to roll over on his stomach. She twisted his arm and folded it up on his back.

"Lacey, he can't move. See how I wrapped his arm? He has no power to get up—it doesn't matter what size I am."

My eyes widened. Tiffany laughed and hopped off him.

"I'm going light on you, T," Jared said. "I'm trying to set a good example for Lacey."

"You're so full of shit," she said as Jared popped her in the stomach.

I gasped as she stumbled backward and then smiled at him. "That didn't even hurt," she said.

Jared grabbed her and pulled her in, but in one swift motion, Tiffany swung her body over his back and landed on the other side of him.

"So, you're playing like that, huh?" he said.

"Yup, whatcha gonna do about it?" Tiffany replied.

Jared responded with a wide kick to her side. In another move, he had her pinned on the floor.

"Aww, man!" she yelled. "I didn't even see it coming. Are you getting faster, old man?"

I laughed as they continued sparring and flinging mild insults at each other. My eyes never left them, soaking it all in. I was amazed to see them in action; they were each powerful and strong in their own way.

I wanted that. I wanted to experience the respect and understanding I saw between them. But most of all, I wanted to know that no one had the power to ever hurt me again.

"Whew! That felt good," Tiffany said as they finished and she reached for her face towel.

"What did you think?" Jared asked, all smiles.

"Can I learn all this?" I replied.

"Hell yeah," Tiffany said. "Since you're training one-on-one, you'll learn even faster. You'll be able to handle any situation that comes at you."

"How long? How long until I can defend myself if someone comes after me?" I asked.

"If you work hard and spar with us, I'd say six to nine months," Tiffany said. "You won't be black-belt level, but Jared and I will teach you things we don't show in class. You'll have shortcuts to knock someone out, and as you show you can handle it, you'll eventually even learn how to kill someone."

"Not that we recommend it," Jared said as he narrowed his eyes at Tiffany.

"No, but if it's your life or theirs, then you need to know," she said.

"What she's saying is if the bastard ever comes after you again, you can take him out for good if you have to," Jared said.

I gasped at the thought of killing someone. It's not what I wanted, but I understood what Jared was saying. If Xander showed up and it came down to it, I could end it for good and never hide in fear again.

"Let's do it then," I said as I stood up.

"You got it," Jared said as he and Tiffany grinned at each other.

"I need to clean everything up and then get home," I said.

"You can clean up tonight or come in around ten tomorrow morning. That'll give you an hour before any classes start."

"Are you sure?"

"Yeah, go get some sleep. We have a lot of training to do tomorrow.

Oh, and bring food. You can keep lunch and snacks upstairs in my fridge. I'll show you around up there tomorrow."

"Sounds good," I said. "Thank you both. For everything."

IT WAS nine thirty by the time I got back to the apartment. I was surprised to see Emma still awake.

"Hey," I said as I closed the door behind me.

"Hi! How'd your first kids' class go?" Emma asked as she muted the TV.

"Good—the kids are really sweet, and it's fun to watch them. But the coolest thing was after class."

Emma swiveled her whole body around on the couch to face me, giving me her undivided attention.

"Jared and Tiffany were fighting," I said. "I mean, I think they call it sparring. They're really good. Tiffany is smaller than I am and she *tossed him on the ground*. They said they can teach me how to do that. Do you know what it would mean? No one could kidnap me or—or— hurt me again. I'd know how to take care of myself."

"Will you show me as you learn? I mean, here at home?"

"Well, yeah, I guess it would be okay. I don't really know anything yet."

"But you will. Every night I work at the hospital, I have to walk through a dark parking garage."

"I don't like that," I said and crossed my arms.

"So, you'll do it? You'll teach me some things here on the side?"

"Yeah, but don't tell anyone, okay? I don't know if there's some rule against it or whatever."

"Scout's honor," Emma said, grinning from ear to ear.

16

The next several days passed in a blur. Jared showed me his apartment and the office. Even though I planned on doing most of the work downstairs, I would still need to go upstairs to eat and grab paperwork and files.

Jared definitely had a bachelor pad, but it was surprisingly spotless. Apparently his training carried over into his housekeeping. That was a good thing.

I was exhausted by the end of the week and ready for the weekend. My body hurt from the training. Jared and Tiffany had stepped it up a notch after my commitment. I was okay with that, but after the months of no real physical activity, I felt like an eighteen-wheeler had run over me, backed up, and then run over me again. I hoped the workouts were enough I'd sleep through the night, but tomorrow was the Fourth of July, and someone was always setting off fireworks early.

"Hey, what are you doing for the Fourth?" Tiffany asked after training.

"No plans. I'll probably just sit on the patio and watch the fireworks."

"Hey Jared!" Tiffany yelled up the stairs.

"Yeah?" Jared said as he walked down the steps and into the dojo.

"We should bring Lacey tomorrow night."

Jared stopped for a moment and then smiled. "I think you're right, T."

"What are you talking about?" I asked.

"We're going to a friend's barbecue on the lake. You should come with us."

"Isn't it rude to just invite me?"

"Nah, he lets us bring whoever we want. We've been friends since T and I moved here. He trains here too. He's a black belt."

I nodded as though his description told me who the guy was. "Well, thank you for the invite, but I wouldn't know anyone except the two of you, and I haven't really been very social since I've been back."

"Perfect! This will be a great place to start," Tiffany replied.

"Can I bring Emma? You guys haven't met her yet, and I think she'd enjoy it. I'd be more comfortable too." Emma going with me also meant I'd stay out of the alcohol.

"Yeah, we have room in the car, right T?"

"Yup, bring her."

"I'll talk to her tonight and let you know tomorrow. Is that okay?"

"Sweeeeeet!" Tiffany said and grinned. "We have so much fun there. You'll even get to see Jared drunk," she said and laughed.

"I don't get drunk," Jared retorted.

"He does," Tiffany said. "He rarely drinks, but he does at Glen's parties. He's pretty hilarious most of the time."

"A happy drunk?" I asked and cocked my head.

"That's right," he said and winked at me.

I couldn't believe I felt comfortable enough making a joke about the day I met him. I didn't remember much of it, but I did remember him commenting about me being a happy drunk.

"Okay, I'm out of here," I said. "See you guys tomorrow."

"Night," they replied.

THE LIVING ROOM lamp was on when I got home. Emma was curled up on the sofa with a box of Kleenex.

"Hey, are you okay?" I asked, dumping my backpack by the front door.

"Yeah. I'm fine. It's this stupid movie," she said and sniffed.

"What movie is it? Is it really sad?"

"No, it's just a Disney movie. *The Little Mermaid.*"

"Emma, you're crying at a Disney movie? Are you sure there's nothing else wrong?"

"I don't know. I'm just having one of those days. I don't want to bother you with it, though. I'll be fine."

"No, you can't do that. I'll just worry."

"Are you sure?" Emma asked and sniffled.

"Yeah. What's going on?" I sat next to her on the couch.

"It's just been a crappy day. When I got to work, I locked my keys in the car and had to pay someone to come out and get them for me. Then I forgot my lunch, so I was stuck grabbing a candy bar and bag of chips from the vending machine. It's just been one stupid thing after another. But, I guess, honestly, I've been worried sick about you since you've been home. I think it's finally just hit me, ya know? I've had to stay strong for you, but this is the hardest thing I've ever been through. Now, at least over the last few weeks, you seem to be doing a little better, and I just fell apart. I sometimes see a little glimmer of my friend again." She hiccupped through her tears.

"Emma, I'm so sorry," I whispered.

"It's just been really hard on this side of things, too."

"I really don't know how I'd feel if it had been you. Devastated, most likely."

"I'll be okay. The better you get and the more you heal, the better I'll be too."

"Alright, but don't keep everything all bottled up inside. It's not fair to you. You have to talk to me, or at least to someone."

"I don't want to put more on you, Lacey. That's not right."

"Well, I'm handling this conversation just fine, so it's a start." I leaned over and hugged Emma. "We'll get there, right?"

Emma nodded as she dabbed the Kleenex on her cheeks.

"I have interesting news," I said.

"Yeah? I could use something interesting," Emma said.

"Jared and Tiffany invited us to a barbecue on the lake tomorrow for the Fourth."

"Oh man, it sounds like so much fun, but I have to work."

I groaned and flopped backward into the couch. "Call in sick," I said.

"I can't. Especially since I'm so new. I need to make sure I show up for all my shifts."

"Dammit."

"You should go, though," she said.

"Emma," I said and shook my head. "I don't think I can deal with a party. I thought if you were with me I'd be okay, but I haven't spent much time with Jared and Tiffany outside the dojo. Tiffany said Jared will get drunk, and . . . I don't know. Just thinking about it totally stresses me out."

"If you trust Tiffany and Jared to train you, you should trust them to go to a barbecue. I think it would be really good for you. Just go for a few hours, and then if you're feeling out of place or really uncomfortable, call Daddy to pick you up."

"Really?" I asked and scrunched up my nose. "I'm not sure I'd feel any better calling your dad."

"Please, it's not like they're going to be doing much tomorrow. And he'd probably really like to see you. Call him and take him out for ice cream or something."

I pondered the idea for a moment. "You're right. I haven't seen your dad in a while. It might be fun. Will you ask him if he's okay with it?"

"Sure, I'll call him now."

I bit my lip as she picked up the receiver and dialed her parents' phone number.

"Hi, Daddy," she said. "Lacey's been invited to a barbecue tomorrow night, and I was wondering, if she starts feeling uncomfortable, do you think you might be willing to pick her up and bring her home?"

Emma paused and then covered the mouthpiece. "I told you he'd be all right with it," she whispered.

I smiled. "Tell him thank you."

"Lacey says thank you," Emma said into the phone. "She thinks she'll be okay, but we wanted to give her a backup plan. This is her first social outing since she's been back. You're the best. Tell Mom hi. Love you."

Emma hung up the phone and smiled. "You're going to have a good time. I know it."

"I hope so," I said as a line of worry creased my forehead.

17

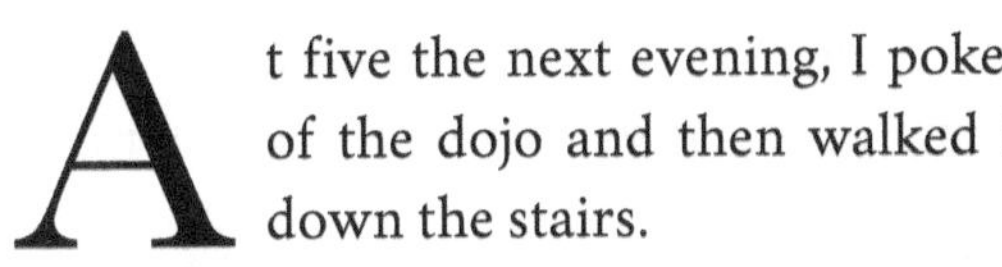

At five the next evening, I poked my head through the door of the dojo and then walked in. I heard someone coming down the stairs.

"T's coming. She's always late," Jared said as he pulled a T-shirt over his head. "Glad you're coming with us."

I bit my lip in order not to gawk. I'd never seen Jared out of his gi, much less without a shirt. His stomach muscles rippled right into his button-fly Levi's. I tried not to stare as he pulled the shirt down, but he filled out every inch of it. That gi didn't do a damned thing for him.

I flushed as I busied myself with something in my backpack. I'd never considered Jared anything other than a friend, and I wanted to keep it that way. But apparently my body wanted something different.

The thought left as soon as it appeared. I hadn't had sex since Xander and losing the baby. The realization was enough to rein in my hormones almost instantly.

Tiffany came downstairs and joined us, and Jared locked the dojo as we left. Tiffany unlocked the car doors, and loaded the bag of food while Jared got in the backseat. Thank God it had been overcast all day so the heat of the car wasn't as stifling as usual.

I slid into the passenger seat and tried to calm my nerves. I wasn't sure how I was going to deal with a lot of strangers at the barbecue.

"Where exactly are we going?" I asked.

"Just off Lake Ouachita," Tiffany said. "It's not far. You'll know the area since you grew up here."

I adjusted my sunglasses as I stared out the window. We had about four more hours before it got dark. I took a deep breath and reminded myself I was with friends. I'd spent almost all my waking hours at the dojo, either working or training. I'd started trusting Tiffany and Jared more. There seemed to be a mutual respect developing among the regulars. I saw it in the students, too. Part of my drive to train was to feel like part of the group. I wanted to belong somewhere, to have friends and a life that was good for me.

Twenty minutes later, we pulled up to a ranch house with a red-and-white brick exterior. I helped grab the food we'd brought and followed them up the sidewalk to the front door. Jared rang the doorbell. I could hear music thumping inside as we waited for someone to answer.

The door flung open as a tall, dark-haired guy answered.

"Jared!"

"Nick!"

I stepped back as the two hugged and smacked each other on the back. Nick held the door and ushered us inside.

I scanned the living room as I followed everyone inside. The large brick fireplace gave a cozy feel, or maybe it was the calico cat curled up in the recliner.

"Nick, this is Lacey," Jared said. "And you already know Tiffany."

"Come here, you!" Nick said as he reached down and wrapped Tiffany in a big hug. She squealed as he lifted her off her feet.

"Lacey, wow. It's truly my pleasure," Nick said as his face lit up.

"Off-limits there, bro," Jared said and patted him on the back. Nick rolled his eyes, punched Jared in the shoulder, and laughed.

"How the hell are ya?" Tiffany asked Nick. "It's been months. How long are you in town for?"

"Yeah, man. I had no idea you were going to be here," Jared said.

"Yup, I'm on summer break from college," Nick replied.

"You still at UCA?" Jared asked.

"One more year left to go."

I listened as I stood next to Jared, hoping I wouldn't feel this awkward the entire night.

"Y'all come on in and get comfortable," Nick said. "I'll take the food from you, T."

"I think it's safer if I take it to the kitchen," Tiffany replied. "You'll finish all the bags of chips before we even get there."

"Ha! Some things never change," Nick said.

Tiffany led the way to the kitchen and Nick followed. Jared waited for a moment and then turned toward me.

"Ignore him. Nick's harmless, I promise."

I nodded.

"And I didn't mean you're mine—I just didn't want Nick to come on to you. So, I hope it didn't upset you. It's just our way of talking. He's a huge flirt, too. I didn't want you to feel uncomfortable is all."

"I appreciate it."

Jared reached out and patted my arm. "You ready?"

"Yeah," I said. I took a breath and turned on the best smile I had.

Jared took me through the kitchen and out the sliding-glass door to the back. There were at least twenty people on the back deck, and the grill was in full use. I took a deep breath and smelled the hamburgers and hot dogs. I noticed the path down to the lake and more people on the dock.

Jared waved at a short guy with a Dallas Cowboys baseball cap on.

"Jared!" the guy said as he walked over. His red hair peeked out from underneath the edges of his hat. "Glad you made it, man!"

"Thanks for having us," Jared said. "I wanted to introduce you to Lacey. Lacey, this is Glen. This is his house and party."

"Thank you for having me," I said, smiling. "And nice hat."

"Are you a Cowboys fan?"

"I'm just learning the game, but I like what I see so far," I replied.

"Well, welcome!" Glen said. "Help yourselves to food and drinks—speaking of which, I'm gonna go check on the keg."

"Okay, we'll catch you in a bit," Jared replied and then turned to face me. "You want a soda?"

"Yeah, that'd be great."

"Coke or Dr Pepper?"

"Coke." Dr Pepper would just make me miss George.

"Hungry?"

"Starving," I replied.

Jared and I made hamburgers and grabbed some chips. We joined several others at a picnic table. He introduced me to everyone, and I waved as I sat down. I was glad Jared was sitting with me since everyone else already knew each other.

Tiffany was on the deck chatting with some gorgeous guy. I remembered her saying she wasn't interested in dating anyone, but I wondered if she had the occasional hookup. Whoever the guy was, they were really flirting.

"It's her ex," Jared said in a low voice.

"Oh," I said and frowned. "She told me she wasn't interested in dating for a while."

"He's part of the reason why," Jared replied. "They broke up a little over two years ago."

"That makes more sense. Did he break her heart?" I asked, glancing over at them.

"Actually, she broke his. She just decided to break things off out of nowhere. She said she didn't want to be in a relationship anymore."

"You didn't find it odd? I mean, she just woke up one day and said it was over?"

"She's funny like that. He's a really good guy, too. I suspect she was worried things were getting too serious."

"How long did they date?"

"Three years."

"Wow. I've never dated anyone that long."

"Not even this last guy? The one that hurt you?"

My eyes widened, and I reached for my soda. "No one," I replied.

Jared nodded and took another bite of his burger, washing it down with a swallow of beer.

"So you're not a big drinker?" I asked, eyeing his beer.

"Nah, not after my dad. Once or twice a year I'll get drunk and just have a good time, but otherwise I don't touch the stuff. T offered to drive tonight so I could relax and not worry about it."

We finished eating, and I stuck close to Jared as he introduced me to more people. I'd lost track of Tiffany and wondered if she and that guy had slipped away for some privacy.

The sun began to set, and the music grew louder. I didn't know how many beers Jared had had, but he was definitely tipsy. But, true to his word, he continued to make sure I was with him as he talked to all his friends. I had to admit it was nice to see this other side of him. He was always in the dojo when I was around.

A few people gathered and began dancing in the middle of the deck as Sinéad O'Connor's "Nothing Compares 2 U" played.

Jared bowed toward me and grinned. "Dance?"

"I . . . uh," I stuttered.

"I won't take no for an answer," he said as he took my hand and led me to join the other couples in the center of the deck.

He slipped his arms around my waist and pulled me toward him, leaving a small amount of space between our bodies. I placed my hands on his shoulders and tried to relax. I'd been this close to Jared every day while we trained, but this was different. We weren't in the dojo.

"I haven't danced in a long time," he said in my ear.

"That makes two of us," I replied.

The smell of beer tickled my nose as he talked. He was definitely loosening up and feeling more relaxed.

"You having fun?" he asked.

"Yeah, it's been nice to get out of the apartment and the dojo. Those are the only places I've really been since I got back.

"When did you come back?" he asked. He took one of my hands in his as he guided us along the edge of the makeshift dance floor. His dancing was as smooth as his karate style. I tried to relax, but this was the closest anyone had been to me since Xander. Panic swirled in the pit of my stomach.

"May," I replied.

"Do you want to go back to Oregon?"

"If the circumstances were right I'd want to go back. I fell in love with it," I said and attempted a smile.

The music stopped, and Jared released my waist. I let out a small sigh of relief as we separated.

"Let's grab a beer, and I'll take you down to the dock," he said. "They'll start the fireworks in a few minutes, and it's the best place to watch them."

"Okay," I said.

Jared grabbed another beer and a Coke for me. We walked down the pathway, reached the dock, and sat on the edge. I slipped off my shoes and socks and dangled my feet in the water.

"Is it warm?" he asked, his hazel eyes dancing in the moonlight.

"Yeah, nothing like a warm lake to cool you off, huh?" I asked and wrinkled my nose.

"How are you doing with training? Are you getting more comfortable?"

This was the Jared I was used to.

"I am. In fact, I don't think you need to tell me when you're going to touch me anymore," I said. "I know you're not going to hurt me."

"Awesome. That's progress."

"It is," I said and nodded.

The darkness had settled in, and the first of the fireworks shot out over the lake. For the next half hour, Jared and I watched the show and sat next to each other in silence. The sky lit up with one spectacular display after another. I'd forgotten how vibrant the colors were over the water.

Everyone cheered afterward and then Jared and I were left alone on the dock.

"How ya feeling?" I nodded toward his beer. I turned to face him.

A warm smile spread across his face as he looked at me. "Good. Real good," he said and laughed. "I'm usually a lot more fun when I'm drinking, but I've just been super mellow tonight."

"It's not a bad thing. I think you're allowed to relax."

"Yeah, it's probably good for me. I get so busy teaching and training I forget to take any downtime."

I paused for a moment. "Can I ask you something? If it's off-limits, just tell me."

"Okay, ask away," he said as he took another drink.

"What happened with your mom?"

Jared hesitated and frowned.

"I'm sorry," I said. "I shouldn't have asked."

"No, it's fine. Don't apologize. It's not a pretty story, though. Are you sure you want to hear it?"

"For some stupid reason, I'm hoping it helps me."

He stared at the water for a moment and sighed. "Dad had a drinking problem. At first, he'd smack Mom around when they'd argue about money. It got worse over the years. Sometimes they didn't fight at all, and he'd just come home and hit her. I tried to intervene, but I was too little. When I was thirteen, he started smacking T. That shit didn't work for me, and I'd pull him off her. He was still stronger than me, but I could take a beating better than T could. She'd run upstairs and hide under my bed until the fight was over, and come out after everything settled down. She tried really hard to help and would bring me ice for my black eye or whatever other bruise he'd given me."

He took another drink from his beer as I continued to listen.

"The time came for me to leave for college. I actually stayed close and came home on the weekends. I was working out on a regular basis and had gotten a lot stronger. When the fights started, I'd antagonize him so he wouldn't go after Mom or T. Hell, I felt more like a club bouncer than a son. But you gotta protect your family, ya know?" He glanced at me.

I nodded.

"T graduated high school and left for college, which meant I didn't need to come home every weekend. I'd begged Mom to leave him, but she never would. I don't know why. I think it was all she knew, and back then when you got married, you just didn't get a divorce . . . no matter what. Anyway, I called one week like I always did, and she begged me to come home for the weekend. I said yes. I hadn't seen her in about a month, even though we talked on the phone all the time. It wasn't that I didn't want to see her—I did. I didn't want to see *him*. She was a great mom, she just wasn't strong enough to leave him.

"I drove home Friday night and pulled into the driveway. As soon as I opened my car door, I could hear the yelling from inside the house. I barged into the front door, and the son of a bitch had a hold of her shirt and was pounding her face with his other fist. I ran to her, whirled him around, and knocked the bastard smooth out. But Mom's face . . ."

His voice dropped to a whisper. "Jesus, she was so bloody. Her entire face was busted, and her eye was swelling shut. I—"

"Jared, it's okay," I said. "I'm so sorry. I had no idea," I whispered and lightly touched his knee.

He grabbed my hand as he buried his face in the crook of his arm. A thick silence hung in the air between us. I felt like shit asking him to talk about it.

"She died right there in my arms," he choked out.

I gasped, pulling him toward me and wrapping my arms around him. He laid his head on my shoulder and slid his arm around my waist. I didn't say anything else.

For the first time, I had a small inkling of what Emma and Walker had felt while going through everything with me. Helpless. I couldn't do anything for Jared except hug him. There were no magic words to take away his pain. I closed my eyes and tried to calm the ache in my chest.

Jared finally sat up, but he didn't pull away.

His fingers lightly traced my cheek as he tilted my chin up toward him and his lips gently met mine. My body went rigid under his touch, and I pulled away.

"Jared," I whispered.

"Sorry, that was unexpected," he said and cleared his throat. The crickets sang in the distance as I struggled with something to say.

"Just forget it happened," he said. "It's the beer."

I bit my lip. Had he meant to kiss me, or was it the mix of alcohol and the emotional moment? My stomach sank. I didn't want anything to get in the way of our friendship.

"I shouldn't have asked about your mom," I said, dipping my toes back in the water.

"Well, I didn't have to tell you, either. I—I see her in you in so many ways. I want better for you, Lacey. I don't want you to live in fear or end up like her. I'd never forgive myself."

"I'll be okay. You and Tiffany . . . you guys mean a lot to me. I mean, shit. I'm a social butterfly tonight," I said and laughed. "You got me out of my apartment and around other human beings. Ask Emma. That's no easy feat these days."

I took a deep breath. I sounded more sure of myself than I felt, but I needed to change the subject for Jared's sake.

Jared smiled as he tilted his beer up and drained it.

"What are you two doing down here?"

My head snapped up to see who was coming down the pathway.

"Hey, T," Jared said.

"What's up? You guys just hanging out?"

"Just talking," I said. I didn't want Tiffany to know about the kiss, and I certainly wasn't going to tell her about our conversation. If Jared wanted to say something to her, he could.

"You guys ready to go?" she asked.

"What time is it?" Jared replied.

"Almost midnight."

"Really?" I said, standing up. "That was fast. It doesn't seem like we've been here long."

"It's all about having fun," she said, grinning.

I wanted to ask her about her ex, but I figured I'd asked enough questions for the night.

We said goodbye to everyone and headed home. Before I realized it, Jared had fallen asleep in the backseat and Tiffany was pulling into my apartment complex.

"Thanks," I said. "I'll see you guys in the morning."

Tiffany reached across the seat and gave me a hug.

"Hey," she said as I stepped out of the car. "Is he doing okay?"

"Yeah. He's good."

1 8

I woke up Saturday morning to the sound of voices on TV. Rubbing my eyes, I tried to clear them, but the smoke from the fireworks last night had dried them out. I enjoyed the Fourth of July, but it always smelled bad, and the smoke just hung in the air.

Thoughts of Jared's kiss lingered while I took a shower. His lips were so soft. But it had happened so quickly—I almost didn't even realize he'd kissed me until it was over. I cared about him, but to what extent I wasn't sure. At this point, I was just trying to pick up the pieces of my life and put them together again. I did want him in my life, but for now he was my friend, boss, and sensei. If he hadn't been drinking, I doubt he would've kissed me. And his mom. I mentally kicked myself. I should never have asked him about it.

The hot water streamed down my body, and I closed my eyes. I couldn't imagine having someone you love die in your arms. I wondered if Walker had experienced the same kind of fear when he found me—horror and anguish mixed into one ball of emotion.

Turning the water off, I grabbed my towel, and got dressed. I pushed the thoughts out of my head as I opened my bedroom door.

"You know you're welcome here anytime," Emma said.

Curious, I continued down the hall. Apparently the voices hadn't been on TV after all. I was thankful I'd showered and put on a bra.

"Make yourself comfortable," Emma continued. "If you're still here when I get home, well, I'll see ya then." She laughed.

"Who—" I asked as I stepped into the living room. "Holy shit. Are you for real?" My eyes widened in shock as I stared at Walker.

"Lacey," Emma chided me. "Be nice. I have to go to work, so I'll see ya later," she said as she opened the front door. "I mean it. Be nice," she said again as she closed the door behind her.

"You can't just show up like this," I said and walked into the kitchen to grab some coffee.

"I wanted to see how you're doing," Walker said. "You look good." He shoved his hands into his front pockets as he stood in the living room.

I blushed as I took a sip of my drink.

"So, what the hell?" I asked, leaning against the kitchen counter. "You have a nasty habit of just leaving. At least this time you didn't show up with an ex-girlfriend on your arm," I said and smirked.

He flinched. "I deserve that. Something came up, and I had to go. You were so pissed at me I didn't think you cared. I was taking a chance of you screaming at me even coming over here this morning, but I needed to see you. I wanted to know how you were doing."

"You were gone for weeks. Emma didn't even know where you were. You practically lived here, Walker. You don't just leave like that."

"Emma knew where I was. We were in touch."

My eyes widened and then narrowed as I glared at him. "What do you mean Emma knew?"

"She knew where I was."

"Then why wouldn't she tell me?" I put my hand on my hip.

"I asked her not to," Walker said. He ran his hand through his hair. It had grown over the last few weeks.

He sat down on the sofa and leaned back. "I'm sorry. You were dealing with enough already, and I didn't want you worried about it."

"Well, will you tell me now?" I asked, dropping my hand from my hip.

Walker nodded as I set my cup on the coffee table and sat on the opposite corner of the sofa. I turned to face him and grabbed the dark-brown corner pillow and put it in my lap. This had better be good.

"I went to Missouri."

"Missouri . . . wait, Garrett?" I asked, sitting up straight. "Is he okay?"

"How'd you know he was in Missouri?"

"He never told you?" I asked, surprised Garrett hadn't said anything to Walker about seeing me at Susan's funeral.

"Told me what?"

"I'll explain later. Is he okay?" I asked impatiently. "That's where you were, right?"

"Yeah. I visited for a couple weeks. He wants to come back to Arkansas, and now that he's fifteen, the judge will take it into consideration. I'm almost twenty-two and I can support us, so I filed for custody. I was working with an attorney, completing papers, and spending time with him. He said to tell you hi."

"He did?" Tears gathered in my eyes.

"He misses you," Walker said.

"Oh God. I miss him too. Fifteen? How? Like, how did that even happen?" I asked and laughed through my tears. "Wait, Walker, you didn't tell him what happened to me, did you? Please tell me you didn't," I pleaded.

"No, not everything. He knows you went to Oregon and it didn't work out. I just said you'd been in an accident, a house fire, but nothing else. He wanted to come home right then, but he obviously couldn't."

"Do you think you can bring him home?" I asked, clutching the pillow to my chest.

"I'm going to do everything in my power," he said and paused. "I didn't just leave you again, Lace."

"But it seemed like you did! I mean, you were here every day for, I don't know, weeks! You can't just keep waltzing in and out of my life. It's not okay."

"Honestly, I didn't think you cared. Shit, you told me every day what a pain in your ass I was. I figured you'd be happy when I left."

"Yeah, but I thought you left because I screamed at you outside the liquor store," I murmured. "I was so pissed at you."

"Yeah you were pretty mad, but I'd do it again. I've been in the military for a while now. Yelling doesn't faze me anymore."

"That's why you could just ignore me when you were watching TV?"

"Pretty much. The military isn't for sensitive people, that's for damn sure. You either toughen up or they ship your ass home."

"I hadn't thought about it."

"You had enough to deal with. And this is our first real conversation since I stopped by to tell you Xander was in prison, and that one only lasted for a few minutes."

I cringed at the memory. He was right, though. I'd been so angry after he saved me I never bothered asking him about the last two years.

"I don't want to talk about anything in Oregon," I snapped.

"I'm sorry. It's just hard for me to know what to say to you anymore."

"Might help if you stuck around for a change, huh?"

Walker rubbed his face and sighed. "Is there any coffee left? I had a long drive from Missouri last night."

"Help yourself," I said. I picked mine up off the table and took another sip.

Walker went to the kitchen and pulled out the empty pot.

"There's none left, do you care if I make more?"

I stood up and joined him in the kitchen, grabbing the can of Folgers from the cabinet. "Not even sure why you bothered asking. You never did when you were here before."

"Lace, I know you're pissed at me."

"I've been pissed at you for two years. You have no idea, do you?" I asked and shook my head.

Anger bubbled up inside me at the thought of him showing up at the mall with Brittany. He'd never bothered to find out why I hadn't visited him in Texas or what had happened. He just took James and Brittany's word for it. The kitchen suddenly closed in on me. I squeezed past him and took a step toward the living room.

"What happened to us, Lace?" he asked softly.

I stopped mid-step and whirled on my heel. Coffee sloshed out of my mug and onto the beige carpet.

"What happened to us?" I asked, my voice rising an octave. "What happened? You. Married. Brittany! That's what happened. You and me? You ruined us," I yelled.

"I know!" he said as he set the coffee can down on the counter harder than he should have.

"No! You obviously have no fucking clue if you're still asking me what happened to us," I spat. My cheeks burned bright red. Before I realized it, I had hurled my coffee mug straight at his head.

"Shit! Lacey, stop!"

"No, I won't stop," I said, grabbing a plastic cup off the kitchen table. I threw it at him and it bounced off his chest. I reached for the glass next and hurled it at him. He ducked as it shattered against the kitchen cabinet.

"Lacey, dammit! Stop!" he yelled as he brought his arms up to protect his head.

"What happened? I'll fucking tell you!" I screamed, grabbing another glass from the table, ready to throw it at him.

"He killed himself right in front of me, Lacey!"

I held the last glass in my hand, ready to throw. My chest heaved as my brain tried to understand what he'd just said.

"What?" I asked, my voice raspy from yelling. "What are you talking about?"

Walker peered through his arms and then slowly lowered them.

"Two days before you were going to come down to visit, one of the guys I was in boot camp with . . . he fucking shot himself in front of me. He blew his brains out, and I ended up wearing them." The color drained from his face as the words left his mouth.

"Holy shit," I whispered, setting the glass down. "Oh my God." I shook my head as I began to grasp what had happened.

"I was completely fucked up, so when you didn't show, I . . . James said you'd kissed him, and I couldn't think straight. And Mom . . . my heart broke. Anything I had left inside me after Jeffrey committed suicide broke when I saw her. I screwed everything up by leaving. I wasted the last few months I had with Mom, you left me, and Brittany was just there at the right time." His shoulders sagged with the weight of his words.

"I never kissed James," I said, still standing motionless. "Walker, I never kissed him. He kissed *me*, right after you proposed."

"Yeah, I know," he said and sighed. "I overheard Brittany and him laughing about it later. I'm so sorry."

Walker glanced down at the floor covered with broken glass, and then his gaze returned to my face. "I'd like to come out of the kitchen without you throwing anything else at me."

Dazed, I sank to the edge of the carpeted floor as I stared at nothing in particular.

"Can I?" he asked.

I nodded while he sat down next to me, and I turned to look at him. Pain flickered across his face as our eyes met.

"I'm trying to piece it all together," I said. "I—I don't know what to say. I had no idea what had happened to you."

"I lost my shit after the suicide," Walker said. "They'd talked to us about combat, but you never think someone you know would shoot himself on purpose."

"What happened?" I asked. My gaze grew more intense as he continued.

"The first day of boot camp Jeffrey and I started chatting. Come to find out I went to school with his younger brother. Everything was so different, and we had no clue of what to expect while we were there. It was nice to connect with someone from back home. We became instant friends. One day we were on the range during M16 training. Jeffrey was standing next to me. I was focused on my own weapon and wasn't paying attention to what was going on. Apparently, he turned the gun on himself and pulled the trigger. The next thing I know, I'm looking at a hole in the back of his head with his blood all over my face and clothes. I just stood there. The staff and the tech sergeant came running toward him. I don't even remember what happened afterward. It's all a blur."

He sighed as he ran his hands over his face.

"I was on my way," I said, my voice thick with emotion.

"You were?"

"I was about to leave my house and meet your mom and Garrett. Mama had found out we were serious and . . . she drugged me."

"What the hell?" Walker asked as his mouth dropped open.

I nodded. "She drugged my food," I said, staring at the floor. "She cooked dinner and said I should eat before the trip. I didn't think anything of it. But before I could even finish my food, it hit me. I fell out of my chair and collapsed on the floor like a rock. She kept me drugged up for days in her bedroom. I'm not even sure how I had the clarity of mind to figure it out, but I finally stopped drinking the water she was bringing me. I was a wreck when I realized what she'd done, and I'd missed the trip to see you."

"My God, Lacey. No one told me."

"No one knew except Emma, and I swore her to secrecy. But for the life of me, I couldn't understand why you showed up with Brittany and never asked me what happened. You just accused me of cheating on you. I never cheated on you, ever. I loved you. You were my everything. My heart fucking broke," I said as the tears spilled down my cheeks. I wiped them away and looked up at him. His blue eyes glistened as he held my gaze. "I never knew about Jeffrey, but it explains why you were so different, so angry. The Walker I knew would've come searching for me. You wouldn't have let me go so easy."

"I'm so sorry," he whispered as he reached for my hand. This time, I let him take it. "I never stopped loving you, Lace. It took me a while to come out of the brain fog from Jeffrey and then losing Mom. I was so pissed at myself for leaving. It was my fault I lost you. I take full responsibility."

"Maybe not," I said, rubbing my thumb over the back of his hand. "I don't know anyone who could go through what you did and not make some shitty decisions."

Walker tilted my chin up toward him. "What are you saying?"

"I'm saying I understand, and I don't—"

"Wait. Please be very careful with what you say next," Walker said, interrupting me. "I'm still so in love with you I can't fucking see straight. Don't give me hope and then take it away. I don't think I could deal with it."

My eyes searched his face, and I nodded. I understood what he was saying. "I'm not ready. I need to heal and be able to stand on my own two feet, Walker. While I'm such a mess, I don't have anything to offer you or anyone else anyway. But I forgive you. I forgive you for letting me go, and I forgive you for marrying Brittany. You went through hell and back, and I don't think I would've done much better. Hell, I didn't." I sighed and wiped the tears away again. "I ran from Mama and right into the arms of a monster who tried to kill me," I hiccupped.

Walker reached around me and pulled me into his lap. I wrapped my arms around his neck as the tears flowed.

"I'm so sorry I wasn't there," he said as he threaded his fingers through my hair and kissed the top of my head. "It's why I couldn't leave you again. I knew I'd screwed up and lost you the first time. It didn't matter what you said or how rude you were after the fire. I swore I'd do everything in my power to make it right. You wouldn't have been there if . . ." his voice trailed off as his arms tightened around me. "If I'd never left you in the first place."

We sat in silence for a while. My tears slowed, and Walker's breathing became normal again. My heart ached about Jeffrey and Susan. I squeezed my eyes shut as the tears threatened to come back. I lifted my head off his shoulder and looked up at him.

"I was at the funeral, hiding in the back," I said and attempted a smile. "I had to say goodbye to Susan and tell her I'd tried to show up for the trip. The thought of her thinking I hadn't shown had torn me up. Dammit," I said as the tears trickled down my cheek again.

"I never saw you."

"I saw you. You were so different, and Brittany was hanging all over you. You were just . . . cold. I didn't understand at the time, but I do now. You were in shock."

Walker nodded.

"Anyway, I waited until everyone had left and then I snuck up to see her before they closed the casket. Garrett caught me. I thought he was going to tell you, but he just wanted to see me. We hurried to my car so no one would catch us. He told me he had to move to Missouri. Then he asked me why I didn't show up. I couldn't tell him my crazy mother drugged me, so I just said I'd been on my way and something had happened with Mama. He believed me, so I left it alone. He didn't need to know the details."

"You did the right thing," he said as he tucked a piece of stray hair behind my ear. "You still have the most beautiful green eyes I've ever seen."

I smiled at him and wiped away my tears.

"I'm glad you were able to say bye to Mom," he continued. "She loved you, Lace. She was so pissed at me about Brittany. She did everything she could to get me to see reason, but she didn't have a lot of strength left."

"I loved her too," I whispered. "You guys were my family."

"I'm sorry I took that away from you," he said as he leaned his forehead against mine.

I squeezed his hand. "At least I understand what happened now. We were both in the middle of hell, doing the best we could."

"I just want you to be okay. These last few months have been a nightmare. I didn't know what to do for you other than talk to the police about Xander. Helping put him in prison was the best thing I could think of. The idea of you facing him again . . . I couldn't stand the thought of it."

"Thank you. I'm not ready to talk about it yet, though."

"Take your time. I don't plan on going anywhere."

Did he really mean it this time? I sighed and looked at the kitchen floor with the shattered glass and coffee cup.

"I don't want to be like her."

"Like who?"

"Mama. She'd get so angry so fast. I've never thrown anything at anyone in my life! Oh my God, I'm so sorry!" I said as my cheeks flushed with embarrassment.

"You've had a lot going on."

"No," I said and shook my head. "There's no excuse. I can't justify it. I'll just start down the same path as her. I refuse to do that."

"Karate should help channel your anger. I know what you're going through. My moods and temper were all over the place after Jeffrey and Mom died. I was sad one minute and pissed off the next. No one even had to do anything. Physical activity and the military kept me focused and probably saved my ass. Once I got out of the slump, I filed for a divorce."

"I bet she loved that."

"She lied and told me she was pregnant. She knew I wouldn't leave her and a baby."

"Bitch," I muttered.

"You have no idea," Walker said and sighed. "Anyway, I found out she lied and filed the next day. Everything was final before I ever left to find you in Oregon."

"Why *did* you go to Oregon?"

Walker paused and took a breath.

"I know you're not ready to hear this, and I'm not expecting anything from you when I explain. But there wasn't a single day that went by I didn't think about you. I never stopped loving you, Lacey. When I realized how badly I'd screwed everything up, I needed to make it right. I went to Oregon to see if we could have the conversation we're having right now. To see if there was any chance you could forgive me and we might be able to fix things. I missed us. You're the best thing that's ever happened to me."

I stared at him, unable to find words.

"You don't have to say anything," he said. "I just wanted to answer your question."

"Thank you," I muttered.

A calm silence filled the air as we both processed what had just been said. Everything had changed in one afternoon.

"I need to clean up the kitchen floor," I said.

"I can help," he said.

"No, I made the mess. I'll clean it up."

My gaze traveled to his face and I allowed myself to get lost in his blue eyes for a moment. I'd missed him more than I'd ever wanted to admit to anyone, even when I was acting like a bitch. I leaned in and lightly kissed his cheek before I stood up and cleaned the kitchen.

Walker went outside while I swept up all the glass and mopped the kitchen floor. I was glad he did. I needed a few minutes to think after our conversation. Maybe he did too.

"How's it going?" Walker asked as he came back inside. He appeared a little more settled. I hoped everything I'd told him about Mama helped him understand what had really happened between us.

"It's almost two in the afternoon. What the hell happened to the day?" he asked.

"Time warp," I said, putting the broom and dustpan away. "But I haven't eaten anything, and I would love some sweet and sour chicken." I grinned and wiggled my eyebrows at him.

A warm smile spread across his face and reached his blue eyes. "I've missed your smile," he said.

"Yeah? Me too. I've missed having something to smile about."

"You seem to be doing a little better than before I left."

"It's probably because of Jared."

Walker's jaw tightened as the words left my mouth. "Who's Jared?"

"You've met Jared, sort of. He's the guy that asked me if everything was okay the day you told the cashier I was under twenty-one. He's my sensei, and my boss."

Walker released a visible sigh. I chewed my lip so I wouldn't blurt out he'd also kissed me.

"You're working?" he asked.

"Yeah, at the dojo. I even help teach the kids' class. Who would've thought, huh?"

"Who would've thought," he said as his eyes searched my face.

"I'm there Monday through Friday for most of the day. I take care of the paperwork, payments, keep things clean, and then I train off and on throughout the day. Tiffany, his sister, is there sometimes too. We're becoming friends."

Walker nodded, and an awkward silence fell between us. My stomach growled and broke the tension.

"Is everything cleaned up?" Walker asked.

"All done," I said, washing my hands at the kitchen sink.

"Let's go grab some Chinese food then."

"Really? Let me grab my wallet."

"I've got it. Let me take you to lunch. We finally got some things settled between us, and it would be nice to get you out of the apartment for a little while."

"Okay. Sounds good to me," I said.

I locked the door and followed him outside. We reached a dark-blue Toyota Corolla. He unlocked the passenger door and held it open for me.

"Thanks," I said as I slid into the seat. "Is this your car?"

"Yup. I haven't had her long. It was a gift to myself for the divorce." He got in and chuckled as he slipped his sunglasses on.

I paused for a moment. I'd forgotten how good he looked in sunglasses.

"It's really nice," I said. "What did you do with your Nissan?"

"I traded it in. I was shocked the car dealership gave me anything for it, but they did."

He turned on the stereo and lowered the volume so we could talk.

"I like it," I said as I pushed buttons, opened the glove compartment, and gave it the once-over.

"I have to try and park in the shade as often as I can. As you can tell, your bare legs will stick to the leather."

"I like the leather, though. I'm happy you have a good car."

"Me too."

THIS WAS the second time in a few days I'd gone somewhere outside of my mile radius.

Walker and I were seated at a corner table, and I sat where I could see everyone around me. Worst-case scenario, I had a knife and a fork. I could do some damage if I had to. But I hated thinking like that. My brain and body were on high alert all the time, like I was just waiting for something bad to happen.

"You alright?" Walker asked after we ordered.

"Yeah. I just struggle getting out around people I don't know."

"It'll get better, but the key is to get out. The more you stay isolated, the harder it is when you're in public. Survey your surroundings, identify your weapons, and locate the exits."

"What?" I asked, tilting my head. "Where did you learn that?"

"The military," he said as a smile pulled at the corner of his mouth.

"What do you do? I haven't even bothered to ask you."

"I'm a security forces specialist. I hated it for a long time. Boot camp was hell, but after Mom died, it gave me something to take my aggression out on. I could train, punch a bag, learn weapons, box."

"Box? Seriously?" I asked, unable to hide my surprise.

"Yeah. I box," he said, smiling.

"That's why your arms are so . . ." I stopped. My cheeks warmed as I realized I'd just admitted I'd checked him out.

"Yeah, I stay in shape."

"I see that." *Shit, what the hell is wrong with me?*

Walker chuckled. I was grateful when our food arrived—it gave me something to put in my mouth besides my foot. Maybe I could manage not to embarrass myself for the rest of the day.

I dug into my sweet and sour chicken and stole a few bites of Mongolian beef off Walker's plate.

"I'm glad you have your appetite back," Walker nodded at my half-empty plate.

"Training has helped. Hell, not drinking has helped," I said while I pushed the remaining food around on my plate. I was stuffed. "Remember the night at the restaurant?"

Walker stopped mid-chew as he waited for me to continue.

"The night I was trying to break up with you," I said.

"And I wouldn't let you," he said and nodded. "I'll never forget it. I got you into my bed that night."

"Ha ha. Yes, you did," I replied. "You thought you were so smooth, too."

Walker wiped his mouth and put his napkin on the table. He signaled for the waitress and ordered two coffees.

"That's the night you told me you were possessed."

"Pretty memorable, huh?" I asked, pulling at a string on my cloth napkin.

"I know it was hard for you, but you trusted me, Lace. Maybe someday you will again."

"Maybe. It was two years ago, but things were so different. I wasn't so broken."

Walker held my gaze. "You're not broken. You'll heal if you keep going. Take it a day at a time, one step at a time, train, spend time with your friends, get out of the house. The memories won't ever leave, and don't let anyone tell you different, but they do fade. And most importantly, you'll get stronger."

"I don't feel strong, Walker. And I can't seem to control my moods. I'm jumpy, and I'm afraid to sleep. I get up in the morning, shower, grab some coffee and go straight to the dojo. I mean, if Xander showed up there . . ." I flinched as I said his name and my heart pounded against my chest. "Well, if he was going to show up, that's where I'd want the motherfucker to be. At least I could watch him die.

Jared and Tiffany would take care of him." My chin quivered at the thought of seeing him again.

"Would you? Watch him die?" Walker asked as he sipped his coffee.

"I think about it. Guess it makes me a horrible person, but he—he deserves to."

Walker reached for my hand, and I tried to focus on the warmth of his skin as I willed my heart to slow down.

"Thanks," I said and looked at him.

"It'll help if you can find something positive to think about or do when Emma and I aren't around. Something to keep your thoughts in the present moment instead of in Oregon."

"That's probably a good idea. I know you and Jared can't be with me everywhere I go."

Walker hesitated as I mentioned Jared's name again.

"I'm going to talk about him, Walker," I said as I pulled my hand away. "He's my friend. He and Tiffany have helped me in ways no one else has. If it bothers you, I'm sorry," I huffed.

Walker raised his hands in surrender. "I get it. I'm sorry."

"Maybe if you met them it would help."

"Let's not push things yet, okay?"

"Yeah." I wasn't ready to drop it, but I did. "It's been a big day. I'm ready for a nap," I said as I stifled my yawn. "My belly is really full."

"You got it," Walker said and signaled for the check.

WALKER PULLED into the apartment parking lot twenty minutes later. The coffee hadn't seemed to do me a lot of good, but a full belly had.

I curled up on the couch as Walker put in a movie and sat next to me. I stretched my feet across his lap and watched the screen light up with the Disney castle as the music began for *The Little Mermaid*. It wasn't ten minutes before my eyelids fluttered closed.

"Hey sleepyhead," Emma said as she came through the front door.

"Huh?" I lifted up my head and wiped the drool from the corner of my mouth. Walker chuckled, and I glared at him. "What time is it?"

"It's a little after six," she replied as she sat her purse on the kitchen table. I didn't miss the glance at my feet in Walker's lap.

"Were you busy?" I asked

"It wasn't too bad tonight. What about you two? Anything good happen?"

"Mm, yes. Walker took us out for Chinese food for lunch, and I ate too much," I said, rubbing my belly. "It was really good."

"You got out of the house? Lacey, that's great! Twice in one week-end," Emma said.

Walker's eyebrow shot up. "Where else did you go?"

"A barbecue for the Fourth," I said casually. I didn't want to get into any details.

"With Jared?"

"And Tiffany," I said as my eyes narrowed.

"Well, I'm sorry I brought it up," Emma said and released a nervous giggle.

Walker glanced at the clock and then at me. "I need to go," he said.

"Oh. Okay. Thanks again for lunch," I said and removed my feet from his lap.

I watched as he stood up and stretched, and then I got up and opened the door for him.

"Bye Emma, have a good night," Walker said.

"You too," she replied.

He stepped outside and turned toward me.

"Thanks for coming over today," I said softly.

"I'll see you tomorrow," he said as he leaned down and kissed the top of my head.

"Yeah?" I asked with a touch of excitement in my voice.

"Yeah." He smiled gently, then turned away and walked down the stairs.

I closed the door and sighed louder than I meant to.

"Alright now, what the hell is going on?" Emma said as she stared at me. "Walker just kissed you goodbye on the top of your head, and you didn't even say anything nasty to him. Come on," she said as she sat down and patted the sofa for me to join her. "Tell me what happened today."

I sat down with her. "A lot happened."

"Start from the beginning so I don't miss anything. Are you two back together?" she asked. I didn't miss the hope in her voice.

"No, and don't go getting any bright ideas, either. Dating someone right now isn't on my to do list. I need to get better first."

Emma nodded and motioned for me to continue.

"We talked. He told me what happened at boot camp. Did you know? About Jeffrey?"

"Who's Jeffrey?" Emma asked.

"One of the guys committed suicide while they were doing weapons training on the range. He shot himself in the head while Walker was standing next to him."

"Oh my God!" Emma gasped. "Lacey, that type of wound is messy. If Walker was standing close enough—"

"Yeah, that's what he said. All the . . ." I paused and pointed to my head. "It went all over Walker, his face and clothes."

"That's horrible!" She covered her mouth with her hand.

"I know. So then when I didn't show up to visit, and his mom was barely holding on, and James told him I kissed him, I guess it was just too much. Something inside him just snapped."

"Is it why he never asked you about it? Because James said that?"

"Yeah, and in one way I get it. He and James grew up together. He never considered James and Brittany had lied to him. And after Jeffrey, he realized Susan was . . .dying" I sighed as the memories of the funeral came flooding back.

"It's okay," Emma said as she reached over and patted my hand. "Wait—James. As in the same James who was at the going-away party?"

"He's the one. I don't think I ever told you what happened. I tried to just brush it off, but I guess he'd planned the whole thing with Brittany, from what Walker said. James kissed me right after Walker proposed."

"What?" Emma screeched. "At the party? Like, right after his best friend proposed to you?"

"Yup," I said and chewed my lip. "Bastard set me up."

"How do you know?"

"Walker said he overheard Brittany and James laughing about the whole thing one day. That's how he found out James had initiated it. Ugggh! He's such an asshole!" I scrunched up my nose in disgust.

"Why am I always the last one to know the juicy stuff?" Emma asked as she rolled her eyes toward the ceiling.

"You were the only one who knew about Mama, so you can't say that."

"You're right. But does Walker finally know? Did you tell him what she did to you, Lacey?"

"Yes. I told him."

"What did he say?" Emma asked in a low voice as she leaned toward me in anticipation.

"That he had no idea. For the first time in two years, we both have answers. Now I understand why he didn't come looking for me. He wasn't himself. He said it was like he was in a fog after Jeffrey, and it just got worse with James telling him I'd cheated on him, and with his mom dying. Brittany just took advantage of the situation and moved right in."

"He does understand you didn't cheat on him though, right?"

"Yeah, and he knows I was on my way to see him."

"How do you feel about it all? I mean, after two years, you finally understand what happened. It doesn't fix anything, but maybe you and Walker can move on."

"I'm processing. You know what it did to me when he married Brittany. You know what he meant to me, Emma."

"He still does mean something to you by the expression on your face," she said.

"I never stopped loving him. I just couldn't deal with it, so I shoved the pain down."

"I know."

"But it doesn't mean we're getting back together. Besides, there's Jared."

"Girl! Did you see Walker's face when you mentioned his name?" Emma squealed.

"I really wanted to kick you for bringing it up."

"I'm sorry," Emma said and groaned. "I realized my mistake after it came out of my mouth."

"I don't really want to talk about Jared in front of him, but he's part of my life, and Walker is going to have to deal with it."

"Yeah, but Jared's your boss and teacher. Nothing more, right?"

I squeezed my eyes closed for a moment.

"Lacey?"

"He kissed me at the barbecue."

"Holy hell, are you serious?"

"I don't think it meant anything."

"How can a kiss not mean something? Even Walker kissing you on the top of your head means something. Love bubbles were floating out of him."

"Love bubbles?" I giggled.

"Don't change the subject," she said and laughed.

"Love bubbles," I muttered and shook my head. "Jared was drunk. It's why I don't think it meant anything."

"Well, there's two sides to that, though. One, you don't care who you kiss because you're too drunk to care, or two, he really wanted to kiss you and his defenses were down, so he went for it. I'm putting money on the second one."

"Hey now, we're not placing bets here. He apologized as soon as it happened and said it was the beer. He fell asleep in the backseat on the way home, so I knew he'd had a lot to drink. I really don't think it meant anything."

"And what if it did?"

"No," I said and shook my head. "We're not going there."

"You might not be, but I am," Emma said. "You've got two men in your life who have feelings for you. You can't deny Jared cares about you. I mean, he trains you for free."

"That's because of his mom, but I know he cares about me as a friend. Besides, we'd just had a slow dance and watched the fireworks from the dock. The kiss was almost Fourth of July protocol or something."

"Seriously? You just keep telling yourself the kiss meant nothing," Emma said.

"I will," I said and folded my arms.

"Is he super hot?"

"Yes," I said and groaned. "Now stop. You're not helping!" I said and swatted her on the arm. "It can't be anything anyway. He's my boss and my sensei. I'm pretty sure sleeping with him isn't a good idea."

"Who said anything about sleeping with him? If he's getting

attached to you, it doesn't matter. I think you just need to be careful. If you care about him, don't lead him on."

"I'm not leading him on. I've been strictly professional during work and training. I haven't given him any signals or anything. Especially after Tiffany said something to me about it."

"What? What do you mean?"

"She just said to be careful because he'd get attached to me. She mentioned something about a savior complex or something."

"Ohhhhhh," Emma said, making her mouth into an O.

"We're done having this conversation," I said and rubbed my face.

"Okay, but I suspect it will come back up soon."

My eyes narrowed at her.

"I have every intention of going to work on Monday and not mentioning it. He already apologized, it's over, we're moving forward. And do *not* tell Walker."

"I'm not that stupid," Emma said. "He loves you so much."

"How do you know all this?"

"Just things he says when we talk. How much he worries about you."

"Well, we're friends. We've never had that between us, and I think it's a good place to be."

"You're right. You guys fell so hard and fast. It was a whirlwind, really."

"We've both changed a lot in two years. I just want to get to know him again. Like, did you know he boxes?"

"He's mentioned it."

"Speaking of, he told me you knew he was in Missouri with Garrett."

"Ohhh," Emma said, grimacing.

"I was mad at first, but he said he made you promise not to tell me."

"Oh, phew. I thought I was going to get my butt chewed out."

"You were, but he explained it was to protect me from worrying about Garrett."

"It was. Lacey, do you realize everything Walker and I've done has been to help you? We love you. We'd do anything to keep you safe," Emma said as her eyes glistened.

"Don't do that. Don't get teary on me. I've cried a lot today," I said. "I know I wouldn't be here without either one of you. And right this minute, I'm okay with being alive."

"Me too," Emma said as a tear snuck down her cheek.

21

Walker showed up at the apartment around eleven the next morning.

"Hey," I said, smiling. It was nice not to be pissed he was here.

"You ready?"

"What do you mean?"

"I'm getting you out of the apartment for the day."

"Oh, I don't know. I'm really tired. I didn't sleep much last night."

"No isn't an option," he said as he grabbed my wallet and sunglasses from the kitchen table.

"Bye, Emma! I'll have her home by eight," Walker yelled down the hall.

"Bye! You two have fun," she replied.

"I'm not sixteen, ya know," I said, following him out the door.

"No, but that was funny."

I couldn't hide my grin.

We reached his car and got in. "Where are we going?" I asked as he pulled out of the complex.

"It's a surprise. Just try and enjoy the drive."

I nodded and stared out the window. Although I was glad to be out of the house, spending time with Walker as a friend was strange.

Thirty minutes later, we pulled into the Lake DeGray parking area.

"Oh my God, I can't believe you brought me here," I said. A shy smile spread across my face.

"I thought a picnic would do you some good. Get some sunshine, be near the water, and just spend the day together. And I packed some food—including strawberries."

"Ha!" I said and laughed. "Do you remember me putting the entire strawberry in my mouth on our first date?"

"Yup," he said and flashed me a smile. My breath caught as the memories returned of our time here. Our first kiss and his hands on my body. Heat stirred inside me for the first time since I'd left Xander. My hand trembled slightly as I tried to shut down all the emotions.

"You okay?" he asked as his eyebrows knitted together.

"Yeah, I was just thinking. It's nothing," I said while I got out of the car and helped him unpack the trunk.

"Holy shit. This is the exact spot, isn't it?" I asked, glancing around. "You remembered? This lake is huge."

"It's impossible to forget," he said as he shook out the blanket and laid it on the ground. "I fell in love with you that day."

My cheeks flushed at his words.

"Hand me the drinks?" He motioned to the brown paper bag full of food and soda.

"Here," I said and passed the soda to him, relieved he hadn't said anything else. Walker was ahead of me on processing his emotions. He knew he still loved me. I was just confused. Some days I didn't know my ass from a hole in the ground, and I was usually riding a crazy roller coaster of emotions.

We sat on the blanket as Walker unpacked the rest of the food.

"This looks good," I said, eyeing the sandwiches. "I guess I'm hungry."

"You still don't eat a lot. I mean, you killed the Chinese food, but I don't see you eat much."

"I've put some weight back on, though, and I eat regularly now.

Maybe I'll be able to sleep through the night again soon," I said, taking a bite of the watermelon he'd cut up.

"Nightmares?"

I nodded as I chewed. "Sometimes they start the second I close my eyes. Or it seems like they do."

"What happens in your dreams?"

I paused for a moment and wiped the watermelon juice from my mouth with a napkin. Was I ready to talk about it? Would it make things better or worse?

"Sometimes it's the fire, sometimes it's Xander, and sometimes it's Mama. I guess I've had a lot of nightmares in my life," I said.

"When's the last time you saw your mom?"

I speared another piece of watermelon with my fork and took a bite.

"At the hospital, right after you were arrested. But she came to Eugene last fall, too."

"What?" Walker asked as his back stiffened. "Why?"

"To free me from the demons," I said and attempted a smile. "She showed up at my dorm and threatened to drug me again if I didn't cooperate. I fought her, but she was too strong. She pulled me right down the damned hall and into the elevator."

"Weren't people around to help you?"

"Not really. Everyone had left for the Christmas break. A few people stayed, but it was pretty quiet. Right before she shoved me into her car, Xander showed up. He was taking me out on our first date."

Walker's jaw tightened, but he remained quiet.

"He stopped her. Xander was my knight in shining armor. He kept me safe," I said and put my fork down. "By the time I realized he wasn't safe, it was too late. I'm not even sure how it all happened, but before I knew it, I depended on him for everything. He was my ride to school, he provided my food, and he kept a roof over my head. I'd allowed him to completely alienate me. I hardly saw my friends at school—he'd walk me to and from class every day and tell me he was protecting me from Mama. And he was—that was the shittiest thing about it. He was so logical about everything I couldn't see through his

BS. He partied and screwed around on me. There were drugs. Hell, I did drugs, Walker. I put cocaine right up my damned nose."

Pausing, I looked down at the blanket. "I'd lost myself, and when I was ready to leave, I found out . . . I found out I was pregnant," I whispered.

"I'm so sorry," he said as he removed his sunglasses. Sadness flashed across his bright-blue eyes. "They told me you'd lost the baby when I arrived at the hospital. They screwed up and thought I was the father."

Tears pooled in my eyes as I struggled to gain control of my emotions. "I barely even remember seeing you at the hospital. I knew you were there, but everything was so hazy. My eyes burned, and I hurt so bad from him beating me."

Walker scooted toward me and took my hand. His fingers intertwined with mine as I continued. "He'd hit me before, but the evening you found me, it was the worst. He came unhinged about the baby and snapped. I'm pretty sure he had a short walk to crazy anyway. It was there all the time, I just didn't see it. He got the duct tape and dragged me by the hair up the stairs and into his bedroom. He was so strong. I gave it everything I could, but he overpowered me so easily," I said, shaking my head. "After he taped my hands and ankles, he kicked me in the stomach over and over again. I figured I'd lost the baby after I saw all the blood." My head throbbed as the words left my mouth.

I released Walker's hand and jumped up. "Oh God." My hands balled into fists as I remembered how hard I had fought to get free. My stomach churned as the nausea came up. "What happened to me? Shit! Shit! Shit!" I gasped for air as panic surged through me like an electric current. I covered my head with my arms.

"Lace, it's okay," he said as he stood up.

"No! No! Don't you get it? I'm not okay," I sobbed.

He reached for me, and I snapped my arm away from him. "Don't touch me. Please just don't," I said as my body trembled and the tears flowed down my cheeks.

"Alright. What do you need me to do?"

"Just listen. Don't touch me, just let me talk. I have to do this."

Walker shoved his hands into his pockets. Inhaling a shaky breath, I made myself feel my feet on the ground. I wasn't in Oregon. I was with Walker, safe and alive. And it was time to tell him the rest.

"After he kicked me in the stomach, he left the room and came back with the gas can. He poured it all over the curtains and floor. I almost gagged from the stench. I was already dizzy from losing blood, but I hung on. And do you know what the bastard did next? He decided before he set the house on fire, he'd do one last line of cocaine with me. You know, for old time's sake," I said sarcastically. "I was on the floor, scrambling for any way to get free. He finally removed the tape from my mouth and let me talk. That's where he screwed up and got too close. I bit his nose, and then headbutted him as hard as possible. Hell, I almost knocked myself out. I did manage to knock him out, though. Somehow, I got to the phone and dialed 911 with my nose. Thank God for push buttons," I said. "That's how I called for help."

A moment of silence hovered between us.

Walker kicked at the ground with his tennis shoe. "You were in bad shape when I got to you, but I didn't know how bad it was. You thought I was your mom. At the time, I didn't care who you thought I was. I was just trying to make sure you didn't die."

I wrapped my arms around myself and willed my body to calm down. Then I reached down for my soda and took a drink. After a minute, my stomach settled.

"He's everywhere I look," I whispered. "I'm terrified he's going to come after me."

"He can't."

"For now," I said. "That's why I have to be able to train. I know you don't like hearing Jared's name, but he's teaching me to protect myself. Not just from Xander, but from Mama too. I'm so tired of being scared all the time."

"Believe it or not, I get it. I can take care of you when we're together, but I can't always be there."

"I know. But part of my problem is I've let everyone else take care of me."

I turned away from him and stared out over the lake. Dragonflies danced across the water as the sun reflected off the water's ripples.

"Sorry, I didn't mean to freak out on you," I said.

"There's nothing to apologize for."

I didn't say anything as I sat back down on the blanket.

Walker leaned against the large oak tree as he glanced out at the lake. I suspected this wasn't easy for him to hear, but he'd seen me at my worst. And as much as he'd gone through, I figured he could handle the full story.

"You're the first person I've told everything to," I said.

"I'm glad it was me," he said.

"You were there, and no matter what, that means I have a connection with you I'll never have with anyone else. You saw the house, me . . . you know how bad it was. No one else will understand it the way you do."

Walker ran his hand through his hair and let out a heavy sigh. "You're right. I saw you bloody and beaten. My heart stopped when I found you. There was a lot of blood, and I wasn't even sure you were alive, but then I found your pulse. The fire was catching so quickly I wasn't sure I could get us out. For a minute, I thought we were going to die together. Then I heard the sirens. I scooped you off the floor and into my arms. The rest is a blur. By the time we got outside I was coughing and could barely see. They grabbed you and loaded you into the ambulance. I tried to go with you, but they wouldn't let me. It took three guys to hold me back," he said.

"Really?" I asked.

"I almost lost my shit."

"Well, you found your way to the hospital because you were there when I woke up."

Walker nodded and shoved his hands back into his pockets.

"Mama showed up after you were arrested. I thanked her for saving me," I said. "That's how I found out I'd been hallucinating. I didn't know it was you, but I found out later from Emma."

"What happened with your mom?"

I reached for a pillow he'd packed and lay down on the blanket.

"Will you lie down with me?" I asked, patting the spot next to me.

"You sure?" His eyebrow arched in question.

"Yeah."

We lay next to each other and stared at the blue sky for a minute without talking.

"She told me the fire was God's punishment for getting pregnant out of wedlock."

Walker sat up. "What the fuck?"

"Yup. That's my Mama. At least that one didn't make sense to me. I mean, I believed all the other shit she ever told me, but not that time."

"I'm so glad to hear you say that." He lay back down with only an inch between us.

A peaceful silence hung in the air for a few minutes.

"I'm tired," I said. "Unfortunately, I stay tired. I'm trying to sleep at night and stay busy during the day. The only reason I know I fall asleep is because I wake up from the bad dreams," I said and yawned. "After I talk or cry about stuff, I'm drained afterward. It's like it just sucks the life out of me."

"I'm here with you if you want to go to sleep."

I turned my head toward him. "You'd do that? You'd just let me sleep next to you for a little bit?"

"I love to watch you sleep," he said. A warm smile spread across his face.

"It's only because I drool," I said and wrinkled my nose.

"You're cute when you drool. But I'm serious, come here," he said and patted his chest. I only hesitated for a minute before I laid my head on his chest and closed my eyes. He wrapped his arm around me, and I drifted off to sleep to the sound of his heartbeat.

2 2

The week passed by quickly. Jared didn't say anything about the kiss, and neither did I. I did my job and trained like it never happened. I was relieved. I didn't want to lose what we had.

"Hey," Tiffany said as she entered the dojo.

"Hi," I replied around the pencil in my mouth.

"I see he's got you busy with paperwork," she said, smiling. She pulled out a chair at the table and sat down.

I paused while I took the pencil out of my mouth. "Yeah, it's a big mess, but don't tell him I said so."

"Oh, he knows. It's why he pays you to do it."

"Well, hopefully I'll have everything straightened out soon and I can keep it that way," I said.

"How's everything else going? You seem to be getting a lot more comfortable in your training."

"I know I'm safe with you guys. Once I realized it, I was able to focus, ya know?"

"I remember what that was like," she said and paused briefly. "Well, Jared asked what I thought about you testing for your first belt."

"What?" I asked, dropping the pencil to the floor. "How? I mean, shit." My eyes widened at my slip. "Sorry."

"No worries," Tiffany said and laughed.

"How does it work?"

"Well, we're open to having a private test until you make some more progress. There are a few other sensei who would come over to the dojo, and you'd go through some moves for everyone. It's low pressure, and Jared will prepare you. It's up to you. We think you're ready."

"I am?" My eyes widened as I leaned back in my chair.

"You can invite a few friends if you want."

"I can?"

Tiffany laughed as she stood up. "Just think about it and let us know in a day or two. Jared will work with you specifically for the test. You'll be more than ready."

"Wow, okay. I'll let you or Jared know before I leave today."

"Awesome! I'm excited for you. You've come a long way in such a short time. Before you know it, you'll be kicking my ass."

"Ha! I wouldn't go that far," I said and shook my head.

"I've got errands to run. Do you have the deposit for the bank ready?"

"I do. It's in Jared's office."

"Perfect. See ya later," she said as she hurried off.

I leaned back in my chair and stared at the dojo. It was nice Jared and Tiffany thought I was ready, but was I? Would I freak out in front of people I'd never met? What happened if I failed? Butterflies stirred in my belly, but even then, I knew I had to test. I had to advance as quickly as I could.

I sighed and focused on the rest of the paperwork. I'd tell Jared yes when we trained this afternoon.

"HEY, I haven't seen you all day," I said to Jared as he walked down the stairs into the dojo. "Guess I've been busy working while you've been teaching."

"Some days are just really busy. I had an appointment with some parents who wanted to see the dojo and grill me with questions for their six-year-old. I'm pretty sure we'll have a new student in the kids' class," Jared said.

"Is he cute?"

"Are kids ugly at that age?"

"Ummm, yes, just don't tell their parents," I said and scrunched up my nose.

Jared's laugh echoed through the dojo. "You ready? I wanted to show you a takedown."

"Seriously? I get to take you down?" I asked, surprised.

"By the end of our training you'll be tossing me on the floor like a ragdoll," he said as a crooked smile spread across his face.

"We'll see about that, but let's do it."

Jared showed me the moves, and I stepped through them on my own as I watched him.

"Okay, so after you bring your opponent down, you're going to pin them to the floor. You have to be precise with this or they can knock you off them, and you'll be the one pinned to the floor."

I frowned, trying to visualize what he meant.

"Let's walk through it. I'll guide you."

We grabbed the mats and lined them up on the floor. Then, I stepped into him and took him down.

"Oh!" I squealed, surprised I'd put him on the floor. "Are you okay?"

"Lacey," Jared said as he laughed. "I'm fine. We need to try it again, but don't be surprised because you can do it."

"I just wasn't expecting it. I've never thrown anyone on the floor before."

"It won't be your last if you continue to train," he said, smiling.

"Okay, let's do it again."

This time I followed the move all the way through without squeal-ing. I brought my knee down gently into his chest.

"Here, you're not in the right spot. Watch what happens."

In one move Jared rolled me over and pinned me underneath him on the mat.

My eyes widened as his body pressed against me, and for a brief moment, his hazel eyes softened.

"Are you okay?" he whispered.

"You just caught me off guard is all."

Jared stood up and held his hand out. I reached for him as he helped me off the floor. I brushed my clothes off and took a few steps around the dojo. What had just happened? If we'd stayed there any longer, I wasn't sure Jared wouldn't have kissed me again, and he was sober. I bit my lip and shook it off.

"Alright, thanks for giving me a minute," I said. "How do I fix it?"

Jared grinned. "Take me down again, but this time put some force into it. I'm going to resist, so you'll need to work for it. When you pin me, I'll show you how to not make the mistake again."

I nodded and stepped into him before he was ready. I took him down and pinned him.

"Good!" Jared said and laughed. "Now you're really close, but move your knee here." He took my knee and nudged it up into the center of his chest. "And it's your other leg that needs to be strong." He patted my calf, and I repositioned my leg. "There, now you've got it."

I couldn't help but smile as I got up.

"Again," Jared said as he stood up.

I threw Jared on the floor for the rest of our training session. He resisted more and more each time, and I had to work harder for it. By the time we were finished, we were both hot and sweaty.

"You did great today. Your technique is really improving, and you're moving from your core more often. It will feel more natural over time."

I nodded, walked over, and grabbed my towel. I wiped the sweat from my face, smiling. "That felt pretty awesome. So if a guy who was about six two and two hundred pounds came at me, do you think I could take him down like that?"

Jared's expression grew serious. "Yes. I have no doubt."

"Works for me. Thanks."

"Did T talk to you about testing?" he asked. "You're ready. You're past ready, actually, but I wanted you to start building some confidence before I put you in front of strangers."

"You'll train me specifically for the test?"

"Yeah. It's all we'll do for the next few weeks."

"Weeks?" I asked as my voice squeaked.

"About that. We'll most likely have about a month. I'll have to contact the other guys to see what night works for them, but we'll have some more time. You already know everything, it's just getting you prepared mentally."

"I'll do it," I said and blew out a big breath.

"Awesome. I'll let you know the date as soon as I find out."

"Sounds good. I've gotta get home. Have a good night," I said.

"You too, Lacey."

2 3

―――――――

Taking my time walking home, I mentally practiced the takedown on the way, but my mind kept going back to Jared on top of me. The way he looked at me. Maybe Emma was right—maybe something was happening with Jared.

I walked up the apartment stairs lost in thought. I opened the door and put my bag and keys on the kitchen table. My nose scrunched as I got a whiff of myself. There was no doubt, I needed a shower.

"You sure do get sweaty for a girl."

"What?" I said and spun around. "Holy shit!" I yelled and ran to Garrett. He wrapped his arms around me, lifted me off the floor, and spun me around.

"Surprise," he said as he set me down again.

I realized I hadn't paid attention to any of them as I'd come into the apartment. I peeked at Walker and Emma on the sofa and looked back at Garret again.

"Oh my God. I can't believe you're here! And what are they feeding you? You've grown a foot since I last saw you," I said as my jaw dropped.

Walker and Emma laughed.

I squeezed his muscular arms and stared up at him. "You're not so little anymore," I said with a hint of sadness in my voice.

"Yeah, I hit a growth spurt."

"And your voice is deep! It was cracking every time you talked a few years ago." I shook my head and hugged him again. "How are you here? Walker didn't have time to pick you up, did he?"

"Nah, Dad had meetings in Hot Springs today."

"I'll take it. I would've been home sooner if I'd known you'd be here."

"It's alright. Walker and I had some stuff to talk about, and we ate dinner at Rod's. We've only been here for about fifteen minutes."

"Oh good. Listen, as you can see and most likely smell, I need a shower and some clean clothes. Are you guys staying for a while?" I asked.

"We have a few hours," Walker replied.

"Okay, I'll be fast," I said as I ran down the hall.

TEN MINUTES LATER, I reappeared with wet hair and fresh clothes. I went to the fridge and grabbed bottled waters for myself and Garrett.

"I'm going to be rude and take Garrett outside so we can catch up."

"You? Rude?" Walker asked and laughed.

I scrunched my nose at him as I handed Garrett his water, grabbed his arm, and led him to the patio.

We both grabbed a chair as I opened my water and took a drink. I stretched out my legs and propped them up on the railing.

"How are you?" I asked, searching his face. Garrett's hair wasn't a sandy blond anymore. It had darkened, and he'd lost the last bit of boyishness around his face. Not only had he gotten a lot taller, but he was no longer a scrawny kid. He'd filled out everywhere. I reached out and placed my hand on his arm. I couldn't believe he was sitting outside with me.

"Honestly?" Garrett asked.

"Nothing but," I replied.

"Shitty."

"Does life just suck in general or is it something specific?"

Garrett cleared his throat as he took a drink of water. "Everything. Missouri is stupid, and everyone who lives there is too."

I tried to hide my smile. "Everyone in Missouri? That's a lot of stupidness," I said.

"When did you turn into a smart-ass?" Garrett said, grinning from ear to ear.

"Ha ha. You have no idea," I said. "But seriously, what's going on?"

"My dad's an asshole, I hate school, and everything has been shit since Mom died."

"I know what you mean, buddy," I said, staring out at the trees.

"I guess my dad's okay, but I didn't even know him. And then, all of a sudden, I'm moving in with him. Walker left for the military, Mom died, you were gone, and the move. It just all went to hell."

"Walker said he's trying to get custody of you."

"Man, I hope it works out. It sucks to be somewhere you don't belong. No matter how hard I try to fit in with my stepmom and half-sister, I just don't. I have two friends at school, and that's it. I keep busy with football, but most of them are assholes too."

"Football is good. Sometimes hitting someone can make you feel better," I said and wiggled my eyebrows at him.

He leaned back in his chair and propped his legs up on the railing. My eyes widened at the size of his feet.

"How tall are you?" I asked as I inspected him again.

"Five eleven."

"Wow. You're gonna be taller than Walker soon at this rate."

"I know. I love it," he said, smiling. "But since he boxes, he can beat my ass, so I won't give him a hard time about it."

"That's funny. I know he wants you to move back here with him. He loves you, Garrett. He has a lot of guilt about going into the military and leaving you. I think he just tried to make the best decision under shitty circumstances. And I can't imagine what it's like for you without your mom."

"I've got this hole inside me I can't seem to fix. At least if I moved in with Walker I'd have my *real* family again. And you."

I smiled at him. "That would be great, buddy."

"It sounds like I'm not the only one who's had a shitty few years."

I hesitated. I couldn't tell him about Xander. He had enough crap to deal with. "I'm taking karate, and I have a great sensei. His name is Jared. He trains me every day," I said, attempting to change the topic.

"Do you like him?"

"Like as in a boyfriend like him? We're just friends. He and his sister really helped me after I came back home. I was a mess. Hell, I still am, but it's getting better."

Silence filled the air.

"What's wrong?" I asked.

"Nothing. I guess I just thought you and Walker were doing well," he said as sadness clouded his features.

"We are. The best we've done in two years. We're friends right now. I need that. So much trust was broken between us I just want to get to know him again. We've been through so much, and we aren't the same people we were back then. He told you I was in a fire, right?"

"Yeah, how are you doing now? Walker wouldn't give me a lot of details, but I got the impression there was more than what he told me," Garrett said.

"There was a lot more, and maybe I'll tell you one day, but not tonight. I just want to spend time with you while you're here. I'm so happy to see you. The day, at your mom's funeral, I didn't think I'd ever see you again."

"Me neither. I was so stoked when Walker said he'd seen you and you guys were talking."

I laughed. "If that's what you want to call it. I wasn't very nice to him at first. Did he tell you he was the person who got me out of the fire?"

"In Oregon? No, he never told me. What the hell?"

"He saved me, and it's all you need to know right now. Whether I wanted him here or not, he's shown up almost every day to help me get better. The only times he's left have been to go to work and to see you."

"Are you sure you won't tell me anything else that happened while you were in Oregon? Why was he out there?"

"That I can tell you. He'd just gotten divorced and he came out to see if we could talk," I said. "But seriously, it's enough for tonight. I promise I'll fill you in sometime soon though, okay?"

"Just take care of yourself, Lacey. I miss you," Garrett said softly.

"Yeah . . . I miss you too, buddy."

"I gotta take a leak. Where's your bathroom?" Garrett asked as he stood up.

"Down the hall on the right," I said as I followed him into the apartment.

He walked down the hall, and I shook my head. I never would've guessed he'd grow up like he did.

"I'm so glad you brought him over," I said to Walker as I plopped down on the sofa between him and Emma.

"You're welcome, but I think he needed to see you even more," Walker said.

"He doesn't seem like he's doing well."

"He's struggling. I'm doing everything I can, but part of life is dealing with shit we don't like."

"Ain't that the truth," I muttered.

"But he's just fifteen, and he's already gone through so much," Emma said. "He seems like such a good kid."

"I am," Garrett said as he came out of the bathroom.

We all laughed as Walker stood up. "We've gotta get going. His dad will be ready soon."

"His dad? You two don't share the same dad?" Emma asked.

"He hasn't been my dad since he walked out on my mom when Garrett was six," Walker replied. "But as long as he's taking care of Garrett, I'm making an effort."

"An effort for custody?" I asked.

"That's funny," Garrett said and laughed.

"You ready?" Walker asked Garrett.

"If I have to be."

I stood up and reached out to hug Garrett again. He wrapped me in his arms and held tight.

"See you soon," I whispered in his ear.

He released me and ruffled my hair.

I turned toward Walker and hugged him too. "Thank you for bringing him."

"I'll try and get him here again soon, okay?" he said.

I nodded as Walker gently kissed my forehead.

Sadness crept over me as I watched them walk down the apartment stairs. I closed the door and ran my hands over my hair.

"That was a nice surprise," Emma said as she walked into the kitchen and grabbed a soda.

I pulled out a kitchen chair and sat down. "Sometimes I wonder what things would've been like if Walker and I had stayed together. Maybe Garrett would already be back home."

"Lacey, you can't think like that. The best thing you can do is to continue to heal and get stronger. That's the best gift for you and everyone in your life."

I nodded. I knew she was right, but my heart hurt. Seeing Garrett tonight reminded me of how terribly wrong it had gone for all of us.

2 4

Over the next several weeks, I worked my ass off. I managed to maintain a steady routine and training schedule with Jared, and Walker continued to come over every day after I got off work and on the weekends.

By the time the day of my test arrived, my nerves were frazzled. It would start at six that evening, and if all went well, I'd receive my yellow belt.

My gi had finally come in, and I unwrapped it from the plastic and shook it out. Jared had taught me how to tie the belt, but I struggled with it.

"Emma!" I yelled from my bedroom.

"Yeah?" she asked as she came into my room. "Oh! You're so cute in your pajama things," she said and laughed.

"Ugh! It's a gi, and I can't figure out how to tie the belt. I would hate to walk in there tonight and ask Jared to help me in front of all the other sensei."

I glanced at the clock, only ten more minutes before I had to be there.

"Walker should be here any minute, and we'll go a little early, okay?"

"Yeah," I said as I hurried to the bathroom and put my hair up into a ponytail. Then I wrapped it up and piled it in a bun on top of my head, securing it with another hair tie. I didn't want it in my face while I tested.

"Are you excited?" Emma asked as she sat down on my bed.

"I'm so nervous. What if I screw up, or worse, pass out? I don't know these people. What the hell did I agree to do?"

"You know Walker and me. You also know Jared and Tiffany. Won't they be on the floor with you?"

"Sort of. They'll be sitting at the front of the room with the other sensei watching every move I make!"

"So, focus on them. You're surrounded by more friends than strangers. Don't forget it. And remember why you're doing this."

I walked out of the bathroom and stared at her. "You're right. I'm doing this so no one can hurt me again," I whispered.

"And to teach me. After you get this belt, I expect lessons."

A giggle escaped me. "Emma, what would I do without you?" I walked over and hugged her.

"I'm so proud of you," she said as she hugged me back. "You've come such a long way already."

"Thank you. I couldn't have done it without your support."

"Well, you sure have been through more than most, but you never fail to have people around to help you get through it."

"Hello?" Walker yelled from the living room.

"Oh! Good, let's go," I said, grabbing my belt and running down the hall. Walker grinned from ear to ear when he saw me in my gi. "Oh shit, my shoes!" I said, tearing back down the hall, rounding the corner to my room. Emma handed me my shoes and laughed.

"Let's go," I said and hopped on one foot at a time and slipped them on.

Walker offered to drive since it would be dark after I was finished. He pulled into the parking lot and I was out of the car before he'd even put it into park.

I walked through the dojo door, belt in my hand, as calmly as possible. My feet stopped short when I saw the group of black belts in the middle of the wood floor.

As everything became more real, my breath quickened, but I was determined to hold on to my promise to myself—to be able to beat Xander Koffman's sorry ass if I ever had to. I took a deep breath and waited at the edge of the floor for permission to enter.

Jared waved me forward. He strolled toward me and smiled. "You ready?"

"No!" I whispered. "I can't get my belt on."

"It's okay, don't stress about it," he said as he placed his hand on my shoulder and guided me toward the side of the dojo. "Let me have it. I'll do it for you this time, and then we'll practice tomorrow. Now that you have your gi, you'll wear it during training."

I nodded as I lifted up my arms slightly and he stepped into me and wrapped the belt around my waist twice. He pulled it tight, and I automatically stepped into him. Our eyes met as a tremble traveled through my body.

"I know you're nervous, but you're going to do great."

"Nervous isn't the right word. I'm scared shitless."

A smile pulled at the corner of his mouth as he finished tying my belt.

"Thank you," I said as I peered at the other sensei. They didn't seem to be paying anyone attention except for Tiffany. I sighed, relieved.

"I need to go talk to my sensei, so why don't you stretch and we'll get started in a few minutes."

"Okay."

I turned toward the back of the room and spotted Walker leaning against the wall next to the front door. He gave me a small wave. Emma grinned as she sat down at the table.

Thirty minutes later, I'd completed my test and was officially handed my first colored belt. For the first time in years, pride coursed through me. I'd accomplished something positive, even if it was only a yellow belt. I'd worked my ass off for it, and I was one step closer to my goal.

Jared introduced me to all the other sensei, and Tiffany took pictures of us together. You would've thought I was the only student who'd tested for a belt by the way they acted, but Jared and Tiffany knew how much I'd struggled over the past several months. I'd gone from drunk to fighter, and they'd helped me every step of the way.

Jared pulled me aside as everyone was preparing to leave. "Tomorrow we have the kids' class, but my sensei thinks you should be in at least one regular adult class a week. I can still train you one-on-one, but he mentioned it's important for you to continue to become part of the larger picture."

"Oh," I replied as my face fell. "But what if I freak out again?" I asked, tugging on my hair and releasing the bun.

"I think you should try the class Tiffany also comes to. Then you can stick close to her, but I also want to introduce you to some of the other guys in there, especially Kasey. I have no doubt he'll really like you. He's a stand-up guy, and you can't have too many friends with black belts."

"Okay," I said. "It'll help since Tiffany will be there."

"And me. I'm always there," he said, smiling. "You can train right in front of me if you want, but I'm hoping you'll get comfortable around the other guys too."

"I understand. Thank you for all your help. I got my yellow belt!" I said, smiling from ear to ear.

"I'm getting a nasty look. I think your friends are waiting for you," he said and nodded toward the back of the room.

"What?" I asked and turned around to see what he was talking about. Walker glared in our direction as he crossed his arms over his chest.

"Guess I need to go. Thanks again, Jared. Bye, Tiffany!" I said, walking over to join Walker and Emma.

WALKER WAS silent on the ride home, but Emma congratulated me and chatted a mile a minute. Walker pulled into the parking lot and Emma

and I got out of the car. Emma headed straight for the stairs to the apartment while I waited for Walker. It took me a few seconds to realize he wasn't getting out too.

"Hey, aren't you coming up?" I asked.

His window rolled down. "I need to go, but congratulations. You did great," he said and attempted a smile.

I frowned. He always came over before he went to work. What was going on?

"You sure?"

"Yeah. I'll see you tomorrow."

"Alright," I said and frowned as I watched him pull away. I ran across the parking lot and up the stairs. Emma was pulling out food for a salad. I'd been too nervous to eat before the test.

"No Walker, huh?" she asked as she pulled out the tomato, lettuce, and cucumbers.

"No, what happened? I looked back at you guys after the test, and he was pissed or something."

"Oh, you should've seen it from my side of the room. Walker and Jared were shooting each other looks all night."

"What kind of looks?" I asked, afraid to hear the answer.

"Not friendly ones. They were more like, 'she's mine, get away from her.'"

"Emma!" I groaned. "That's not funny."

"I'm not trying to be funny. In fact, I think there were lightning bolts shooting out of their eyes too," she said and grinned.

"Really? Shit, that's not good. I was hoping they might get along."

"Wouldn't count on it. They have a mutual interest named Lacey Anne Beaumont."

"You're so dramatic," I said, sitting down at the table.

"I told you this was going to come up again. When Jared was helping you with your belt, I thought Walker was going to walk right over there and smack him."

"Well, Walker boxes, so I doubt it would be a smack. And Jared's a fifth-degree black belt. He'd block any punch before it ever reached him."

"It would probably be a well-matched fight, if you ask me."

"No! I don't want them fighting. I don't want them to act like cavemen, either. What is wrong with them? Can't they get along?"

"What's wrong with them is they're both in love with you."

"Jared is not in love with me," I huffed.

"Oh yes he is. I saw how he looked at you, and so did Walker. You can't blame Walker for being upset. He's here almost every day, and he told you he's still in love with you. I'm not sure what you think is going on with Jared, but it was very clear to everyone else who was there tonight."

"Shit, shit, shit. What am I going to do?"

"There's nothing you can do tonight, so get some food and some sleep. You can figure it out tomorrow."

I leaned back in my chair and let out a heavy sigh. She made it sound so easy.

The next evening, I arrived ten minutes early for the kids' class. Parents huddled in groups and chatted about how well their kid was doing and what belt they'd test for next. I'd never realized they were so competitive. What happened to the kids learning to protect themselves from bullies and having some confidence?

I went to the bathroom and changed into my gi. I'd decided I didn't like walking to and from the dojo in it. Too many cars honked at me, and the guys whistled. I'm sure they thought it was funny, but I wasn't interested in the attention.

Stuffing my clothes into my backpack, I joined the kids on the floor. I stretched for a few minutes while the parents tied belts and straightened little gis. The kids were full of energy tonight; they were jumping all over the floor.

I turned as I heard someone come down the stairs. Jared waved, but he didn't smile like he normally did. I frowned as he walked right past me without saying anything. *What the hell?* Jared had never acted like that with me before.

The class seemed like it lasted three times longer than it should have, but I was busier worrying about why Jared had given me the cold shoulder than helping the students. At least the kids hadn't noticed. As long as they got to kick or punch something, they were happy.

I changed my clothes and hung back after everyone had left.

"What's going on?" I asked, approaching Jared in the middle of the floor. "You seem like you're mad at me," I said softly.

"Nope. Not mad."

"Then why didn't you talk to me? You basically ignored me unless you needed me to do something in class."

"I'm just in a bad mood. Can't I have a bad day sometimes?"

"Of course you can, but if it's not my fault you're having a bad day, it would be nice if you didn't treat me like it was."

My stomach flipped and I stared at the floor. Although I suspected something was up, I didn't really want to know what it was.

"I wouldn't go so far as to say it's your fault," he said as he began a kata. I moved out of his way. He snapped out a punch and a round-house kick as I watched. I'd never seen Jared irritated before, but I was pretty sure he was pissed about something.

"Did I screw up the books or the checking account?" My heart began to pound with each second he didn't respond. Whether or not I wanted to admit it, Jared was the one person I didn't want mad at me. I spent most of my time with him.

"Nope," he said.

"Okay, well, you obviously don't want to talk to me, so I'll leave," I said, biting my bottom lip. I turned away from him, slipped on my shoes, and grabbed my backpack.

"Wait," he said.

I slowly turned to face him. He rubbed his hand across his jaw as he searched my face.

"It's been a shitty day."

"Jared, just talk to me. Please. If I've done something . . ." my voice trailed off. "Just give me a chance to fix it."

His eyes softened as we walked toward each other. I stopped a few steps before I reached him, but he didn't. His arm slipped around my waist as he pulled me into him. His fingers threaded through my hair and then cradled the back of my neck as his lips met mine. His mouth was warm and gentle, and I leaned into him as everything inside me melted. Heat stirred in my body as his kiss deepened and his hold on my waist tightened. I'd forgotten what it felt like to be wanted. My body responded with a deep longing as I slid my hand inside his gi and touched his bare chest. Our lips parted, and he groaned as our tongues met.

Xander's face flickered through my thoughts as Jared continued to kiss me.

I quickly pulled away.

"Oh my God," I whispered. "I'm . . . Jared, I . . ." I stammered, struggling for words.

He stepped backward, regret filling his handsome face.

"I need to tell you something," I said.

"Shit," he muttered as he peered up at the ceiling.

"Can we go somewhere? If I fall apart on you, I don't want anyone to see me."

Jared frowned and then took my hand and led me up the stairs to his apartment.

"I need a minute," I said and attempted a smile.

"Okay, I'm going to change." His shoulders slumped as he walked toward his bedroom.

I grabbed a bottled water from his refrigerator and sat down on the dark-green love seat. The kitchen and living area were one open room, with the bathroom down the hall. The office and Jared's bedroom were the only other rooms.

I sighed and rubbed my forehead. What had I been thinking? I couldn't have feelings for him. It was too soon. His kiss had surprised me, and so had my reaction.

"Alright, let's talk," he said as he came out of his bedroom. My breath hitched as he walked out in his Levi's and no shirt. My eyes traveled across his muscular chest and arms and down his rippled stomach. I stared as he opened the hall-closet door and grabbed a T-shirt off a hanger. He joined me on the love seat and slipped it on.

"Your kiss," I said as my cheeks warmed. "Was amazing. You completely caught me off guard, though. I need to tell you some things, and I hope you can understand. So, just please let me talk and then I'll answer any questions you have."

Jared nodded.

"Do you remember the first time you met me?" I asked. "I barely remember it because I was so drunk."

"Yeah, you walked in front of a car."

I glanced down at the love seat, trying to choose my next words. "My last boyfriend beat me, taped my hands and feet, and kicked me in the stomach until I lost our baby."

"What the fuck!" Jared exclaimed.

"There's more," I said. "He poured gasoline all through the house and set it on fire. Then, he left me there to die."

"Jesus, Lacey," Jared said as his brows knitted together. "It makes sense now. You mentioned a fire the first day we met."

"It's why you saw me so drunk. I'd only been home for a few weeks. I couldn't sleep, I wouldn't eat, I hated everyone, and I didn't want to be alive. My emotions still tend to run off the charts. Some days I feel better, other days I'm angry and depressed. I didn't know what to do with those emotions until you invited me to train. But as you saw, being around a lot of men still rattles me really bad. Jared, I care about you so much. You're the reason I get half a night's sleep, but I haven't been with anyone since I lost the baby, and I mean in every sense of the word. And I hate to be cliché right now, but my life is complicated. I can't drag you into it. You're my boss, my sensei, and more than that, my friend. I don't want to lose what we have. I feel safe with you."

Jared sat quietly as we held each other's gaze. "How long has it been since it happened?"

"It feels like yesterday," I whispered. "Almost three months."

"I didn't know," he said.

"Walker saved me," I blurted.

Jared's eyes widened in surprise.

"He flew out to Oregon and came to find me. But what he found was me beaten and bloody inside a burning house."

Jared's jaw tightened and his hands balled up into fists. I couldn't tell if it was the mention of Walker's name or imagining me like that.

"You mentioned he was your ex-fiancé."

"Yeah, and he flew out to see if we could fix things. He just hadn't counted on me being what needed to be fixed."

I bit my lip, closed my eyes, and took a deep breath.

"Do you still have feelings for him?" Jared asked.

"Jared," I said, my voice barely above a whisper. "He's back in my life. I'm not sure what it means exactly, except he got me through some very dark days after the fire. I don't know how to answer your question. We have a past, and I think part of me will always care about him. The last thing I ever imagined was sitting on this love seat having this conversation with you, though. I don't want things to change between us. I love training with you. I love helping with the kids, and I love seeing you every day, but it's all I can give you right now."

Silence filled the air, and my hands trembled as I took a sip of water. The next words out of his mouth would be the deciding factor. If he couldn't handle being friends, I would no longer have a job or a sensei, and I couldn't deal with losing them both.

"Lacey, I wouldn't have kissed you if I'd known. I knew someone hurt you, but I had no idea. I'm sorry. I'll tell you now, though. I *will* kill him if I ever see him."

"No way. You can't get involved."

"Too late. I already am. As your sensei, it's my job to train you to protect yourself. I'll teach you everything I can, but I promise you if he shows up, I'll make sure he never hurts you again," he said as his jaw tightened again.

I paused for a minute.

"Are we okay?" I asked. "I should've stopped you when you kissed me. I was just surprised. I don't want to lose you, but I don't want to hurt you either."

"We're good, Lacey. Please, don't be concerned about anything."

"You're sure?" I asked.

"Promise," he said and stood up. He held his hand out and pulled me up for a hug.

"Thank you," I whispered. I stayed in his arms for a moment, and then we let each other go.

Confusion clouded my thoughts as I left the dojo and started walking home. Jared's kiss still lingered on my lips. Did he really understand where I was coming from? Or was this the beginning of our relationship falling apart? Less training, awkward silences, little lies about our feelings? Unfortunately, the only way I would find out was to go back to the dojo tomorrow.

"Hey," I said to Emma as I walked into the apartment. I scanned the living room for any sign of Walker, but I didn't see him.

"He's not here," Emma said and laughed as she rinsed a plate off and loaded it into the dishwasher. "He got called into work early. He said to tell you he'll be here tomorrow after you're finished at the dojo."

"Oh thank God," I said and dropped my backpack by the door.

"Well good grief, what's that all about?" Emma asked. "I thought you guys were working things out."

I pulled a chair out and slid into it.

"Are you alright?" Emma asked as she dried off her hands on the dish towel.

"No clue. I just had this amazing kiss with Jared and . . ." I covered my face with my hands.

"What?" Emma squealed. "Lacey, you didn't."

"I did!" I exclaimed. "Shit," I said as a tear snuck down my cheek.

"Oh no," Emma said and pulled out a chair to sit with me. "What happened?" she asked as she patted my hand.

"I'm so confused, and I shouldn't be confused about a guy. It's only been three months since the fire, and"—I hiccupped through the tears—"And I don't know what I feel right now. I don't want to feel anything. All I really want right now is to train and get a full night's sleep. I want the nightmares to stop, and I don't want to be afraid when I turn the corner, Xander or Mama will be standing there. This isn't a good time be confused about guys," I said and sniffled.

"Have you considered maybe the reason you're attracted to Jared is because you feel safe with him? I'm not trying to be mean, but I think, at least in the past, it's how you've chosen the guys you're with. Now, don't get me wrong. Jared's gorgeous, and any girl would be blind not to notice. But you spend a lot of time with him, and he's giving you something you've never had before. He's teaching you to protect yourself. There has to be a part of you that's afraid to lose him for that reason alone."

I frowned at her and brushed the tears from my cheek. "You sure you didn't get a degree in psychology instead of nursing? What the hell, Emma?" I said and let out a little laugh.

"No, but we did study psychology, and one of the nurses I work with has a degree in it."

"You told her about me, didn't you?" I asked. My heart dropped at the idea someone else knew what I'd been through.

"Lacey, I'm sorry. I did. I needed to know how to help you. And honestly, I don't talk to anyone but her and Walker about everything you've been through. It breaks my heart, and I just need to talk to someone. She won't tell a soul. I promise. Ya know, I really don't even give Mom and Daddy details."

I rubbed my forehead. It wasn't fair to ask Emma not to talk about it. I couldn't imagine how she must feel. "I get it."

"Oh gosh, I'm sorry."

"Don't be. I can't imagine how hard this has been for you. You talk to whoever you need to," I said and attempted a smile.

"Thank you. Now, let's get back to more interesting things, like Jared."

I groaned.

"So, what did you do?"

"What do you think I did? I kissed him back!" I said and cringed.

"Was it good?" Emma asked as her eyebrow rose.

My face reddened as I remembered the kiss.

"You don't have to say a word—it's literally written all over your face," Emma said.

"It freaked me out. He took me totally off guard, and then I melted. I mean, into a big puddle on the floor. But seconds after, I saw Xander's face, and it was over. I pulled away and told him we needed to talk."

"What did you say?"

"There wasn't anything I could say except the truth. I told him about Oregon and what happened. And then I said I could only be his friend—I didn't have anything to give him anyway."

"Was he upset?" Emma asked, her eyes intent on my face as she waited for my reply.

"I was shocked, but he actually apologized. He said he had no idea what I'd been through, and if he had, he'd never have kissed me. I think he felt bad, but then he told me if he ever saw Xander, he'd kill him."

"Oh geez! I mean, I'm not on team Xander by any means, but killing someone is a big deal. I have a feeling he'd know how to do it, too."

"Yeah, but what are the chances Jared and Xander would ever meet? Right?" I asked, trying to convince myself of the impossibility.

"He's in prison. Walker made sure of it."

I nodded.

"You know what? I'm proud of you." Emma said.

"For what? Screwing up my life and everyone else's too?"

"No, for talking to Jared. For being honest and not just running to him because he's there."

"Sometimes I wonder if it would help me to be with someone again. I mean, maybe it would give me something good to think about. I'm not explaining it well. When I close my eyes at night, I see Xander's sneer as he watched me and lit the house on fire. I feel his hands on my body, his kiss, his threats whispered in my ear at night. If I was with Jared, it would be his hands, his kiss, his whispers. I know it's terrible to say, but sometimes I want to be with him because I can't get away from Xander," I said softly.

"I know you, Lacey. You don't have a mean bone in your body. You'd never lead someone on just to make yourself feel better. Do you really want to be with Jared?"

I tapped my fingers on the table and sighed. "I don't know."

"Well, you don't have to figure everything out today. Just get to know him, train, get healthy, laugh more," she said, smiling. She couldn't hide the hint of sadness in her eyes. "Sometimes, the best we can do is just keep things simple and focus on one thing at a time. What's that one thing for you?"

"I don't ever want to let anyone hurt me again."

"Then that's it. That's the reason you get up every day, that's the reason you train, eat, and sleep. And every time you get scared or overwhelmed, remember your reason."

"I'm glad Walker wasn't here tonight. This was much needed girl time," I said, smiling.

"Me too. I don't get to just hang out with you very often. Although I love having Walker here with us, sometimes I just miss you and me. You were gone for nearly a year, and we lost touch. I don't ever want it to happen again," she said.

"Agreed," I said. "He'll be back tomorrow?"

"That's what he said, and I don't have any reason to not take him at his word."

"Emma, can I ask you something?"

"Of course!"

"Do you have feelings for Walker?"

Her mouth dropped open. "What? Are you serious?"

I searched her face for a minute. "Yeah, I'm serious. You talk about him all the time, and the guy can do no wrong."

"I had no idea you thought that. I'm actually embarrassed."

"Why? Are you in love with him?" I asked, straightening in my chair.

"No, no! You've got it all wrong. Just calm down."

I wasn't sure I could. I hadn't really thought much about it until it came out of my mouth. Emma talked about him all the time, defended everything he did, and giggled when he was around. *Shit, shit, shit.* My eyebrows knitted together at the thought.

"Walker and I are just friends. He is in love with you, not me!" she explained quickly.

"Him being in love with me has nothing to do with whether or not you have feelings for him," I said.

"I care about Walker as a friend. I couldn't have made it through these last few months without him. Have you ever stopped to think I might be scared your mom or Xander might knock on this door someday? When Walker's here, I feel safe. He takes good care of you, he's protective of both of us, and as long as he's here, I don't worry about you or who might show up at our apartment."

"Emma," I said, feeling like a horse's ass. "I had no idea."

"It'll freak you out if I tell you this stuff. I talk to Walker about it. He knows I get scared sometimes."

"I'm so sorry," I said as my hands dropped into my lap. "I never realized how much I've not only screwed up my life, but everyone else's too. It never crossed my mind I was putting you in danger," I said as my eyes grew wide. "Maybe I should leave and go somewhere else. I don't want you to be scared all the time. It's not fair." A heaviness settled into my chest as I finally realized how far the consequences of my relationship with Xander had reached.

"No, it's not what I'm saying at all. You're not going anywhere—this is your home too. I would never ask you to leave."

"But I would. I would leave to keep you safe," I whispered, closing my eyes and willing the tears away, but they spilled over anyway.

"You're not leaving, and this is not your fault. You didn't tell Xander to be a monster. You can't control him. And this is the end of this conversation. The only reason I said anything was so you know there is nothing between Walker and me. We have a good friendship and it's entirely based on you. Nothing else. I think he's grown up a lot since you two were together. And I don't know what's going to happen with Jared, but I do hope you won't close the door on Walker."

I stared at her for a moment and wondered what in the hell I ever did to deserve such a good friend. Emma loved me no matter what I got into. She had always been there for me, and I'd just accused her of having feelings for Walker. I felt like shit.

"What time is it?" I asked.

"Almost ten."

"Come on," I said and stood up. I walked into the living room and waited for her.

"What are we doing?" she asked as she joined me.

"You can't be scared to open the door. I know how it feels. It sucks. I told you I'd teach you a few things to help you feel safer, so here we go."

"Ninja Emma," she said and gave her best *Karate Kid* impression.

I giggled and then showed her how to knock someone out with one strike.

I took Emma's advice and concentrated on my goal over the next few weeks. September had finally arrived, which meant the weather would cool off soon. It also meant I'd somehow managed to make it through another month without coming unhinged.

Jared kept his word, and we continued to train and get to know each other as friends. I didn't bring up Oregon again, and neither did he. But I didn't miss the affectionate looks from him, or the catch in his breath when our bodies touched while training. I'd ended up on top of him or underneath him more times than I could count. Sometimes I thought he chose the training moves based on how close we could be to each other without crossing the line.

I'd also started a group class. I stuck close to Tiffany the first few times, but then I trained with Kasey for a night. I giggled most of the class as he cracked jokes under his breath.

"Listen, you can hit me as hard as you want. Don't hold back. But this—" he said as he knocked on his cup, "please, be kind to the real estate."

My eyes widened and I burst into giggles. I'd never heard a guy refer to his dick as real estate.

"I give you my word I won't wreck your real estate on purpose," I said, holding up my hand in a Scout's honor.

"Awesome, then we're best friends for life."

Kasey had been training for five years, and he showed me techniques Jared hadn't yet. I knew Jared had talked to Kasey about my past, but Kasey never said a word about it. It was almost like there was an unspoken understanding between us; he would be there if I ever needed him. I hoped to God I'd never have to take him up on it.

After class finished, I ran to the bathroom and changed clothes. I returned to the dojo and had just said goodbye to Kasey when Jared walked over to me.

"Hey, you seem to be doing well with Kasey," he said, smiling.

I wasn't sure if there was a hint of jealousy there or if he was serious.

"He's hilarious," I said and tossed my backpack over my shoulder. "I feel good working with him. I appreciate it."

We held each other's gaze for a moment, and his eyes softened. "You wanna grab something to eat?"

"I totally would, but it's my birthday and Emma and I have plans tonight."

"Shit, are you serious?"

"Yeah, I don't like to announce it, but you probably saw it on the paperwork I filled out when you hired me," I said and laughed.

"I didn't even really pay attention to the month or day, just that you were over sixteen and could work," he said. "Happy birthday," he said and gently squeezed my arm. My stomach fluttered with his touch.

"Thanks," I said softly. "I need to go. See you tomorrow?"

"Have a good night," he said.

I gave him a small wave as I left the dojo.

MY STOMACH GROWLED as I raced home. Emma and I usually ordered in since she was at the hospital so much; she liked to be home when she could be. I didn't like crowds much, so it didn't bother me. But tonight we were going out, and I couldn't wait to get some sweet and sour chicken. Chinese food and pizza had become my favorite food groups.

I opened the door and froze. "What the hell?" I said as my backpack slipped from my hands.

"Happy birthday!"

My mouth dropped as tears pooled in my eyes.

"We didn't want to yell happy birthday right as you came in. We were afraid we'd scare you," Emma said as she hugged me.

"Oh my God," I said, running to Garrett and hugging him.

"Joss!" I said and wrapped my arms around her and the tears slid down my face.

"Happy birthday, Lacey," she said.

I hugged Emma's parents, who'd also shown up.

"Happy birthday, Lace," Walker said as he kissed my cheek.

"Thank you," I said, glancing up at him.

"I have a surprise for you," he whispered in my ear.

My face lit up. I loved birthday and Christmas surprises because they were always good. "What?" I asked, grinning.

"Turn around."

I slowly turned around. My mouth dropped as I stood speechless.

"So this is what happens to you when I'm not around? Don't stand there gawking with your mouth hanging open, Hillbilly," George said.

I nearly knocked him over with my hug, and before I could stop it, I broke down and sobbed all over his shoulder.

"Girl, it's okay. I'm here for the night. We can snuggle up like old times, and you can fill me in."

"George, I've missed you so bad," I whispered, still unwilling to let him go.

"You too. You too," he said as he hugged me back.

My tears finally slowed, and I pulled away from him. "How? How are you here?" I asked, touching his cheeks.

"That hunk of a man right there," he said and nodded toward Walker, who was talking with Emma and Garrett.

"What?"

"Mmmhmm, he paid for my ticket and asked Emma if I could stay. I fly back tomorrow, though. That's the shitty part. But hey, let's not waste a minute," he said.

"Okay. Best birthday present ever," I said and hugged him again.

"Save some of that for Walker. Girl, you didn't mention how hot he was. Are you . . . ?" He wiggled his eyebrows at me.

My cheeks reddened. "No, it's too soon," I said and scrunched my nose up at him.

He hung his head as he rubbed my arm. "It's okay. Just keep him on reserve."

"George!" I whispered. "Come on, I want you to meet Joss and Garrett," I said as we took each other's hand.

"Joss," I said and hugged her again. "This is George. He's from Oregon."

"We've met already, but it's nice to meet you again," Joss said and laughed.

"Who organized all this?" I asked.

"Walker," Joss said and held my gaze.

"Oh," I said and frowned. "That was super sweet of him. I'm so happy to see everyone."

"Happy birthday, old lady," Garrett said and pulled my hair.

"Ouch!" I said and smacked him. He laughed as he hugged me.

"Emma said you're working?" Joss asked.

"Ooh, really? Do tell," George said.

"It's up the street at the dojo. I've been taking karate there too," I said.

"That's great! You seem like you're doing better than the last time I saw you," Joss said.

"It started that night, actually. What you said to me in the parking lot . . . it stayed with me."

Joss smiled. "Glad it did. Hang in there. Everything will be okay."

"Thanks. I'll catch up with you in a minute."

I pulled George over to chat with Jim and Linda.

"George, these are Emma's parents," I said, smiling.

"Hi, honey. Happy birthday," Linda said as she hugged me and kissed my cheek. "You're looking better than when you came home."

"Thank you. Your daughter keeps me fed. Oh shoot," I said, searching the kitchen. "Emma, did we get Chinese food?"

"I'm sorry, Lacey. We got pizza instead, but I promise we'll go out for Chinese food sometime soon. I figured you'd want to spend time with everyone. Especially George," she said as she winked at him. "But we do have pizza and cake." She beamed.

We all followed Emma to the kitchen table, and someone gently squeezed my shoulder. I turned around and let go of George's hand.

"I'll catch up with you in a minute," I said to George.

"Take your time," he said as he eyed Walker.

I laughed. I wondered if Walker realized George thought he was beyond gorgeous.

Walker took my hand and led me over to the patio door. "I just wanted to tell you happy birthday."

"Thank you for flying George out, Walker. I can't tell you how much it means to me."

"You don't have to. I saw your expression when you saw him here. You haven't let go of his hand this whole time," he said, smiling.

"He's the best birthday present I've ever had."

"He has to leave tomorrow morning though, and I have to run some errands for work after I drop him off at the airport, so you won't be able to go with us."

"Oh," I said as my face fell. "Dammit. Well okay, at least I know. I'll just plan on not getting any sleep tonight then," I said, smiling up at him.

Walker's fingers trailed softly down my cheek.

"Do you remember the last party we were at together?" he asked, his voice husky.

I nodded, unable to find my voice. My stomach flipped as the memories of that night returned.

"It seems like a lifetime ago," I whispered.

"I took you home that night and made love to you after you accepted my proposal," he said, his eyes filling with need.

My breath caught and my chest ached. Moments like this threw me back to the days we were together, and every part of me wanted to run back into his arms. But things were different now. I took his hand and squeezed it. Then I stood on my tiptoes and kissed his cheek.

"I should get back to George. I'm glad you're here." Slowly, I took a step backward, and his blue eyes filled with sadness as I released his hand.

I wondered if he was going to give up on me. Was it too painful for him? Would he eventually come to the realization he needed to move on, and I might not ever be able to?

EVERYONE LEFT AROUND ELEVEN. I hugged them all and thanked them for coming. Although I loved seeing everyone, I was ready to have George to myself.

"Girl, you've lost weight. What the hell?" he asked as we lay on our sides facing each other in my bed.

"I've actually gained weight since I've come home. I was on a liquid diet for a while, until Emma told me to knock it off or get out."

"What? She didn't! After everything you'd gone through. No, that shit's not okay," he said.

"She wasn't mean. She had to leave for a week, and when she got home, I was passed out. Walker said I was probably close to alcohol poisoning. And at that point, I wanted to die."

"Lacey, don't say that," he said as his eyes glistened.

"I couldn't sleep, I was afraid to leave the apartment, and the only thing that helped was the rum," I said and shrugged. "But I scared the shit out of her and Walker that night. Emma called him, and he put me in the shower. He stood in there with me the entire time. He said I drifted in and out of consciousness. Emma dressed me and then he put me to bed and stayed up watching over me all night."

"Shit, that's the sweetest thing I've ever heard."

"Really? You're feeling romantic while I was on the brink of death?" I huffed.

I laughed while he rolled his eyes at me. I'd missed him so much.

"Don't be mad at me, but I went to see him in prison," he said.

I sat straight up in my bed.

"What the hell? George, are you serious? Why?"

"I had to see it for myself. I had to see him behind bars," he replied. "I kept thinking he was going to be back on campus, and I couldn't get past everything. You were there one minute and gone the next. And the quarterback who everyone thought was so amazing tried to kill you." He paused as his eyes widened. "I just needed to see the bastard behind bars."

"Did it help?"

"Yeah, once I saw it with my own eyes. Once I saw him there, I was able to start dealing with everything. And girl, orange does *not* look good on him."

I couldn't hide my smile. George would notice. "How are the girls?"

"Adalyn and I are roomies. We're off campus now, and we love it. You know there's no one better to party with," he said and grinned. "And Megan found herself a man, so she's living with him. We don't see her much anymore."

"I miss everyone."

"Adalyn said to tell you hi, and to get your ass out there to visit soon."

"Maybe. I miss Oregon, and now that you've been to the South, you know why."

"Shit, I almost melted on the sidewalk of the airport," George said and fanned himself. "How do you do anything with your hair? It's so humid."

"Right? I hate it," I said, wrinkling my nose.

"Do you want to come back? You could stay with Adalyn and me. She'd love it too."

"She was so good to me when I told her about Xander. That girl is a wicked mastermind."

"Right?" George asked. "She's super smart and fun. Get a few drinks in her and you've got your entertainment for the rest of the night."

I laughed. "I do want to come back, but I don't know how or when."

"I get it, but just know you have two roomies waiting for you."

"Thanks," I said and reached for his hand.

"I miss this," he said. "Staying up all night talking."

"Me too."

"So, tell me about this karate class. Walker actually mentioned it. He said you tested for a belt last month."

"I did. It's just my first one, but I'm taking a class, and I have one-on-one training with Jared."

"Oh, I heard that name too."

"What do you mean?" I asked as I frowned at him.

"It was more about how his name was said."

"Walker?" I asked.

"Mmhmmm. Walker wasn't saying anything bad, just that Jared was training you and helping you with your test. It was more the tone of his voice."

"Yeah, from what Emma said, there was a pissing match going on during my test."

"Over?"

"Me," I said and sighed, rolling over on my back.

"Well, anyone with eyes in their head can see Walker is in love with you. And I don't mean he loves you, I mean he is *in* love with you. Big difference."

"Jared and I have gotten closer too," I whispered.

"What? Girl, what the hell. I can't leave you alone for a second without you stirring up shit." He laughed.

"I know. I didn't mean for anything to happen."

"What did happen?" George asked and leaned closer to me.

I turned my head to face him. "He kissed me."

George's eyebrows shot up, and his mouth formed an O.

"Yup," I said. "And I had to tell him about the fire and how we had to just stay friends. He's been good about it."

"But? Do you like him?"

"Yeah, I do. But I'm not sure how deep it goes."

"What about Walker?"

I shrugged.

"You don't know if you still have feelings for him, or you don't know if you want to talk to me about it?"

"Both," I said.

"Oh, well let me help you with that."

"What?" I asked. "Help me with what?"

"You definitely still have feelings for him. I saw you over by the sliding-glass door tonight. I thought he was going to pick you up and take you to your bedroom."

"Oh, you're just being dramatic."

"No, like, if you can't see it then I don't know what to do with you."

"I don't want to see it," I said softly. "I'm scared to fall in love again. Last time it almost killed me."

"Ah hell, I'm sorry."

"Don't apologize. But it's why I don't want to see how much either of them really care about me. I don't want to love anyone again."

"It'll get better."

"That's what they say, but what if it's too late? What if everyone has moved on with their life and I can't? What if Xander ruined me?"

"If he ruined you, you wouldn't be taking karate classes, you wouldn't be hugging your friends tonight at the party, and you wouldn't be torn between two guys."

"You think so?" I asked.

"I know so."

"Thanks."

"I might be in another state, but I'm always here with you."

"I love you, George. I never thanked you for coming to check on me that day at Xander's. So, thank you."

"I love you too, Hillbilly."

I CRIED my heart out when George left the next day. We made promises to see each other soon and call once a month. I hugged Walker goodbye as they left for the airport.

2 8

I didn't get out of bed the next day. As great as seeing everyone was, I couldn't get past George leaving. Seeing him again brought up a tangle of positive and dark emotions, and I couldn't shake the depression.

Emma checked on me a few times. I made an excuse my stomach hurt. Although I don't think she believed me, she gave me some space.

I dozed off and on as I tried to sort everything out that was going on in my head. A soft knock at the door woke me.

"Yeah?"

The door opened enough for Walker to peek his head through. "Can I come in?" he asked, his forehead creased with concern.

"Sure," I said, sitting up, grateful I'd put on a tank top and pajama shorts before crawling into bed.

"Was the party too much too soon?" he asked as he shoved his hands into his pockets. His shoulders slumped as he waited for me to respond. I knew he wanted to make me feel better.

"It's okay," I said. "It was just a lot seeing George, but I wouldn't change any of it."

"You wouldn't?"

"No. I'm just having a really tough day. George and I stayed at Xander's house together sometimes. He was a really big part of my life there."

"I knew you guys were close," Walker said as he leaned against the wall. My heart skipped a beat as I watched him. Was George right? Was I still in love with Walker?

"Do you want to sit down?" I asked and patted the bed next to me.

"You sure?"

"Yeah, I'd like the company," I said and attempted a smile. I scooted over on the bed, and Walker sat down.

"Get comfy, you don't have to hang off the edge. You've been in my bed before. Hopefully I smell better this time," I said.

Walker chuckled and leaned against the headboard, his long legs stretched out in front of him. "Yeah, that wasn't your best moment."

I scrunched up my nose, imagining what I smelled like the day Emma had found me passed out.

"How are you doing?" I asked softly.

Walker's eyebrow arched.

"Pretty shitty I haven't asked you before," I said.

"Lace, you don't have to right now."

"Tell me. I want to know how you're doing."

"I'm doing good. Work's fine. Garrett's case is dragging out, though. I'm not sure I have much of a chance since his dad is married. The judge views us both as relatives and has to evaluate what he thinks is best for Garrett. I guess two parents is better than one."

"He has three more years before he's a legal adult. Raising him would be a big responsibility."

"I know. I've thought about it a lot. Am I the best thing for him? Should he get through it until he turns eighteen? Everything keeps running through my head. But I think he'd be better off with me. His home is in Arkansas. It's familiar to him. I think that's what he misses. Hell, I get it. I left for Texas and I hated it. I was surrounded by screaming jerk-offs and I couldn't even scratch my ass without permission."

"It was that bad?" I asked and laughed.

"Worse, but it got better after boot camp. When I finally got my shit together, I started to like the military. I feel good about serving my country and what I do."

"Thank you."

"For what?"

"For taking care of us and our country. I mean, don't people thank you when they find out you're in the military?"

"No."

"They should," I said and folded my hands in my lap. Silence hung in the air for a moment.

"How's training going?" he asked.

"Good. I like the adult class. I've gotten used to working with other people, which is a really big deal. I never thought I'd get out from Tiffany's shadow, but I have."

"I know you're having a rough day, but you've made a lot of progress from when you first came back home."

"Even when I don't think I can any longer, I just get up every day and put my feet on the ground," I said.

"Some days it's all you can do. But the difference between you and others? You keep putting your feet on the floor. Once you made up your mind to train and get better . . . I've never seen so much raw determination before."

"I highly doubt it. You're in the military."

"Yeah, but we signed up to be there. You didn't ask for any of this."

"No, I didn't," I said and held his gaze.

Walker reached out and took my hand in his. I closed my eyes as the warmth of his skin calmed me. I hadn't realized how much I'd looked forward to those small moments with him.

"George knew who you were because I told him," I said.

"What do you mean?" Walker said as his thumb stroked the back of my hand.

"The day Mama showed up at the dorm I was supposed to go on a date with Xander. When Xander got there, he told Mama to leave. I was so upset about seeing her I didn't want to go out, so instead, he suggested George and I come over and hang out at his house. We did, and we ended up spending the night. We were all in separate bedrooms until I had a nightmare. George ran in and woke me up. He said I was screaming your name," I mumbled as my cheeks reddened.

"You were? Even after what I did to you?"

"Guess so. I don't remember any of it, but I guess a part of me was still trying to reach you."

"I don't know what to say," he said as our eyes met again.

"It's okay. We've already talked about what happened. I just wanted to tell you how George knew who you were that day you showed up in Oregon. After he woke me up, he wanted full details about you. I gave him the short version of falling in love with you and Mama drugging me."

"What did he say?"

"Something about the Mother of God, which wasn't funny since I'd just told him I used to think I was possessed." I chewed my lip in an attempt to hide my smile. "Yeah, maybe it was kinda funny."

Walker chuckled. "At least you're smiling a little," he said as his fingers intertwined with mine.

"No plans today?" I asked. "Do you not have much of a social life? You're either at work or here."

"Those are the two most important places to be," he said. My stomach fluttered with his words.

"I'm sorry I was such an ass to you after the fire. I'm still emotionally all over the place about everything, but I know you were doing the right thing."

"I'd do it again."

"That's what I'm afraid of, though. What if I make a mistake again? I thought Xander was a good guy. I obviously can't trust myself to make good decisions. What if I go back out there and screw up again?" I asked as my eyes dropped to my lap.

"Hey, you won't. You're surrounded by good people. Emma would say something . . ." His voice trailed off.

I looked up and met his intense gaze. He frowned as he searched my face. "Are you looking?" he asked softly.

"No! No, that's not what I meant at all," I said and shook my head.

He leaned forward, released my hand, and rubbed his face.

"Walker, I didn't mean it like that. I'm sorry, I thought I could talk to you about it."

"I don't think talking to me about a possible relationship with another guy is a good idea."

My head snapped up as I glared at him, and my cheeks flushed with anger. "Stop! Dammit, just fucking stop! This isn't about you and whether or not I care about you. This is about me not being able to trust myself. How do I not fuck up again? That wrong choice almost cost me my life. I almost died!"

Walker looked away. A chill filled the room.

Fear gnawed at me as I realized what I'd just done. Had I crossed a line with him? I hadn't considered it would hurt him when I asked the question. Why had I said those things to him? This couldn't be happening. In a split second, I'd managed to jeopardize what we'd worked so hard to rebuild.

I scooted across the bed toward him. "Look at me."

He turned to face me, and the sadness in his eyes pierced my heart. Tension filled the space between us. Had I just lost him? My insides cringed at the idea, and my heart pounded against my chest.

"Walker," I whispered. "I'm sorry. I don't know why I just went off. I'm really scared."

His blue eyes softened as his fingers lightly traced my cheek. He slowly closed the gap between us and gently pressed his lips against mine. I didn't move away. I didn't want to. He pulled away slightly and searched my face. My arms wrapped around his neck, and I pulled his mouth to mine. He picked me up, and I straddled his lap. He groaned as I sat on top of him.

"I need you," I whispered in his ear.

"Jesus," he said as he grabbed my waist. Warmth spread through me as he gently kissed me again. My lips parted, welcoming him as his tongue swept over mine.

Heat traveled through my body, and I released a sigh. His hand ran up my back, and my nipples hardened and pressed against my tank top.

I gasped as he adjusted me on his lap and I could feel his desire through his jeans. His hot breath caressed my skin as he trailed kisses down my neck. He gently took my nipple in his mouth, and my back arched as I rocked against him. His fingers cupped my neck as he continued to tease me.

"I need you," I whispered again.

"You're going to make me come just saying that," he said, his voice thick and heavy as he leaned in to kiss me again. His thumbs grazed my nipples, and he cupped my breast through my tank top. My body ached for him.

I tilted my hips forward and rubbed against him. My thin pajama shorts rode up my butt as he slid his hands down my back and grabbed my ass cheeks.

"Off," I whispered, tugging at his shirt. He released me and pulled his shirt over his head.

Walker wasn't nineteen anymore. There was nothing about him that said teenager. His broad shoulders and chest had filled out, and his stomach rippled as he leaned forward to kiss me again. His hands slid up the back of my tank top as I wrapped my arms around him.

His kisses left me breathless and needing him more than I'd thought possible.

I reached down and grabbed the hem of my tank top, slipping it over my head.

Walker's eyes traveled down my body, and my defenses melted. I wanted him, and I needed something good in my life again.

"Are you sure?" he whispered as he held my gaze.

I nodded, flipping open the button on his jeans. "Are you?" I asked and slid my hands into his jeans and freed him.

A guttural moan escaped him as he closed his eyes. Suddenly, I wanted to take care of him for being there with me the last several months. I scooted down on the bed as he opened his eyes. I peered up at him and ran my tongue along his shaft.

"Oh shit," he said as I took him in my mouth. "Oh God," he

groaned as I flicked my tongue across his tip. I'd forgotten how good he tasted. Suddenly, everything else drifted away as I stroked him. Only Walker and I existed. Nothing and no one else.

He gently pulled my hair as I took him into my mouth again. I dug my fingernails into his side as I picked up the rhythm.

"Stop," he said. "It feels too good."

A shy smile eased across my face.

I rolled off his legs and onto the bed. He sat up and tugged on my pajama shorts. He slid them down my legs and tossed them on the floor. My black G-string was the only piece of clothing left.

"You're so beautiful," he muttered as he leaned forward and placed soft kisses down my belly. His tongue flicked at the edge of the lace. I groaned as my hips lifted toward him.

He gently rubbed me through the soft material as I grabbed his arms. His fingers slid underneath the material and tentatively massaged my center.

"Walker," I gasped as my back arched off the bed. He slid my G-string off, parted my legs, and ran his tongue over my core. I gripped his arms as his tongue flicked across my clit. He slid his hands under my ass and tilted my hips up as he sucked me. His tongue swirled against my sensitive skin as I rocked against him. I dug my fingers into the mattress as the familiar swell began to build. Walker eased a finger inside me, and I lost control. Black dots danced across my vision as he continued to massage me with his tongue.

I gasped, pulling his head away from me. He stood up and slid his jeans off. He grabbed a condom out of his pocket and rolled it over the hard length of him. I ran my eyes up and down his tan body. Muscles rippled in his legs as he stepped toward me. I needed him. I wanted him inside me again, to erase all the horrible things that had happened when he wasn't with me. I wanted his arms around me and his lips against mine. This man still had the ability to undo me.

He lowered himself carefully as he lay on top of me. "Are you okay?"

I nodded and wrapped my arms around him. He throbbed against me as I leaned up to kiss him. I could taste myself on his lips.

I released him as he repositioned himself and pushed slightly against my core.

"Lace," he said as he slid inside me.

I gasped as he filled me and moved in and out slowly. I sighed and closed my eyes, but in that split second, Xander's face flickered in front of me and fear shot through my body.

"Stop!" I gasped. "No!"

"What's the matter?"

"I can't," I said and pushed against him. "I can't!" I pounded against his chest. No!" I cried.

"Lace, hey, it's okay," he said and pulled out of me. "Look at me." He gently grabbed my shoulders.

Violent trembles traveled through my body as I shook against him and tears streamed down my cheeks. Walker pulled me into his lap and wrapped his arms around me.

"It's okay. I'm here. You're safe with me," he said as he rocked me back and forth. I curled into a ball as the sobs tore through my body. He smoothed my hair and kissed the top of my head. I grabbed his arm and held on with everything inside me. The sound of his voice finally calmed me, and my tears slowed.

"Hey, I've got you," he whispered.

"I'm sorry," I said. I tilted my chin up and searched his face. Was he mad at me?

"You don't ever have to apologize when you get scared. I should've known it was too soon," he said as he tucked a piece of hair behind my ear. "I don't ever want to hurt you. Guess my dick got the better of me today. I'm sorry. I'm afraid I hurt you more than I helped you this weekend."

"I was okay. I wanted to be with you," I hiccupped. "And then when you were inside me, it wasn't you anymore. It wasn't you," I said, crying and tucking my head into his chest.

"He can't hurt you anymore."

"What if I can't get past it? What if it doesn't get better?"

"Shh," he said as he rocked me. "Just take a deep breath."

Silence fell between us as I melted into his arms. Dammit, I'd screwed up. I'd wanted the memories to be replaced so badly I had hurt Walker in the process. Stabs of pain and hollowness threatened to settle inside me. I couldn't hurt him any more than I already had.

"I'm going to take a shower," I whispered, getting out of bed without looking at him.

"I love you, Lace."

I didn't respond. I just shut the bathroom door behind me.

29

The next day, I opened the door to the dojo but didn't see Jared or Tiffany anywhere. I ran up the stairs and found Jared in his kitchen.

"Morning," he said as he poured coffee into his cup.

"Hey," I said and attempted a smile. I couldn't push the thoughts of Walker out of my head, and there was still a hollow ache inside my chest. I'd hoped hitting something, or someone, would help.

"How was your birthday weekend?"

"Good and bad all at once. One of my friends from Oregon came to visit."

"That's great. Did you know they were coming?"

"No, Walker surprised me and paid for George's ticket," I said, walking to the office and grabbing the files I needed. I sat down on the love seat, and Jared joined me as I rifled through the paperwork.

"George?"

"Yeah. We went to school together out there. He's one of my best friends."

"It sounds like a great weekend. What was bad about it?"

I paused. I couldn't tell him about me freaking out on Walker. Or how confused I was about my feelings.

"George leaving," I muttered. "I cried when I saw him, and I cried when he left. He was a part of the . . . he knew Xander."

Jared's jaw tightened. "You doing okay?" he asked.

"No. Not today," I said and sighed. "It's like my skin is crawling and I have all this shit running through my head, and I can't make it stop." Frustration filled my voice. "I don't know how to make it stop."

"We'll train this morning. That'll help. You can do the paperwork later."

"You sure?"

"Yup. Let's go downstairs."

"Thank you," I said and put the stack of papers on the kitchen table, following him.

❦

THIRTY MINUTES LATER, I was sweaty and sore from punching and blocking Jared. He'd raised the intensity of our training and now he resisted me more. I swept his legs out from under him, tossed him down on the mat, and twisted his arm, forcing him onto his stomach.

Sitting down on his back, I let out a Tarzan call and banged my chest. I could feel Jared's chuckle rumble through his body. A giggle escaped me. He was right—beating someone up had lifted my heavy mood.

I didn't hear the front doorbell jingle. Someone cleared their throat, and I turned to see who it was. Walker was standing by the door. His body went rigid as he saw me straddling Jared. Had he also heard my Tarzan call? My cheeks flushed as I stood up, offering my hand to Jared as he got up off the mat.

Walker's gaze turned stony as he and Jared glared at each other. I dropped Jared's hand and approached Walker. My stomach fluttered. Nothing seemed right about him showing up like this.

"Hi," I said, wiping the sweat from my forehead and approaching him. "What are you doing here?"

"I won't be over tonight," he said quietly.

I stared at him. "Why not?"

"I have some things I need to do before work."

"Is it for Garrett?" I frowned.

Walker didn't respond right away.

"I'm sorry about yesterday," I mumbled.

"I know, but I need some space."

"What? You said you wouldn't leave again," I said as a pang of fear flowed through me.

"You're not suicidal anymore, Lace. I think you need some time without me around. It's making things more difficult for both of us. Maybe you should figure out what you want, and who," he said as he nodded toward Jared.

Tears threatened as I bit my lip to control them. "This is about yesterday, isn't it?" I asked, my voice cracking with emotion.

"It was my fault. I shouldn't have gone there," he said. "I love you. You know that, and hopefully I've proved it to you over the last several months, but I know you're not ready. And honestly, it's killing me." He ran his hand through his hair. "Honestly, I thought I could handle it, but I need a break. And being with you again yesterday . . . it's too much right now."

"Walker," I said softly as tears streamed down my face.

"If you need me, you or Emma can call. But I think for now I'm going to focus on my job and what's right for Garrett."

"Walker, don't. Please," I pleaded, reaching for his hand.

He squeezed it, leaned down, and gently kissed my cheek. "See you soon," he whispered as he dropped my hand and walked out of the dojo. My heart split open as I watched him walk away.

I wiped the tears from my face and took a deep breath.

"That was intense," Jared said from behind me.

I turned around slowly and stared at my feet.

"Are you two trying to work things out?" he asked.

"No," I whispered.

"That's not what it looked like from over here."

I searched his face as my forehead creased. Was he really trying to have this conversation with me? "I can't talk to you about this right now. There's work to do, and I need to focus on my training. That's it."

Jared stared at me for a moment and then nodded. Maybe he figured this wasn't the right time to push me. "Okay. Then let's finish training," he said.

I followed him back to the mat and punched him with everything I had. He flinched as my fist made contact with his stomach.

"Sorry, that was out of line," I said and took a deep breath.

"Let me get the bag. I think it will work better for you to really put some power into it."

Jared held the bag for me as I punched and kicked it with as much strength as I could find. Anger flowed through me as I imagined Xander's face on the bag, Walker's pain-filled expression when he told me goodbye, and my own face for hurting everyone around me.

AFTER I FINISHED work at the dojo, I took my time walking home. My chest ached as I realized Walker wouldn't be waiting for me.

Mentally, I kicked myself for sleeping with him. I never meant to hurt him. I didn't know what I'd been thinking, but all of the sudden I needed to be in his arms, feel his hands on my skin, and be with him. Maybe I'd thought it would erase some of the bad things or give me something good to think about, but it hadn't worked out like I thought it would. I'd pushed him away without realizing how close I'd let him get again.

I opened the door to the apartment, closed it behind me, and leaned against it. It felt empty without him. My eyes squeezed shut, and I willed myself not to cry. There were no choices left, I had to give him what he'd asked for. Maybe he was right, and some time apart was what we both needed.

The door moved and knocked me forward.

"Oh, sorry!" Emma said as she pushed it open. "Did I hit you?" she asked and laughed. Her voice faltered as she saw the expression on my face. "Lacey, have you been crying?"

"Earlier. And I was about to again until you smacked me with the door," I said.

Emma came in and put her purse on the table.

"He told me," she said. "Walker, I mean. I'm guessing it's what you're upset about?"

"He stopped by the dojo and told me he needed a break," I said softly.

"Did he say why?" Emma asked as she sat down.

"Just that he thought it'd be best to give us some space. He said it was tearing him up being around me all the time," I said and leaned against the living room wall. I didn't want to sit down.

"It has been hard on him, and he's been here a lot. He got up early every morning to be here for you. He only got a few hours of sleep, and I suspect it was right here on our couch."

"What am I going to do?"

"Do you have an option?" Emma asked.

"What do you mean?"

"Do you know how you feel about him? Or Jared, for that matter?"

"Walker mentioned the same thing. He said it would give me time to figure out who I wanted to be with."

"I doubt you'll know until you start feeling better. Don't get me wrong, you're doing great, but you're not just gonna instantly get over what happened in Oregon. If you ask me, Walker's timing is off, and I do think you two need some space. He's so head over heels for you that his emotions are getting in the way of his common sense."

"Yeah, maybe. It doesn't matter anyway. He made it clear. He's going to focus on his career and Garrett."

"It'll be okay. I don't know how, but it will be."

I nodded. "Are you going to be alright without him not around? I mean, you mentioned you felt safe with him here."

"I'll be all right as long as you keep teaching me some things in case I ever need it."

"No time like the present," I said, pushing off the wall and walking into our living room. "Chop chop," I said as I clapped my hands together and Emma joined me.

"You want a what?" Jared asked me the next morning.

"You heard me," I said, putting my hands on my hips. "I need your help because I don't know what the hell I'm doing."

"Have you asked Emma how she feels about it?"

"She doesn't need to know. This conversation is between us," I said. "Promise me, no one else will know. You'll take me to buy a gun and some bullets, and it stays between us."

"Fine," he said. "But I also need to teach you how to use it, clean it, and the basic safety rules."

"Alright. So, when and where?"

"You're really serious about this, aren't you?"

"You have no idea."

"Okay, I don't have a class for a few hours so let's go."

I followed Jared out of the dojo as he locked the door behind us.

A FEW HOURS LATER, we walked back into the dojo, and I owned a Smith & Wesson 686 revolver. I had no idea how easy it was to buy a gun. Jared helped me narrow down the choices and the rounds to go with it.

"I hope I never have to use it," I said, pulling it out of my backpack.

"Don't ever draw it on someone if you're not going to use it."

"Really? I don't want to shoot anyone!"

"Then why did you buy it?"

"For protection! I mean, don't people run if you pull out a gun?"

"Sometimes, but if they're mean enough to hurt you in the first place, they won't necessarily be scared off by a tiny blond waving a gun around."

"Really? I can look mean when I want to," I huffed.

"Yeah, you can, but that's not the point. Carrying a gun is just as much a mental game as a physical one. Don't wave it around unless you can pull the trigger."

I sighed and rubbed my forehead. Was this really what I wanted?

"Fine, then show me what the hell I'm doing. I have to figure out where to hide it since I don't want Emma finding it."

"Does she go through your stuff?" Jared asked.

"I don't think so. If she does, I'm obviously not there to see it," I said with a hint of sarcasm.

Jared showed me how to load it, turn the safety on and off, and clean it. We made plans to shoot instead of train that afternoon. I guess he figured target practice was a type of training too. I'd take it. I just wanted to feel safe, especially now since Walker was gone.

3 0

Jared kept his word, and we incorporated target practice into my training routine. I also passed the test for my orange belt, but this time I tested in front of the adult class as well as the group of other sensei. Emma came to watch, but I hadn't heard from Walker since the day he'd said goodbye to me at the dojo. I wanted to pretend it didn't bother me, but it had been almost seven weeks without him.

After careful consideration, I'd located a good hiding place for my gun and rounds in one of my many shoe boxes. Emma rarely went in my room anymore now that I was sober and staying out of trouble. I didn't want her to freak out about it, so I kept my mouth shut.

Jared, Tiffany, and I wrapped up training early since it was the day before Thanksgiving. Emma and I were going to her parents' house. I agreed to meet Jared and Tiffany afterward since they didn't have family around either. I'd bring a movie, and they'd provide the popcorn.

"Hey hey," Emma said as she walked into the apartment.

I muted the TV and hopped off the sofa to help her with the groceries.

"Can you believe tomorrow is Thanksgiving?" she asked as she put the bags on the kitchen counter.

"No, not really," I said and began unloading the food and putting it away.

"I have to make the pies tonight. Do you wanna help? I promised Mom and Daddy I wouldn't forget."

"Yeah?"

"Yes! Let's get started early and turn on the Christmas music too!"

"Emma! You can't, it's not Thanksgiving yet," I said, giggling.

We both loved the holidays, no matter how shitty they actually ended up being.

"Go turn it on—I'll get the ingredients out, and we can sing off-key at the top of our lungs as we peel apples."

"I'm not sure our neighbors will appreciate it." Laughing, I ran into the living room and pulled out the Christmas CDs.

I joined her in the kitchen again as each of us grabbed an apple and began the long process of peeling and slicing them.

"I'm so glad you're here this year," Emma said as she glanced at me.

I stopped peeling my apple. "I was with Xander last Christmas. Mama had taken all my clothes and stuff out of my dorm room, and he'd gotten it back for me. Then he bought me this beautiful butterfly necklace. I had no idea I was sleeping with a monster."

"Well, you're not there anymore. We're gonna have so much fun together you won't even have time to think about last year. You've made it through another one and look at you! You're a true badass."

I couldn't help but laugh. "Just because I got another belt in karate doesn't mean I'm a badass."

"Please, I see how you throw those guys down on the floor."

I shook my head and grinned as I started peeling my apple again.

"I've met someone," Emma said softly.

My hand slipped, nicking my finger with the knife. I stared at her as a few drops of blood landed on the apple.

"Oh, Lacey! Shoot!" Emma said as she put her knife and apple down on the table, grabbed me, and led me to the kitchen sink. "I'm so sorry. My timing was awful." She turned on the water and rinsed my cut.

"It's nothing. I just grazed it a bit."

"It doesn't look too deep, but we should toss the apple," she said as she made a disgusted face.

"Definitely," I said as I wrapped a paper towel around the cut. "So, who is he? Where did you meet him? How long have you been seeing him? What's his name? How old is he?" I giggled. "Now you know how I feel," I said as my face lit up. If anyone deserved to be happy, it was Emma.

"Hang on," she said as she disappeared down the hallway. She returned with a Band-Aid. "Finger, please." I held out my finger as she wrapped the bandage around it.

We sat back down at the table again and, I tossed my apple in the trash can, grabbing another one.

"I'm waiting," I said, teasing her.

"Well, he works at the hospital, he's twenty-five, married, and has five kids."

I dropped my knife on the floor as my mouth hung open.

"I'm kidding! Oh my gosh, the expression on your face," she said, laughing.

I laughed with her, shaking my head. "I was about to give you a seat next to me on the crazy train," I said.

Her face lit up as she smiled. "He's taken me out to lunch a few times, and he wants to take me to a movie this weekend."

"Emma, that's wonderful. What's his name?"

"Nathan."

"That's a good name. When do I get to meet him?"

"Well, I'd like to go out with him a few more times before introducing him to everyone."

"That's fair. I get it. But I don't count," I said and wiggled my eyebrows at her. "I'm going to call Jared, and we're going to follow you guys on your date."

"Lacey Anne! You wouldn't."

"Don't put it past me. If you're not going to introduce me, then I'll just stalk him. I have no shame, and you know it."

"You wouldn't!" Emma replied, exasperated.

"No, I wouldn't do that to you. It was funny, though."

"Oh gosh, you had me for a minute."

"I'd love to meet him when you're ready. And just so you know, I'll break his kneecaps if he hurts you."

Emma's eyes grew wide.

"Just sayin'," I said and shrugged. A small smile pulled at the corner of my mouth. This would be fun.

"I love you too," Emma said, grinning.

We finished peeling the apples and made the pies over the next few hours. We even grabbed the Christmas decorations and put everything up. It was after one in the morning by the time I crawled into bed, and it was the first night I didn't have a nightmare and wake up in a cold sweat.

ONE OF THE skills I'd learned over the years was how to fake a good mood. I smiled and laughed as Emma and I loaded the pies into the car and drove over to her mom and dad's. They hugged us, fed us, and asked a ton of questions about our jobs, guys, and anything else they could think of. But sometimes, as much as I loved them, it was a reminder I didn't have my own parents.

An emptiness seeped inside me. I wondered where Mama was and if they fed Xander turkey in jail. I pushed the thoughts aside, but Mama always seemed sane during the holidays, and those were the few good times I kept tucked away in my heart.

I ate too much turkey and fell asleep on the couch while everyone watched the football game. Emma woke me around six and we hugged everyone goodbye. An hour later, I pushed open the door of the dojo and jogged up the stairs to Jared's apartment.

"There she is," Jared said as a warm smile spread across his face.

"Hey Tiffany," I said as I gave her a little wave.

"What movie did you bring?" she asked.

"*National Lampoon's Christmas Vacation*," I said, handing it to her.

"Sweet! That movie is hilarious," Jared said as he took my coat.

Jared and I settled into the love seat, and Tiffany sat in the recliner.

"How was your Thanksgiving?" she asked.

"Good. I fell asleep during the football game."

"You didn't," Jared gasped.

"I know, total loser," I said, grinning. "I ate too much," I said, pooching my tummy out.

Jared and Tiffany laughed as I relaxed my stomach.

"Alright you two, hush up. It's starting," Tiffany said as she turned up the volume.

I leaned back into the love seat and propped my feet up on the coffee table, grateful I didn't have to pretend to smile for a little while. I didn't even care Jared's leg was touching mine during the movie. I wondered if he'd kiss me again if he knew Walker was gone. But for whatever reason, I hadn't told him yet. Maybe it's because I didn't want to admit he was really gone.

After the movie was over, Jared drove me home. "Did you have a good day?" he asked as he pulled into the apartment complex.

"Helluva lot better than last year," I said.

"You were in Oregon last year, right?"

I nodded. "Does it really get better? The bad memories?" I asked softly, leaning back into the seat and turning my head toward him.

"Do you want me to be honest or lie?"

"Honest. Always be honest with me. I don't want a bunch of sugar-coated bullshit."

"Some days it gets better and others it doesn't."

"How long did it take you with your mom?"

Jared paused as a frown line creased his forehead. "I don't remember how long. Maybe a year or two before they weren't as frequent. But everyone processes differently, so it's hard to give you a time frame."

I nodded.

"Well, thanks for letting me hang out with you guys tonight."

"Anytime." Jared's hazel eyes softened.

A smile eased across my face as I opened the car door and stepped out into the cold night air. "See you tomorrow." I closed the door and walked up the stairs and into the apartment, without glancing back at him.

Emma and I had begun the countdown to Christmas. She invited me to the Christmas party at her work and introduced Nathan to me. She was all smiles as he held her hand. I'd never seen her so happy. He stood about six feet tall, and his dark hair was cut close to his head. His eyes were a smoky gray, and he kept them on Emma unless he was speaking to someone else.

They were kind enough to introduce me to their other coworkers and not ditch me. It wasn't Emma's style anyway, but I wasn't sure about Nathan yet. He probably wasn't excited about a third wheel.

"What do you think?" Emma asked when Nathan left to use the men's room.

"He seems really nice," I said and smiled, nibbling on my cookie.

"Do you like him?" she asked. She couldn't contain the excitement in her voice.

"I do so far."

Emma frowned at me. "That's not what I expected you to say," she said.

"I just need time to get to know him is all," I said and patted her arm. "You have to keep in mind my judgment of guys isn't too good."

"Don't say that."

"Say what?" Nathan asked as he joined us again and took Emma's hand. He dried his other hand on his pant leg. At least we knew he washed his hands after he took a leak.

I smiled at Emma, hoping Nathan was going to be perfect for her, but only time would tell.

"Hey, some of the staff is going out for a few drinks, do you care if I go?" Emma asked.

"No, of course not. I think it would be really good for you."

"You're sure?"

"Yes! Please go. I'll enjoy some much-needed alone time."

"Okay, we'll drop you off at the apartment then. We're meeting them at eight, so we should leave soon if you're ready."

I agreed, and Nathan and Emma dropped me off at the apartment. Actually, I was looking forward to curling up on the sofa and watching some mindless TV by myself. Between Emma and all the time I spent at the dojo, it was a rare luxury. At least she trusted me enough now. It was progress for both of us.

We'd forgotten to leave any lights on, so it was pitch-dark when I entered the apartment. I closed the door behind me and stood still, running my hand up the wall, attempting to find the light switch.

I froze—feeling something cold against my throat.

"If you scream, I'll slit your throat right here. Emma will never get your blood out of her floor."

I gasped as his body pushed me backward into the door.

"Hello, Lacey from the South," Xander said as he flipped on the light.

I squinted, temporarily blinded by the sudden brightness.

"You're still so beautiful," he whispered.

My heart hammered against my chest as I stood paralyzed. Xander Koffman was in my apartment with a knife to my throat. How? How was he here?

"I bet you're just full of questions, aren't you?" he asked, sneering. "You always were. It drove me fucking crazy. Would you like me to start at the beginning?"

"Yes," I said, my voice cracking.

I racked my brain for anything Jared had shown me concerning a knife, but we hadn't done any weapons-defense training yet.

"Well, as you can see, I'm out of prison. I can't say the stay was pleasant," he said. His eyes traveled across my face and to my chest. "It's been a while," he said as his finger trailed down my neck, collarbone, and to the edge of my top. "You were such a good fuck, too."

"Please, don't," I whimpered. I swallowed against the knife and the bile that rose in my throat.

"We'll save that for later," he said, laughing.

"Why are you here? What do you want, Xander?"

"Such a good question. I actually came here to catch up with your boyfriend."

"I don't have a boyfriend," I replied.

"Hmm. I did wonder, since I haven't seen him around the last few weeks."

My eyes widened. He'd been watching me for weeks?

"He probably didn't mention that even with his firsthand account, they only charged me with domestic battery. And as you know, I'm well connected. My attorney found a technicality, and they couldn't exactly prove it was me who set fire to the house. Unfortunately, too many people saw you beaten up, though. That was a detail I hadn't counted on. You getting out alive. So instead of years in prison, I only got a few months, and then they released me for good behavior. Not to mention the overcrowding is ridiculous. But it worked out well for me in the end. So here I am, Lacey."

He paused for a moment and licked his lips. "I think we'll start with dessert first. When I'm finished with you, I'll hunt Walker down and finish him too."

He moved the knife against my throat as he grabbed my breast through my shirt. I squeezed my eyes closed as tears trickled down my cheeks. My mind scrambled for any training I'd learned, but my brain refused to cooperate.

Xander flicked open the buttons on my blouse and pulled it back, revealing my black lace bra.

"You definitely have an amazing pair of tits," he said, moving the material away and exposing me. His thumb flicked across my nipple. He leaned in, his erection pressed against me.

Closing my eyes, I forced myself to try and calm my racing thoughts, feeling feet on the floor. I imagined the ball of energy swirling in my abdomen and remembered that every move I made came from that power.

Pain shot through me as Xander took my nipple between his teeth and pulled. My eyes shot open. *Fuck him. I'm not going down like this.*

Tiffany's voice floated through my terrified thoughts, and I slowly slid my left arm in front of me, biding my time. Then in one swift move, I grabbed his nuts through his jeans, squeezed with every bit of strength I had, and twisted.

"Ah! You stupid bitch!" Xander said as the knife clattered to the floor and he stepped backward. I released his nuts as I brought the heel of my right hand up and struck the soft tip of his nose. He stumbled backward and fell to the floor. I pushed off the door and ran past him.

"I'm going to kill you, but this time, I'll really finish the job. You just fucked up, little girl!" he said as he grabbed my ankle and I went tumbling to the floor. I kicked at his hand as he started to regain his strength. I rolled over on my back and snapped a kick to his face. He screamed as he released me.

I scrambled to find my footing. I ran to my bedroom door, slammed it closed behind me, and locked it. The flimsy door wouldn't hold against his weight for long; I only had a few seconds.

I pulled my closet door open and threw the shoe boxes out until I found the one I needed.

"Open the goddamn door, Lacey!" Xander screamed as he kicked it.

The door rattled. My hands shook as I tried to shove the rounds into the cylinder. I cursed as the first one fell to the floor, but I managed to slip two others in. My legs trembled as I stood and walked over to my window. I faced the door and took a deep breath as I heard Jared's voice in my head. *Don't draw your gun unless you're ready to pull the trigger.*

I jumped as the door flung open. Blood trickled down Xander's face as he bolted into my room.

"Stop right there, motherfucker. I've had about enough of your shit." I glared at him, pointing the gun at his chest. I refused to go down again. This man had stolen my life from me, and I was about to take it back.

Xander's laugh ripped through me. "Please. Who are you kidding? You won't shoot me."

"You forget I was born and raised in the South," I said as I held it on him. "When someone breaks into our house here, we shoot them." I tried to hide the tremble in my hands.

He grinned and took a step toward me.

Closer. Just a few steps closer.

"You think you're hot shit because you have a few belts in karate? You'll never get rid of me. I'll fucking haunt your dreams for the rest of your days. Lucky for you, you only have one left. This time, I won't leave until I've finished the job."

He took another step toward me. I didn't hesitate as I stepped in and turned the gun in my hand as I moved. A crack ripped through the room as the butt of the weapon made contact with his temple. Xander dropped to the floor unconscious.

"That's for calling me a bitch," I said, standing over him. I held the gun in one hand and stepped over him into the doorway. Grabbing a handful of his hair, I tugged on it as I tried to move his body down the hallway, but he was too heavy. I didn't want to put my gun down in case he regained consciousness. I tucked it into the back of my slacks and prayed it wouldn't fall out.

Lifting his upper body, I slipped my arms underneath his armpits, and pulled. His arms flopped around as I dragged him down the hallway and dropped him in the middle of the living room. I searched the room for something to tie him up with, but the only thing that crossed my mind was the string of Christmas lights, and it wouldn't work.

I ran into the kitchen and rifled through the tool drawer that contained a hammer, screwdriver, nails, and some tape. I shut it and then pulled it open again. My eyes narrowed, and I grabbed the duct tape, running back into the living room. I reached for my gun and laid it on the floor next to me, grabbing his wrists and wrapping the tape around them as tightly as I could. He moaned.

Shit. He was waking up.

My hands trembled as I finished with his hands and moved to his feet. Sweat dripped from my forehead onto the floor. I tore one more piece off and placed it over his mouth as his eyes fluttered open.

As his eyes focused on my face, I took a deep breath. They darkened with hatred as he realized his hands and feet were bound.

I kneeled next to him and picked my weapon up off the floor. The cold metal felt good against my sweaty palm.

"Who's a bitch now, Xander?" I cocked my head as he tried to talk against the tape. "Mm, sorry, I can't understand a word you're saying."

I flashed the gun in front of him. He glared at me. "Still don't think I'll shoot you?"

I held it close enough for him to see. His eyes followed my hand as I lowered it and then nudged his crotch with the barrel.

"The laws in Arkansas are pretty clear, Xander," I said, applying more pressure to his dick. "Rape is illegal. Beating a woman is illegal. Killing your unborn baby is illegal. Breaking into someone's apartment is illegal. Doesn't sound like you have a lot in your favor right now."

I paused as Xander tried to pull his wrists apart and struggled to say something against the tape. A cold mix of fear and rage swirled inside me. A part of me wasn't sure I'd have an ounce of remorse if I killed him right now.

"Unlike you, I don't have a huge ego, and I don't give a shit what you're trying to say. I'm not taking the tape off your mouth, so shut the hell up."

I stood up, brought my foot back, and delivered a snap kick to his ribs. He doubled over in pain. I kicked him again and again until I heard a rib crack. His eyes glistened with tears as I took a step back and stared at him. My eyes never left his face as I raised the gun and aimed at his head. His eyes widened with fear. Maybe he'd finally realized I wasn't the same Lacey he'd left in Oregon to die.

"I have the legal right to kill you," I said. "You beat me until I lost our baby and you left me to die in a fire. If I call the cops now, you'll just get out and come after me again. I'll never be free from you unless I put a bullet in your brain. At least then I'll know you'll never hurt me or anyone else again. I'm pretty sure I can live with that."

Xander's chest heaved as he struggled to get free. Sweat trickled over his brow and into his eye.

I stood and stared at him as I thought about a bullet piercing his brain. I'd worry about the carpet later. Emma would freak when she saw it, but she'd have to deal with it. I refused to live in fear any longer.

And then a thought flashed through my mind. I continued to hold the gun on Xander as I stepped toward the small corner table that held our telephone. I'd almost forgotten it was there since I never used it. I dialed the number as I held it in my other hand.

"Hey, I need you, now. Can you get over here as fast as you can?" I asked. My voice didn't sound like my own anymore. I tried to hang the phone up, but it bounced off the corner of the table and clattered to the floor.

I walked to the front door and waited, jumping as the knock at the door finally came.

"Who is it?" I asked, trying to calm the fear in my voice.

"It's me. Open up."

I opened the door and ushered Jared in.

"Lock it," I said.

"What the fuck?" he asked as he caught sight of my gun. His eyes followed it to where it was pointed. "Shit, Lacey. What the hell is going on?" he asked as he ran his hands through his hair. His eyes widened as he took everything in.

"Jared, meet Xander Koffman from Oregon," I said.

"What?" He glanced back and forth between the man bound on my living room floor and me.

He rubbed his chin and took a deep breath. "Have you called the cops?"

"No. I was about to unload my gun on him when I called you."

"Holy shit. Give me the gun."

I didn't move. Part of me had called Jared to stop me from killing Xander, but now that he was here, I wasn't sure I wouldn't pull the trigger anyway.

"Lacey, listen to me. You don't want to do this. Trust me."

"If I don't, he'll just come back. I can't live like that anymore."

"You won't be able to live with it if you pull the trigger, either. I don't give a shit what you're feeling right now. As soon as you kill him, you'll regret it. You'll never be able to take it back."

"How would you know?"

"Because. I didn't tell you everything."

My eyes left Xander's face and cut over to Jared.

"What do you mean?"

"My dad's not in prison. I killed him."

"What?" I asked as my arms faltered.

"Everything else I told you was true. Mom died in my arms, but I didn't just hit Dad once. All my anger over the years came rushing out, and I beat him as many times as he'd hit her. I killed him. And you don't forgive yourself for something like that, even if they do deserve it."

My arms trembled from his words and the exhaustion that was setting in.

"Why did you lie to me?" I asked as tears slipped down my cheeks. "I trusted you."

"You'd been through so much and you needed something and someone to believe in. I protected my mom, and I'd do the same for you," he whispered. "I'm the same man you've known all these months. The same guy who taught you to fight, protect yourself, and to use that gun. But you can be pissed at me later. Just give it to me."

I stared at Xander's bloody face and slowly lowered my weapon.

"Give it to me, Lacey," Jared said softly.

I frowned and handed it to him. He released a loud breath as he took it from me. He sat down on the sofa and rubbed his face with his free hand.

"Sit down. You're in shock."

I did as he said, but my eyes never left Xander.

"We have a few choices. First, we can call the cops, and you can give them your statement about Xander breaking in and attacking you. You'll have to provide full details of the attack. They'll question you several times, and they might be dicks about it and drag it out. You most likely won't be charged, but sometimes it happens."

"I could get charged?" I asked as my eyebrows rose.

"I really doubt it. You know I'll testify for you, give my account, anything to get things cleared up. But there will be a lot of questions."

"What's the other option?"

"I make a few phone calls, and then you and I leave."

"Why would I leave him here?"

"Because you don't want to see the people who would come in here and pick up this sack of shit. What I promise you, though, is he won't ever be able to hurt you, or anyone else, ever again."

My eyes widened in surprise as I realized what he was saying. His friends would finish Xander and feed him to the gators. There would never be a trace of him to be found.

I glared at Xander for a moment and tilted my chin up. "Make the call."

"You sure?"

"Yes," I said, turning to look him in the eye.

I jumped up off the sofa at the sound of the front door opening.

"Hey," Emma said as she closed the door and froze. Her mouth dropped as she saw Xander on the floor, Jared with a gun, and my disheveled clothes and hair.

"What the hell is going on?" she asked me.

"Emma, meet Xander," I said.

She stood still as her purse dropped to the floor.

"Emma?" I asked softly. "I can explain."

"Oh, I think I already got it," Emma said as she stared at Xander. Silence hung in the air as I waited for her to say something else.

She surprised me as she stood up straight, threw her shoulders back, and marched across the living room. She swung her leg back and kicked Xander in the nuts.

He doubled over in pain.

"There's more where that came from, you bastard," she said as she kicked him in the stomach.

Tears spilled out of his eyes.

"That's for hurting my best friend. That's for all the hell you've put her through," she said as she delivered another kick to his ribs. "And this one is for trying to hurt her again. I hope you rot in hell!" she yelled as she delivered the final blow to his crotch.

Xander's eyes rolled back in his head as he lost consciousness.

Emma straightened her shirt and glanced at me. "Well, that was unexpected," she said as she walked over to the phone, picked it up off the floor, and dialed 911.

I shot Jared a look as Emma gave them the address to our apartment.

"They'll be here in a minute," she said as she glanced at Xander, who was still passed out.

"I'll make some coffee. It's going to be a long night," she said as she walked away and into the kitchen. I'd never seen Emma in this mode. I assumed it was part of her job as a nurse.

"Jared, give me the gun," I whispered. "Emma can't realize it's mine. I need to hide it."

Jared nodded and slipped it to me. I crept down the hallway and tucked it back into its hiding place. Fortunately, I returned to the living room before she'd realized I was gone.

My eyes focused on Xander lying motionless on the living room floor, and suddenly a cry snuck out of my throat and my knees buckled. Jared caught me and pulled me against him as we fell into the couch.

"I'm so proud of you," he whispered as he stroked my hair. "You fought back and took care of yourself." I grabbed his hand as sobs shook my shoulders. He rubbed my back as he held me.

The cops arrived and arrested Xander. He could barely walk as they dragged him out of the apartment. Jared was right—the cops asked us all a ton of questions. I told them the truth, and all our stories matched. I hoped it wouldn't take long for them to look up Xander's record and learn about the assault in Oregon. It would most likely save me from any charges.

After the apartment had cleared out, Emma excused herself to take a shower. I glanced over at the floor where Xander had lain. Drops of blood dotted the light-beige carpet. I was exhausted, but I had to clean it up before Emma saw it.

"Where are you going?" Jared asked.

"I need to clean the carpet," I muttered and walked into the kitchen for the cleaner.

"I've got it," he said as he took it from me. "That won't work anyway." He returned it to the cabinet as he rifled through the other bottles. He grabbed a wire brush I didn't know we owned, a bowl, a white dish towel, and the Dawn dish detergent.

I sat at the kitchen table and watched him scrub the floor. My mind and body had gone numb from the shock. I wasn't sure when I'd be able to process the fact I'd kicked Xander's ass and almost shot him.

Jared finished and returned everything to the kitchen. He'd worked magic on the carpet.

"Thank you," I said, standing up.

Jared wrapped his arms around me and pulled me into him for a hug. "I'm so glad you're okay," he whispered.

"I'm not sure I am," I replied.

"But you beat his ass. You found your power and all the training kicked in."

"It saved my life," I agreed, pulling away, rubbing my forehead, and staring at the floor for a minute. "What you told me earlier," I whispered as my gaze drifted back to his face. "About your dad. Were you telling me the truth, or were you just trying to get me to come to my senses?"

"It's true," he said softly. The strain around his eyes tugged at my heart.

"Did you go to jail?"

"No, the court viewed it as self-defense since I had to fight him off my mom. Technically, we don't know which blow killed him. It could have been during our fight or the extra one I gave him after he was already on the floor. But I have to live with it for the rest of my life. I didn't want the same for you."

I nodded. "I understand. I get why you didn't share it with me the night we were on the dock," I said, unable to keep eye contact.

"But?" he asked as he tucked a piece of hair behind my ear.

"But I'm not sure I can trust you anymore." I bit my lip as the tears threatened.

"Please don't say that," he said as he cupped the sides of my face and leaned his forehead against mine.

I grabbed his hands as my tears fell.

"I care about you so much," Jared said, his voice cracking with emotion. "You brought something back into my life I thought I'd never feel again. I felt worthy. I had a purpose."

"Oh, Jared. You gave me that too. I just don't know how I'm going to feel about all this later. I don't know if things will ever be the same between us," I hiccupped.

"Can we try?" he pleaded.

"I need some time," I whispered.

Jared squeezed his eyes closed for a moment. "Then I'm not going to leave without telling you this. I love you, Lacey. I've tried not to overwhelm you with it as you healed, but shit. You walked right into my heart, and I'd do anything for you. Take some time if you need to, but please, don't let us go," Jared whispered.

He tilted my chin up and brought his mouth to mine. I could taste our tears as he wrapped his arms around my waist and kissed me. My arms around his neck. I kissed him for loving me. I kissed him for saving me when I couldn't save myself. I kissed him for giving me a piece of my life back.

We slowly pulled away from each other. He stepped back and opened the front door.

"Goodbye, Jared," I whispered. His eyes darkened with sadness, and then he walked out the front door.

I sat down at the table and sobbed until I had no tears left.

"It would be stupid to ask if you're okay, so I won't," Emma said as she came out of the bedroom. Her hair was still wet from the shower, and she'd put her pajamas on. "We probably won't sleep, but we should at least try. I just don't want to be in my room by myself tonight. I know that sounds real brave after kicking Xander until he passed out."

"It's okay. I don't think I could be alone right now either," I said. "You did surprise me tonight, though."

"Hell, I surprised myself. But when you told me who he was, I had this rush of anger for everything he did to you. And since he couldn't hurt me, I figured I could get a few kicks in. It apparently wasn't an opportunity I could pass up."

I would have smiled if things weren't so serious.

"Want some tea?" she asked. "This one's supposed to relax you," she said as she pulled the box out of the cabinet.

"I'd love some rum right now. Not to get drunk, but shit, my nerves are shot."

"Ya know, I wouldn't blame you this time. Do you really think you can just have a little?"

"Yeah, but I don't have any. I haven't drank anything in months," I said.

"I do," Emma said.

"What?" I asked as my mouth hung open. "You drink?"

"Lisa and I used to have a drink every once in a while. I'd just bought a new bottle before you came home. When I realized how wrecked you were, I hid it and never opened it."

"Well, shit. I think we can handle a few drinks. Go get it."

Emma's cheeks reddened as she hurried down the hall and into her bedroom.

I grabbed two glasses and the Pepsi out of the refrigerator.

"Okay, I know it's been a hell of a night. Well, technically it's morning," she said as she nodded toward the clock that read 2:37. "Anyway, you promise you can handle this?"

"Yeah, I don't want to get drunk. I don't ever want to be out of control again," I said as I looked her directly in the eyes.

"Good, give me the damn glasses," she said and opened the bottle. She poured the rum, and I topped it off with Pepsi.

"Here's to kicking Xander's sorry ass and staying alive," she said as she raised her glass.

"I'll drink to that," I said. Our glasses clinked, and we both took a long swig.

"Let's go crawl into your bed," Emma said. "You have more room than I do. We can just talk until we fall asleep." She grabbed the bottle of rum, and I grabbed the Pepsi and followed her down the hall.

We fluffed up the pillows and got settled. I took another drink and let the alcohol warm me. I missed drinking, but I didn't miss feeling out of control. Oblivion wasn't all it was cracked up to be.

Emma took a sip of her drink and turned to face me. "Can you tell me what happened?" she asked.

"Yeah. I'm not sure if I'll ever talk about it again, so I might as well tell you now."

I paused for a minute and collected my thoughts. As tired as I was, my brain was wired.

"When you and Nathan dropped me off, I thought we'd forgotten to leave a lamp on. When I opened the door, it was pitch-black inside, and I had no idea he was waiting for me. He pinned me against the door and held a knife to my throat." I stopped and took a sip of my drink.

"He started telling me how his attorney got his sentence reduced to months instead of years, and he was out early for good behavior. He said some really nasty things I won't repeat. Then—then he started unbuttoning my shirt," I whispered.

"Oh my God," Emma gasped.

"When he started to kiss me and take off my bra, something in me snapped. I heard Tiffany's voice in my head, and I grabbed him by the nuts and squeezed. If you hold on long enough, it'll make a guy pass out. It's difficult to do, but I couldn't think of anything else. Jared hadn't taught me how to deal with a knife against my throat. When Xander doubled over and stepped back, it gave me the space to bring the heel of my hand up, and I hit him underneath the tip of his nose. I thought it would knock him out, but the bastard is stubborn. He hit the floor, and I tried to run past him. He grabbed my ankle, and I fell. I gave him a kick straight to his face. He let go, and I scrambled into my room and locked the door. I had a gun and ammo ready to go in a shoe box in my closet."

"Lacey Anne! That was your gun?"

"Yeah."

"Where is it now?"

"Jared gave it back to me, and I hid it again before the cops showed up. You were making coffee or something."

"Why did you have a gun?"

My eyebrows rose as I looked at her. "Because I was terrified something like tonight would happen. And it did. That bastard came after me. Thank God I'd had some training and the gun. I'd have been dead otherwise."

"I know," Emma said and held her hand up. "I don't like guns, but I can't argue with you. The facts are in front of me."

"Sorry I didn't tell you, but I was afraid it would freak you out. I was trying to move forward and feel like I could protect myself. But it was more than me. After Walker left, I had to keep you safe too."

"Well, you did."

"Anyway, I ran in here and loaded the gun. When he broke the door open, I was standing by the window. I had it pointed right at his chest. He said I wouldn't shoot him, but I was prepared to. He came toward me, and I took the butt of the gun and knocked his sorry ass out. I don't remember how, but I managed to drag him down the hall and into the living room. Remember the tool drawer your dad started when we moved into the apartment? I grabbed the duct tape and used it on Xander's hands and feet. I slapped a piece over his mouth, too. I wanted him to know what it felt like to be terrified he was going to die. Emma, I almost pulled the trigger, but then I realized I was about to lose control. The adrenaline was running through me, and I wasn't thinking clearly. I was terrified. I picked up the phone and called Jared instead. By the time you got home, he'd talked me into giving him the gun."

"Thank you Jesus," she said. "Lacey, you would've never gotten over it if you'd killed him. I'm so glad Jared stopped you. Oh my gosh," she said and leaned her head against the wall. She closed her eyes, opened them again, and took a long drink. "Oh my God," she whispered as the tears gathered in her eyes. She covered her face with her free hand and broke down into tears. "Oh my God" she hiccupped.

"I'm so sorry, Emma," I said softly as I scooted over and pulled her into a hug, her head resting on my shoulder. I knew she'd never be the same after tonight.

Emma took a few days off work, and we spent a lot of time together. We talked to her parents and told them the calmer version of what happened. Neither of us mentioned the gun. Jim went straight to the hardware store and bought us a new lock, bolt, and chain. After he'd installed them for us, he suggested we consider moving. I wasn't sure it would help. Even though Xander was in prison again, he hadn't had any problem finding me this time.

I never returned to the dojo. I tried—I even walked to the parking lot and stared at the door. I willed my feet forward, but they refused to carry me through the front door. Even if I could go in, I'd never look at Jared the same way. It would always linger in the back of my mind that if he were angry enough, he might snap and turn violent. I was no longer willing to live in fear of anyone. Not even someone I cared about deeply.

Although I didn't sleep much, I hadn't started drinking again. After Emma went to work, I trained myself every day in the living room. I loved it and wanted to continue, but not with Jared. Even though I would always be grateful for him taking me in and giving me a reason to live again, but I'd have to figure out another option.

Christmas was only eleven days away, but for the first time in years, I didn't care. I'd taken Emma to work and gone grocery shopping. I was trying to get out more and help with the errands. I wasn't as scared of being in public now I knew Xander wouldn't be showing up again. Even if he did, I'd proved to myself and him I could take care of myself. I was no longer an easy target.

After I had put the groceries down on the kitchen counter, a knock sounded at the door. My heart skidded to a stop. I wasn't expecting anyone.

I opened the tool drawer and grabbed the hammer just in case. I'd learned that anything could be used as a weapon.

I unlocked the door, leaving the chain attached, while I peeked through the opening and gasped. I tossed the hammer on the couch, unchained the door, and opened it wide.

"Hi," I said.

"Hey," Walker said. "Emma called and told me about Xander. I wanted to see for myself you were okay."

"Do you want to come in?" I asked.

"No. I don't think it's a good idea."

I bit my lip and nodded.

"I didn't get custody of Garrett," Walker said as he ran his hand through his hair.

"Oh no," I said. "Is he okay?"

"Yeah. I think it's the best place for him right now."

"I'm sorry."

"Well, I wanted to see you and make sure you were okay. I'm sure it was scary as hell. I would've been here sooner, but I was in Missouri again," he said as he kicked at the ground with his shoe.

"I'm okay. As okay as someone can be after something like that. Thank you for checking on me."

He took a deep breath, and then his eyes locked with mine. His forehead creased and a surge of sadness spread across his face. "I'm leaving, Lace."

"Already?" I asked. "Will I see you again soon?" My heart pounded against my chest as I waited for him to answer.

"No, that's not what I mean. I got my PCS orders. I'm getting transferred in a few months."

"Wait, what? What does PCS mean?"

"Permanent change of station."

"Where are they sending you?"

"California."

My stomach dropped.

"Shit," he said as he ran both hands over his face and blew out a breath.

"Are you sure you don't want to come in? It's cold out there."

"No, thanks." His gaze drifted back to my face. "Come with me. Come with me, Lace. We can start over in California. I know it's not Oregon, but it's closer than we are here. We can live together."

He shook his head and let out another heavy sigh. "I love you. I want to spend the rest of my life with you. I just need you to want the same thing. I had to try one last time, but if you say no"—his voice trailed off for a moment—"you'll never hear from me again. These last seven months have been some of the hardest I've gone through. Seeing you torn up and angry was awful, but when I had to take a break, I was just hoping like hell you'd miss me. It fucking tore me up, and I can't do it again. If I walk away, I'm done. I've gotta try to move on. Please tell me you'll go with me."

I was speechless. He was leaving again. California. Everything we'd ever gone through together came crashing down.

"Say something," he whispered.

"Walker. I—" I suddenly took a step forward, grabbed his shirt, and brought his mouth down to mine. He paused for a moment and then slid his arms around my waist. He lifted me up as I wrapped my legs around him, and he walked into the apartment and kicked the door closed behind him.

"Is that a yes?" he whispered between our kisses.

"Yes. I love you so much. Please don't leave me again."

"Never," he said as he brought his mouth down on mine again. My lips parted as I invited him in, and our tongues danced as he walked us toward my room.

"Is Emma home?"

"No, she's working and then she has a date with Nathan."

Walker trailed kisses down my neck as he sat me down on my bed. His eyes were heavy with need, but it was more than that. "I love you so much, Lace. You're sure? You'll come with me to California?" he asked. A hint of fear flashed in his voice.

"Yes. I've never stopped loving you. I just didn't realize it. I was so scared," I said. "Everything that's happened . . ."

"That's all I needed to hear," he said as his soft lips brushed mine again.

"Walker?"

"Yeah, babe?"

"I need you," I whispered.

"You sure?"

"Very."

"I'll stop at any minute. You have full control," he said as he smoothed my hair.

I took his face in my hands and kissed him. His hand cupped the back of my head and then moved gently down my back. I moaned into his mouth as I scooted closer to him, sliding my hand up his shirt and running my hands over his muscled back.

He tugged at my top, and I sat up long enough for him to slide it over my head. Then I lay down on my back as I gazed into his eyes.

"I love you," I whispered.

"I've waited so long to hear you say it again," he said as he dipped his head between my breasts. He teased my nipples through the thin fabric of my bra with his thumb.

"So beautiful," he said as he released the front clasp on my bra. My nipples hardened as the cold air brushed against my skin. His tongue flicked across my breast, and then he took me into his mouth. My back arched off the bed as I grabbed the back of his head. His hand moved lightly down my side, and I reached for the top button on his jeans. I flicked it open and unbuttoned his 501s. He moaned as I wrapped my hand around him.

"You feel so good," I said as I stroked him. "I've missed you so much."

He pulled away long enough to remove his shirt and then he undid my jeans, sliding them down my legs and onto the floor. I sat up on the bed as I pulled his jeans down. He stood in front of me fully erect. I leaned forward and slipped him into my mouth.

"Jesus," he said as he grabbed my hair.

I ran my tongue along the length of him and then moved my hand in rhythm with my mouth. My nails dug into his ass as he moved with me. I got wetter with each moan he released.

"Babe, you gotta stop," he panted.

I glanced up at him and smiled.

He reached down to grab a condom out of his wallet. My eyes lingered on him as he rolled it on. He smiled as he leaned over me.

"This needs to go," he said as he tugged on my G-string.

I lay back and lifted my hips off the bed as he slowly pulled it over my legs.

"I just want to see you," he whispered as he joined me on the bed. He trailed his finger between my breasts and down my stomach. I sucked in a breath as he continued down my inner thigh.

I reached for him again and wrapped my hand around his erection, gasping as his thumb moved to my core and then massaged my clit.

"You're so wet," he said as he leaned down to kiss me. Our kiss deepened as I rubbed the tip of him. He moaned into my mouth as he massaged me and then eased his finger inside me. I melted against his hand as that sweet sensation built inside me.

His tongue grazed my nipple, and then he took me into his mouth as he gently sucked my breast. I rocked my hips to the rhythm of his hand. I squeezed him as I took my other hand and pulled his finger out of me.

"I need you inside me," I said.

He paused and searched my face. "If you need to stop—"

"Shh. I'm okay," I said.

He moved between my legs and lowered himself down. I took him in my hand and guided him to my entrance. I closed my eyes.

"Look at me," he whispered.

I opened my eyes and focused on his. We held each other's gaze as he slowly entered me. He began moving, and I sighed as he consumed every part of me. I wrapped my legs around him, the heat between us growing more intense. I leaned up to kiss him as we rocked together. He reached for my arms and moved them above my head, our fingers intertwining.

"I love you so much," he whispered.

"I love you too."

He picked up the pace, and our bodies melted together as our hearts reconnected. I had loved this man since I'd met him. He'd broken my heart, but then he'd given it back to me again. I never wanted to let him go. I wanted to share everything I had with him— my fear, my love, my strength, and my body. I'd never truly belonged to anyone else.

Walker stopped for a moment and sat on the edge of the bed. He pulled me over to him, and I straddled his lap. I guided him back inside me as he pulled me flush against him. My breasts warmed against his chest as I wrapped my legs around his waist. I rocked against him as he thrust deeper. My body trembled against him as his mouth found mine again. He guided my hips and buried himself inside me.

I threaded my hands through the back of his hair and leaned my forehead against his as he filled me. With each intoxicating move, my heart softened. My walls started to crumble as he kissed and caressed me.

"My heart has always belonged to you," I whispered. "I'll never let you go again."

I bit my lip as I stilled against him.

"Are you okay? What's the matter?" he asked as he tilted my face toward his.

Tears spilled down my cheeks.

"No, no, it's okay," he said as he kissed my cheeks. "It's okay," he whispered as he stopped moving. We stayed still for a moment as my emotions overwhelmed me and I tried to collect my words.

"I'm fine," I said softly. "I just realized I'm finally home."

34

I'd never loved a weekend more than this one. Walker didn't have to go back to base until Monday evening. It was the first time I'd willingly slept next to him since before he'd left for Texas. We giggled under the covers and agreed we wouldn't discuss the move yet. I just wanted a few days to enjoy him again and be happy.

We heard Emma come in around midnight; hopefully she'd had a great evening. We figured we'd surprise her in the morning, and Walker made love to me again before we drifted off to sleep in each other's arms.

WALKER MADE breakfast the next morning while I got the coffee started. We laughed quietly as we kissed while he was making the pancake batter. He chuckled as he picked me up and put me on the counter.

"I bet I can get you off before I have to turn this first pancake," he whispered in my ear.

"Walker!" I said quietly. I gasped as he slid his fingers into my shorts and panties and began massaging me so lightly I leaned into his hand, signaling him to increase the pressure.

"There's my baby," he said and peeked over at the pancake in the pan.

"You can't do it," I panted. "It's gonna burn."

A mischievous smile spread across his face as he took my clit between his fingers and gave it a gentle pinch.

My eyes rolled back in my head and I gasped. I grabbed his arms as he pinched me again and his hot breath caressed my neck. "I want inside you so bad right now," he whispered. "I want to fill you up and come with you," he said with one more light tug on my clit.

My fingernails dug into him as I exploded against his hand.

"That's my baby. I love to watch you. I love to make you feel good. I love it so much I almost get off myself," he whispered.

He slid his hand out of my panties, grabbed the spatula and flipped the pancake. My eyes widened. It was a perfect golden brown.

"Told you," he said and winked at me.

I flushed a deep red as I realized he'd gotten me off in an incredibly short time.

He chuckled again as he washed his hands in the kitchen sink. I wrinkled my nose. I definitely smelled like sex.

Ten minutes later, Walker had just finished cooking the pancakes when Emma walked into the kitchen.

"Oh! Walker!" she said and grinned.

"Hungry?" Walker said as he pulled the plates down from the kitchen cabinet.

"Starved, but I need some coffee too."

"Go sit down, I'll get you some," I said.

"Well aren't you being a sweetie this morning," she said as she walked toward the kitchen table and yawned.

I winked at Walker as I hopped off the counter and filled a cup for Emma. He leaned in and kissed me quickly while she wasn't looking. I smiled at him as he took the plate of pancakes to the table. I grabbed the butter and syrup as well as Emma's coffee.

She took a sip and rubbed her eyes.

"How was your night?" I asked.

Her face lit up.

"Great. I think it's getting serious."

"Really?" I squealed. "Emma, I'm so happy for you. When is he coming over? I can cook for everyone."

Walker and Emma responded with silence.

"Seriously? My cooking is that bad?" I asked.

"Your cooking is that bad," they both responded in unison.

I groaned and glared at them. "Fine, Walker can do the cooking then."

"Well you can't just volunteer him," Emma said. "He has a life, ya know."

"I'd love to meet him, Emma. Besides, I'll be around again for a little while," Walker said.

Emma leaned back in her chair. "Really? You kinda disappeared on us, you know."

Walker glanced at me, and I nodded. He sat down at the table and reached for my hand. Our fingers intertwined.

Emma's eyes grew wide as she covered her mouth. "Does this mean? Are you two?"

"Yes. We're together, but this time for good," Walker said.

Emma searched my face for confirmation, and I grinned from ear to ear. "It's true. We are. I'm not letting him go again," I said.

"Oh my God! I'm so happy for you both. I knew it!" she said and slapped her leg. "I knew you still loved him, Lacey."

I rolled my eyes and smiled at her.

"I told you to hang on, Walker," Emma said. "I told you she was still in love with you. What you two have doesn't come along very often." She paused as her expression grew serious. "Don't either of you screw it up again. Do you understand?"

I tried to hide my smile but failed. "Yes ma'am," I said. I eyed Walker as a big smile spread across his face and reached his eyes. My heart swelled as I realized his smile was for me. It had been a long time since I'd seen it.

We all sat there with stupid grins on our faces for a moment and then Walker's stomach growled.

"Dig in," he said as we all laughed.

WALKER and I cleaned up the kitchen as Emma went into her bedroom to call Nathan. We wanted to plan a night with everyone, and Walker was eager to meet him.

Walker and I crept down the hallway and back into my bedroom. I shut the door and locked it.

"I need a shower. Wanna join me?" I asked and pulled my tank top over my head. Walker's eyes drifted down to my breasts as my nipples hardened against the air. I put my thumbs into the waistband of my shorts and slowly lowered them down my legs, stepping out of them as he stood watching.

"I don't know what the hell you do to me, Walker," I whispered and slid my hand down my stomach and between my legs.

His eyes widened.

"But I can't get enough of you."

His jeans bulged as his eyes grew heavy.

"Maybe we should wait on the shower," I said, stepping backward until I reached the bed. I sat down and spread my legs apart.

"Take your clothes off," I whispered.

Walker didn't hesitate as he removed his clothes and dropped them on the floor, his arousal firm against his stomach. He stepped toward me.

"Nope, stop right there," I said and smiled mischievously. "You get to watch," I said, leaning back on my elbow and running my hand between my legs.

Walker moaned as I massaged my clit for him. "My God, you're so wet," he whispered. I watched as his hand closed around his shaft.

I picked up my pace and moved my hips against the motion of my fingers.

"Jesus, you're going to drive me crazy," he said as his voice cracked.

I stopped right before I exploded. He grabbed a condom, put it on, and in three steps he had picked me up off the bed and slid into me. I gasped as I wrapped my legs around him. His fingers dug into my ass cheeks as he thrust inside me.

"Oh God," I whispered, trying to be quiet with Emma in the house.

"I'll never get enough of being inside you," he said as he walked with me and leaned me against the wall.

I moaned as he gained more leverage and pushed deeper inside me.

"Shh," he said, grinning. He kissed me as we groaned into each other's mouths. I dug my fingernails into his back as he quickened his pace.

"Don't stop, baby," I said.

He held me as he turned us back toward the bed and laid us down gently on it. "You doing okay?" he whispered.

I nodded as he slowly pushed inside me. He pulled almost all the way out and then pushed deep inside me again. My back arched off the bed as he continued. He moved his hand in between us and found my swollen clit.

I grabbed the sheets as his pace quickened, gasping for air as my body tingled. The familiar feeling swirled inside me and built with each of his movements.

"Baby," I gasped.

"Yes?" he asked. "Are you ready?" His finger rubbed my clit. "Come for me," he panted. "I want to feel you tighten around me."

I bucked my hips against him and surrendered.

He pushed inside me one more time as he came with me. I grabbed his back as his body tensed and then released.

He stayed inside me as our bodies went limp.

"What are you doing to me?" he asked and smiled.

"Loving you," I whispered as I ran my fingers down his cheek.

35

We reappeared in the living room showered and dressed an hour later. We snuggled on the couch as Emma joined us in the living room.

"I'm off to the store to grab ingredients for our dinner," Emma said. "Nathan will be here around six tonight if it works for you two?"

"Works for me," I said.

"Perfect. What's for dinner?" Walker asked, smiling.

"I thought I'd make meatloaf, mashed potatoes, and some mixed vegetables," Emma replied.

"Ooh, you're going all out!" I said and grinned.

"Oh gosh, I just want everything to go okay. I'm so nervous."

"I'll be on good behavior, Emma," Walker said.

"It's not you I'm worried about," Emma said and shot me a look.

We laughed as she gathered her purse and grocery list. "I'll be back in about an hour," she said as she closed the door.

I sighed as I snuggled into Walker.

"Babe, we need to talk," he said as he stroked my hair.

"Mm, do we have to right now? You've worn me out," I muttered.

"We need to talk about the move."

Shit. I'd gotten lost in all the make-up sex we were having, and I'd forgotten about the move. My heart sunk at leaving Emma again.

I sat up and looked at him. "When?" I asked.

"We have about three months. It'll be toward the middle of March."

"That soon?" I asked as my face fell.

"Lace, have you changed your mind?" he asked. A worry line creased his forehead.

I sat up, crawled into his lap, and placed my hand on his cheek. "Never," I said and gazed into his eyes.

Walker sighed as he covered my hand with his and planted a kiss on the inside of my palm.

"I want to go with you," I said. "I just wish I could move Emma with us, but she has her family and Nathan here."

"I know she's your best friend, and I'm so sorry they're moving me. I don't have any control over it. And if you go with me, you won't either. We could move anytime they tell us to."

"Really?"

"Yeah. I just wanted to explain more to you."

"Okay, what else do I need to know?"

"I'll have to live on base a little while longer, but it will help you connect with the military wives . . ." His voice trailed off. "Shit."

"What?" I asked as my eyebrows knitted together.

"We're not married. You can't live with me on base."

"Why?" I asked, a touch of fear in my voice.

Walker ran his hand through his hair.

"Dammit. I was so nervous about asking you to go with me I didn't think about the housing. As far as the military is concerned, you have to be enlisted or married to live on base."

My back straightened. "What are you saying, Walker? I can't go with you?"

"We can't live together. We would have to get married." He stared at me, waiting for my response.

I wasn't sure what to say. I struggled to wrap my mind around what he'd just said.

"Do you love me?" he whispered.

"Yes, more than I've ever loved anyone," I said and smiled softly.

"Will you marry me, Lacey? Not because of the military, but because you want to be my wife? Because you want to spend the rest of your life with me?"

The longing in his eyes pierced my heart. My pulse quickened as I searched for the right answer, but I already knew what it was.

"Yes. I'll marry you because I love you, and I want to spend the rest of my life with you," I whispered.

Walker's face lit up, and he grinned.

"Really?"

"Yes," I said and laughed. "I'm not letting you leave again without me."

He leaned over and kissed me. "Then guess what we're doing tomorrow?"

"What?" I asked.

"Ring shopping."

My eyes lit up. "Walker Farren, you're getting me all turned on again with this wedding talk," I said, giggling.

He laughed and kissed my cheek. "Emma will be back soon, so just keep thinking about my tongue running all over your body and I swear I'll take very good care of you tonight," he whispered in my ear.

I sighed and nestled against his chest. "What about a date? And are we going to keep the wedding small? We'll do it in Hot Springs, right?"

"Yeah, we'll do it before we leave. We don't have much time to plan, though," he said as he tucked a piece of hair behind my ear.

"Let's not tell Emma until we have the rings and we've applied for the license. This is her night tonight," I said.

"Agreed. I want to check out this Nathan guy anyway. Especially since we won't be here as their relationship continues."

A pang of sadness spread through me. I wanted to see Emma happy in a relationship. I wanted to talk with her into the wee hours of the morning, but I wanted to be with Walker too. We'd have to figure something out.

"How about March tenth? It's about six days before we head out."

"That's fine. I'll just be a crazy lady trying to plan everything."

"I have a church in mind if you're okay with me picking it out?"

"Yeah. I don't have a church, so that works. Ummm, wait. It's not where you and Brittany got married, is it?" I asked, scrunching up my nose.

"Hell no. I wouldn't do that to you."

"Good. I didn't want to have to smack you upside the head."

Walker chuckled. "Okay, I'll file the papers, call the pastor, and submit the announcement to the newspaper. And tomorrow we can go shopping for rings and a dress?"

"I'd love to."

⁂

NATHAN KNOCKED on the door at exactly six o'clock. I opened it and accepted the bottle of wine he'd brought.

"Hi, Nathan! Come on in. Hey Emma, Nathan's here," I said.

"Oh hi," Emma turned toward Nathan. A warm smile spread across her face, and her eyes lit up. I moved out of the way as he hugged her. I glanced at Walker and winked at him.

"Nathan, you've met Lacey, and this is Walker, her boyfriend," Emma said.

Walker stepped forward, extended his hand, and shook Nathan's.

"Nice to meet you," Nathan said.

"You too," Walker replied.

Walker eyed him as I slipped my arm around his waist and gave him a little squeeze. I didn't want him scaring Nathan. Walker was definitely taller and more built than he was.

Against Emma's wishes, Nathan insisted on joining her in the kitchen to finish cooking dinner. Walker and I watched them from the sofa.

I slipped my hand between Walker's legs and massaged him through his jeans. His eyes rolled back in his head, and I giggled softly. "Lacey, stop. I'm going to be so hard I won't be able to walk to the dinner table," he whispered.

"Well, I have no problem with that," I said, continuing to rub him.

"I'll take care of you tonight," he said, grinning. He grabbed my hand and held it in place on his knee.

"Y'all ready to eat?" Emma asked.

"It smells great," Walker said as we stood up and joined them at the table.

Dinner went well, and it was obvious to both Walker and me that Nathan and Emma were head over heels for each other. I wondered if it would ease the news of my leaving. I dreaded the conversation, but there was no way around it.

After dinner, I volunteered to clean the kitchen since Nathan was taking Emma to a movie. As soon as the door closed, Walker locked and bolted it. The dishes stayed on the table as our clothes littered the kitchen and living room floor. If we kept up at this pace, Walker would need more condoms by tomorrow.

36

The next day consisted of ring and gown shopping. I made Walker go into other stores as I looked through the wedding dresses. Since we were getting married in March, I could get away with a backless gown.

I finally found one I fell in love with and tried it on, turning in the mirror, I took it all in—the deep V-neck, the mermaid fit, and the bare back. It was exquisite. Then I peeked at the price tag and grimaced. I'd been without a job for a while, and I wasn't sure how I'd pay for it. My shoulders slumped as I took it off.

I joined Walker an hour later.

"What's wrong, babe?" he asked as he kissed me on the top of my head.

"I can't afford the dress I want," I said.

"Where is it?"

My finger pointed toward the wedding store.

He pulled out his wallet and handed me his credit card.

"What's this for?"

"Go buy the dress," he said.

"Walker it's expensive, like several hundred dollars."

"I don't have anything on this card. I want you to wear the dress you want. We're only doing this once," he said.

I bit my lip and thought about it. We were about to be married, which meant I'd help pay off the credit card. I could deal with that.

"You'll have to go with me, though. I can't sign your name,"

He took the card and put it back in his wallet. Then he grabbed my hand and walked me to the store.

"Which dress is it?"

"I can't tell you!" I said.

"Fine," he said, grinning as we walked up to the lady at the front counter. "Excuse me. My fiancée wants to buy the dress she just tried on. Can you ring it up so I can give you my credit card?"

"He can't see it, though," I said quickly.

"Of course," she said and beamed at us. "Miss, why don't you come with me to make sure I get the right one. Then I'll just put it in the back, and after he leaves, we'll get it fitted for you. I think you were really close in size already, though," she said.

I kissed Walker on the cheek as we left him standing at the front of the store.

We pulled the dress out, and she copied the information down to enter into the register. Within five minutes, Walker had paid for the dress and I'd sent him to the tux shop at the end of the mall while I got fitted for my gown.

I WAS EXCITED but exhausted when we got back to the apartment.

"Where have you two been all day?" Emma asked as I flopped down on the sofa and Walker headed for the kitchen. He was always hungry.

"Shopping," I said and gave her a tired smile. "How was your day with Nathan?"

"I think I'm falling in love with him," Emma said.

"It's funny how it sneaks up on you," I said, glancing at her. "I'm so happy for you. Does he feel the same way?"

"He told me he loved me tonight," she said, grinning.

"That's wonderful," I said as a warm smile spread across my face. "You deserve nothing but the best," I said softly so Walker couldn't hear.

Silence hung in the air and I frowned at how to tell Emma the news.

"Mm, I know that look, Lacey Anne. Spill," she said.

"Walker?" I called.

"Yeah," he replied as he took a bite of an apple and walked over.

"I think we need to have the talk now."

Walker smiled as he joined us in the living room. He swallowed his food and cleared his throat. "Emma, I'd like your permission to marry Lacey."

Emma's mouth hung open as she looked at Walker and then me. "You're serious?" she asked.

"With all my heart," he said.

Emma clapped her hands together and jumped off the couch. "Yes! Yes!" She reached for me and grabbed me off the sofa. She hugged me so hard I couldn't breathe. Then she let go, took a step toward Walker, and stopped.

"Lacey, I'm going to hug your man now, so deal with it," she said, giggling.

Walker wrapped her up in a big hug.

Emma stepped back as tears glistened in her eyes. "I'm so happy you two have finally figured out what I've seen all along."

"There's more," I said as I patted the sofa for her to sit down. "Emma, we're getting married in March before Walker is relocated."

Emma's face fell as she realized what we were saying. "Where?"

"Fairfield, California," Walker said gently.

"Dammit. you're leaving again, Lacey?"

"Emma, I'm so sorry. I don't know what to say," I whispered.

Tears streamed down Emma's cheeks. "I'll get over it. I'm still so happy for you both, but I've gotten so used to you being here again. You too, Walker. What am I going to do without you?"

"First, be my maid of honor," I said. "Second, if things with you and

Nathan don't work out, consider coming out to California with us," I said as I glanced at Walker. He nodded in agreement.

"But Daddy and Mom are here," she muttered.

"I know, but there are options. We'll figure something out. It won't be like it was last time. And if you and Nathan get married, Walker and I will fly back."

"You will?"

"Hell yeah!" I said, leaning over to hug her. "We're family, remember?"

"Oh my gosh, it's only like two-and-a-half months away, plus Christmas is in a few days. We have a lot of planning to do!"

WALKER'S CHUCKLE filled the room as Emma and I wiped our tears.

"If anything changes, you'll come out there with us, okay?" I asked.

"Okay," Emma promised.

BY THE TIME CHRISTMAS ARRIVED, my engagement ring was ready. Nathan, Walker, and I spent the day with Emma and her parents. I asked Jim if he would walk me down the aisle and he'd wrapped me up in a big hug.

"I'd be honored to walk you down the aisle," he said, misty-eyed. Linda teared up as we talked about the plans. They welcomed Walker into their home like he already belonged. I loved them for that.

It was the best Christmas I'd ever had. It wasn't about the gifts or the food—my heart was overwhelmed with the love that surrounded me.

37

March arrived quicker than I'd expected. We'd agreed to keep the wedding small and intimate. Walker struggled with it being his second wedding, but I didn't care. As far as I was concerned, his marriage to Brittany was made from a place of brokenness after losing Jeffrey and his mom. He hadn't done it with a clear head or heart like he had with me.

My heart fluttered as Jim walked me down the aisle. Walker's mouth dropped open when he saw me. His face filled with emotion, and I almost cried before I reached him. Somehow, his eyes were even bluer against his black tux.

Jim kissed my cheek as he handed me off, and I grinned at Emma. George had flown in from Oregon, and he stood next to Joss as one of my bridesmaids. I've never seen him smile so hard, and he looked gorgeous in his tux. I'd let the girls pick out their light-lavender dresses. I wasn't going to torment them with something ugly. They were beautiful, and I didn't miss how Nathan looked at Emma.

I smiled at Garrett as he stood next to Walker. It seemed like he'd grown another three inches since I'd seen him last. Some girl was going to snatch him up soon.

Jim and Linda sat in the front pew along with Nathan. Walker's aunt, Linda, sat with them as well. She'd been thrilled to hear we'd worked things out. The only person missing was Susan. I'd wanted her to be with us the first time we'd planned to get married. My heart stuttered for a moment. If my heart ached, I couldn't imagine what Walker was feeling. She'd been an amazing mom to him and Garrett, and to me during our brief time together.

Warmth flowed through me as Walker took my hand and we faced each other.

"I love you so much," he whispered.

"I love you more," I replied. I bit my lip as the tears threatened, but this time they were for a good reason.

The pastor cleared his throat. "We are gathered here today to join Lacey Anne Beaumont and Walker Tate Farren together in holy matrimony," he said.

I gazed into Walker's eyes as the pastor continued. My heart filled with so much love for him I thought it'd burst. I'd never felt more sure about any other decision I'd made in my life.

Suddenly, the front door opened and a voice yelled from the far end of the church.

"Wait! Stop this wedding. It's a disgrace to God's name!"

My eyes narrowed as I recognized Mama's voice.

"Lacey? What's this?" the pastor asked, wide-eyed.

I looked at Walker and searched his face. "If you don't want her as your mother-in-law, you'd better back out right now," I said.

"Not a chance in hell. Sorry, Pastor," he said quickly. "I'm marrying you today."

"Okay, then please excuse me for a moment," I said to Walker and the pastor.

I handed my flowers to Emma and gave her a reassuring smile. I squared my shoulders, picked up the front of my dress, and walked down the aisle.

"What are you doing here?" I asked as I approached Mama.

"I saw the announcement in the paper, and I'm stopping this marriage. It's not ordained by God!" she yelled.

"Mama, you either hush your mouth or I'll have you escorted right out of this church. I'm a grown woman and I'm capable of making good decisions. I'm choosing to marry Walker right now, with or without your blessing. I don't need your approval. I love you, but you either shut your mouth, sit down and join us, or leave. It's your choice, but I'm getting married today," I said, looking her straight in the eye.

"It's those demons," she spat.

"Stop!" I said. "That is *enough*. You are not allowed to speak to me like that again. I have never been and never will be controlled or possessed by demons. Think what you want, but I'm finished here."

"You'll pay for this," she hissed.

I turned and looked over my shoulder at Jim and Nathan and nodded toward Mama. They stood up and walked down the aisle.

"Would you two be so kind as to escort this woman off the church grounds?" I asked calmly. "Mama, if you don't go quietly, I'll call the cops and press charges for drugging me and holding me against my will," I said and gave her a firm look.

"You wouldn't!"

"Oh, I would. Don't give me a reason to prove how serious I am."

Jim and Nathan each took one of Mama's arms and ushered her down the aisle and out the front door.

"You'll be sorry for this!" Mama screamed as she walked out of the church.

I closed my eyes, took a deep breath, and made my way back down the aisle toward Walker.

The men returned shortly and took their seats. The pastor continued the ceremony without any further interruptions.

Ten minutes later, Walker gave me my first kiss as Mrs. Walker Farren. Everyone clapped and cheered as he escorted me down the stairs. I stopped him in the middle of the aisle and kissed him.

"Thank you for never giving up on me," I said as I gazed up into his eyes. My heart sang as I realized I'd never again have to be apart from him.

"I love you, Lacey Farren, and nothing will ever change that," he said, picking me up and twirling me around.

Portland, Oregon

My Louboutin heels clicked against the dining room floor.

"Don't you look professional," Garrett said as he walked into the kitchen and raided the refrigerator.

"You're up early." I smiled at him as I put my earrings on.

"It's because he never went to bed. He walked in the front door a few minutes ago," Walker said and laughed as he joined us. "Mmm, you look good." He slipped his arms around my waist and pulled me in for a long kiss.

"I can't focus when you kiss me like that," I whispered as my face flushed. "Besides, it's an important day. I want to put the asshole behind bars, and I can't walk into the courtroom rattled," I said, smiling. "It does help that whether we win or lose, he can't hurt Valerie again. Maybe we'll have something to celebrate tonight." I winked at him.

"You're going to be amazing. I'm so proud of you. You've already won this case, don't forget it."

"I love you. I wouldn't be here today if it weren't for you. You've saved me so many times."

"And I'd do it all again," he said and kissed the top of my head.

"Shit, man, will you two knock it off? I'm trying to eat over here," Garrett said.

"If you don't want to see us in the morning, get your ass home at a decent hour," Walker said, chuckling. "Besides, if you remember, Lace and I talked to you about this before you moved in. You should be focusing on finding a job, not chasing women all night."

Garrett flipped Walker the bird and grinned.

"Alright guys," I said, grabbing my briefcase. "I'm off to hopefully put another abuser behind bars. Wish me luck."

"Kick their ass!" Garrett said around a mouthful of cereal.

"I love you. You've got this," Walker said as he kissed me.

I took a deep breath and walked out the door.

MY HANDS TREMBLED as I pulled the courtroom door open and walked in. I'd done this numerous times, but it never stopped being difficult.

I eyed the defendant as I made my way down the aisle. My chin tilted up, and I walked straight to my seat as my client, Valerie, followed and sat down next to me.

"Remember, we have a backup plan, so no matter what, you'll never have to live this way again. We've got this," I said. I smiled and remembered Megan's words to me all those years ago.

Valerie nodded, and I patted her arm. I remembered how terrifying this was, but she had the strength to testify.

Thirty minutes later, Valerie and I watched as her ex-boyfriend was handcuffed and escorted out of the room. I hugged her, and then we walked out of the courtroom together. Nothing compared to the high of winning a case against an abuser and putting his sorry ass in jail.

"You ready?" I asked Valerie.

A shy smile pulled at the corner of her mouth as she nodded.

"My car is this way," I said.

Minutes later, I pulled my Lexus into the downtown traffic.

"How are you doing?" I asked, turning down the volume on the radio.

"Scared, but I know it's the right thing," she said.

"I remember. It's terrifying, but this organization is run by top-notch people. You have an opportunity most will never have. I'm proud of you for taking it."

Valerie's big brown eyes brimmed with tears. "Thank you," she said softly.

"Just stay strong. Don't come back. Give yourself some time to heal. Promise?" I asked.

"Promise."

I slowed and then exited off the highway and continued a few more miles. Ten minutes later, I pulled the car into the driveway of a big brick house.

"This is it."

Valerie and I got out of the car, and I rang the doorbell.

"Lacey!" Joanna said as she opened the front door.

"Hi," I said as I smiled and put my hand out to usher Valerie through the door.

"Oh, it's always so good to see you, even if the circumstances do stink," Joanna said as she gave me a warm hug.

"You too," I replied. "Joanna, this is Valerie."

"Hi, hon. I'm so glad you're here," Joanna said and hugged her.

"Thank you for your help," Valerie whispered.

"Come on in, you two. Chuck will be home shortly, and we'll all eat."

"I wish I could stay, but Walker will be waiting for me. We have a date," I said and grinned.

"You've got a good husband, Lacey."

"Yes, ma'am, I do. I'm very blessed." I turned to Valerie. "Valerie, take care of yourself. You're in good hands," I said as I hugged her goodbye.

My heart sank a little as the front door closed behind me. I remembered talking to Mrs. Walters and planning my own escape. Valerie would do well with Chuck and Joanna until it was time to move her to another state. She had a long journey ahead as she shed her past and became someone new. I was just proud to be part of it.

"Lacey?"

"Yeah, I'm home," I said, dropping my car keys on the table next to the door. I slipped off my jacket and hung it up in the hall closet.

Walker poked his head out of the kitchen.

"Well, don't keep me waiting any longer. Did you win?"

My shoulders sagged as I walked into the kitchen, put my purse on the table, and wrapped my arms around his neck. I laid my head on his shoulder.

"Oh, babe. I'm sorry," he said as he returned my hug. "At least she's still going to be safe. You're doing amazing work in court and with the organization. I love you so much." He tilted my chin up toward him and kissed me softly. I parted my mouth and welcomed him, his warmth, and his heart.

My hands slid slowly down his chest and stomach, and then I unbuttoned his jeans. I loved him in his Levi's, but I was about to love him even more out of them.

"Lace?" he asked as he pulled away, his brow creasing in confusion.

"I won," I whispered. "I put the bastard behind bars."

"What? That's amazing!" he yelled. I giggled as he picked me up and twirled me around. "Shit! You had me going there for a minute."

He stopped swinging me, and my feet touched back down on the floor.

"This means we celebrate," he said as he picked me up and put me on the kitchen table. "You look so damned hot in that suit, too," he said as he slid the skirt up to my thighs.

"Yeah?" I asked, grinning. I moaned as Walker trailed hot, wet kisses down my neck.

"This is just in the way," he said as he slipped the buttons open on my blue silk blouse.

His tongue grazed the top of my breast as I slid my hand into his jeans and wrapped my fingers around him.

"Dammit," I said as my cell phone buzzed.

"No, do *not* answer," he said as he flicked his tongue across my nipple.

"Shit. I have to, it could be about Valerie," I replied, fumbling for my phone in my bag. Walker stopped and sighed while I pulled it out of my purse.

I glanced at the screen and looked up at him. "Krissy?" I asked, shock filling my voice.

"Are you serious? You haven't talked to her since they moved out here a few years ago," Walker said, his eyes widening in surprise.

"I know," I said and frowned as I answered it. "Hello?"

"Hi, Lacey. It's Krissy. Listen, Mama's in the hospital."

"Krissy, I've made it clear to everyone I'm not interested."

"Yeah, I know, but she's not going to make it. She's on life support right now. There's no chance of recovery. She had a massive heart attack, and I just wanted to give you the opportunity to say goodbye."

My face froze. *What? Mama is on life support?*

"Lacey? Are you there?" Krissy asked.

"Yeah." My voice was husky with emotion.

"Babe?" Walker asked. His eyebrows knitted together as he waited for my reply.

"What hospital?" I whispered.

"St. Vincent's."

"I'll be there in twenty." I hung up the phone and sat still for a minute. Dazed, I looked up at Walker.

"Lace, what's wrong?" he asked as he tucked a stray piece of hair behind my ear. His thumb gently caressed my cheek.

"Mama. She's on life support. Krissy called to see if I wanted to say goodbye."

Walker's face fell. "I'm so sorry," he said as he pulled me into him. "I'll drive you to the hospital."

"I can drive."

"No, you can't. You're shaking," he said as he rubbed my back.

I nodded, realizing he was right. My body trembled at the thought of seeing her again after all these years.

Walker released me, and I slid off the table. I grabbed my purse and phone and started toward the door.

"Babe?"

"Huh?" I asked and turned back toward Walker.

"Hang on," he said as he approached me and buttoned my blouse.

"Oh, shit. I was about to flash the entire neighborhood." I glanced up at him, wide-eyed.

"It's okay, I'm here. I've been through this before and no matter what your relationship is, losing a parent sucks. This is going to be hard, but I'll take care of you. You're not alone."

I nodded as he kissed me on top of the head, grabbed my hand, and led me out to the car.

⁕⁂⁕

PORTLAND WAS WET, but I'd grown to love the rain. I almost grieved the absence of it during the sunny summer months, and I counted down the days until fall every year.

"You ready?" I asked Walker while I adjusted my dress in front of the bedroom mirror. Krissy had scheduled the funeral for a few days after Mama died. I'd been shaken to my core when I'd seen her lying motionless in the hospital bed. I had tucked her away in the back of my mind so I could live my life, but I'd never forgotten her. I'd never forgotten all the hell she'd put me through, but I held onto a few good memories too.

"Lace, I'm so sorry," Walker said as he embraced me.

I melted into his arms and buried my head against his chest as a burst of grief consumed me. I crumpled against him as we sank to the floor together. Sobs racked my body as he gently rocked me and I released all the pent-up pain and emotion I'd carried over the years.

"I wish I could tell you this was going to be easy, babe. I wish I could take the pain from you, but I can't. I can hold you while you cry, listen to you when you're angry about the years you lost, and help you remember the good times. It's been a hell of a ride, but she's gone. You no longer have to look over your shoulder," he whispered.

I couldn't say anything, but my grip on his shirt told him I needed him. There was nothing left inside me. I'd experienced guilt, relief, and grief all within a few days. Exhaustion filled me inside and out, but his presence never ceased to calm me, no matter what was going on in my life.

Walker gently lifted me off the floor and set me on my feet. I stood on my tiptoes, kissed him, and then went into the bathroom to pull myself together.

KRISSY HAD TAKEN care of the funeral arrangements since she was the oldest child. She'd forever remained Mama's number-one fan, too. No matter how hard I'd tried to make things right over the years and explain what happened, it had never made an impact on Krissy. Nothing changed, and I finally had to accept not only was Mama gone, but this was goodbye to Krissy as well.

Walker and I showed up at the funeral a few minutes early. Krissy looked beautiful as she spoke fondly of Mama to everyone. People would've thought we'd grown up in two different homes the way she talked about how wonderful Mama was. In a way, we had. Krissy was away at college when things got bad, and she only heard Mama's version of what happened, which was rarely the truth.

The spring day loomed dark with thick clouds as we gathered under the tent. Mama loved spring, so regardless of the weather, Krissy had chosen to hold the funeral outside.

A rare echo of thunder rumbled in the background as the minister began speaking.

"Lynn Beaumont was one of the most gifted and spiritual women I've ever met. I had the honor of meeting and praying with her on several occasions, and every time I did, I learned something new."

In an attempt to shut out the minister's words, I squeezed my eyes closed. I wondered if he knew the truth about what Mama had really been like. Walker squeezed my hand—his way of letting me know he was on my side. I glanced at him, my heart fluttering. I loved him so much.

The rain pelted off the tent as the service came to a close. Umbrellas popped open as everyone walked back to their cars. I didn't move. The craziness of the years flashed through my mind, and my feet were cemented to the ground. I didn't know how to walk away again.

"Lace, we should go," Walker said as he kissed the back of my hand.

"Okay," I said in a daze. He held the umbrella over us as we walked toward the car. Walker opened my door, folded the umbrella, and tossed it onto the back floorboard. A moment later, he slid in the driver's seat.

A sharp laugh escaped me.

"What?" Walker asked.

"It stopped raining. The moment the funeral was over and we all left, it stopped."

"Lace, look over there." Walker pointed.

I followed his finger, and my eyes widened. A brilliant double rainbow filled the sky.

"It's going to be okay," he said. I looked out the window and said goodbye to Mama one last time as we pulled away.

Don't miss the international bestselling Love & Ruin series FREE in Kindle Unlimited. Click here to fall in love with Gemma and Hendrix.

SIGN UP FOR J.A. OWENBY'S NEWSLETTER and receive exclusive bonus scenes, updates on upcoming releases, and more. Just click here.

. . .

I APPRECIATE your help in spreading the word online as well as telling a friend. Reviews help readers find books they love so please leave a review on your favorite book site.

255

YOU CAN ALSO JOIN my Facebook group, J.A. Owenby's One Page At A Time, for exclusive giveaways and sneak peeks of future books.

LET'S GET IN TOUCH! CONNECT WITH ME HERE:

Author J.A. Owenby Website
Join my Newsletter
Follow me on Facebook
Join my Facebook Group
Follow me on Amazon
Join me on Goodreads
Follow me on BookBub
Follow me on Twitter
Follow me on Instagram
Join me on Pinterest

ALSO BY J.A. OWENBY

OTHER BOOKS BY INTERNATIONAL BESTSELLING J.A. OWENBY

New Adult Romance

The Love & Ruin Series

Love & Ruin

Love & Deception

Love & Redemption

Love & Consequences, a standalone novel

Love & Corruption, a standalone novel

Love & Revelations, a novella

Love & Seduction, a standalone novel

Love & Vengeance

Love & Retaliation, coming June 2021

Romantic Mystery

The Wicked Intentions Series

Dark Intentions

Fractured Intentions

Coming of Age

The Torn Series, inspired by True Events

Fading into Her, a prequel novella

Torn

Captured

Freed

Standalone Novels

Where I'll Find You

This book is dedicated to Jeremy Hand, who was an amazing friend and author. The world lost you too soon.

ACKNOWLEDGMENTS

The outpouring of support for the first book in The Torn Series, *Torn*, has been amazing. I'm so grateful to all the readers who reached out to me personally, and to everyone who took the time to give the book such thoughtful reviews.

Brett, I couldn't do this without you. I love you so very much.

My friends are amazing, and I get misty-eyed when I think about all the love and support they give me. Thank you to Sheri Kaye Hoff, Jeannie Kemper, Kara Long, Sarah Jones, Nancy Schnauefer, Cristel Olive, Pat Harvey, Rochelle Miller, Savannah Earnst, Shannon Barnard, Bonnie Gortler, Vivienne Smith, Aubrey Minear, Angela Fowler, Brittney Valencia, Gabriel Jones, Dawn Plummer, and the fantastic people from Lake Hamilton High School who shared posts, left reviews, and recommended my novel to others.

ABOUT THE AUTHOR

International bestselling author J.A. Owenby grew up in a small back-woods town in Arkansas where she learned how to swear like a sailor and spot water moccasins skimming across the lake.

She finally ditched the south and headed to Oregon. The first winter there, she was literally blown away a few times by ninety mile an hour winds and storms that rolled in off the ocean.

Eventually, she longed for quiet and headed up to snowier pastures. She now resides in Washington state with her hot nerdy husband and cat, Chloe (who frequently encourages her to drink). She spends her days coming up with ways to torture characters in a way that either makes you want to throw your book down a flight of stairs or sob hysterically into a pillow.

J.A. Owenby writes new adult and romantic thriller novels. Her books ooze with emotion, angst, and twists that will leave you breathless. Having battled her own demons, she's not afraid to tackle the secrets women are forced to hide. After all, the road to love is paved in the dark.

Her friends describe her as delightfully twisted. She loves fan mail and wine. Please send her all the wine.

You can follow the progress of her upcoming novel on Facebook at Author J.A. Owenby and on Twitter @jaowenby.

Sign up for J.A. Owenby's Newsletter:
BookHip.com/CTZMWZ

Like J.A. Owenby's Facebook:
https://www.facebook.com/JAOwenby

J.A. Owenby's One Page At A Time reader group:
https://www.facebook.com/groups/JAOwenby

Edited by Molly McCowan

Cover Art by iheartdesigns

Second Edition

ISBN-13: 978-1-949414-75-2

ISBN-10: 1-949414-75-2

Click here to gain access to previews of J.A. Owenby's novels before they're released and to take part in exclusive giveaways.

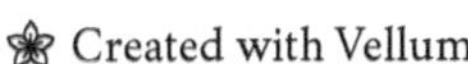 Created with Vellum